Growth

A Short Story Collection

by
Elin Olausson

www.DarkInkBooks.com

"Roadkill" (originally appeared in *Nightscript 7*, Chthonic Matter, 2021), "The Courthouse" (originally appeared in *Curiouser Magazine*, issue 1, 2021), "Uncle" (originally appeared in *Shadowy Natures: Stories of Psychological Horror*, Dark Ink Books, 2020), "Mother Spook" (originally appeared in *Night Terrors Vol. 4*, Scare Street, 2020), "Chalk" (originally appeared in *The Half That You See*, Dark Ink Books, 2021), "Razor, Knife" (originally appeared in *Unburied: A Collection of Queer Dark Fiction*, Dark Ink Books, 2021), "Swan Song" (originally appeared in *Chiral Mad 5*, Written Backwards, 2022), "The Moor" (originally appeared in *Luna Station Quarterly*, issue 45, 2021)

Dark Ink and its logos are trademarked by *AM Ink Publishing*.

www.AMInkPublishing.com

Contents

To my family

Between the dark and the daylight,

When the night is beginning to lower,

Comes a pause in the day's occupations,

That is known as the Children's Hour.

I hear in the chamber above me

The patter of little feet,

The sound of a door that is opened,

And voices soft and sweet.

From my study I see in the lamplight,

Descending the broad hall stair,

Grave Alice, and laughing Allegra,

And Edith with golden hair.

A whisper, and then a silence:

Yet I know by their merry eyes

They are plotting and planning together

To take me by surprise.

(From *The Children's Hour* by Henry Wadsworth Longfellow)

Roadkill

When a car approaches, things can go one of two possible ways. If Dolores is in a good mood, she puts on that smile-but-not-really-a-smile of hers and says that Christmas has come early. When she's down, she steps into her boots and heads out with the shovel and the lantern without saying a single word.

I know which Dolores I prefer, but it's not for me to pick and choose. I sit on my bed while the nightlight paints the world red, and I know that no matter which Dolores went out the door, the one who comes back won't be a lot of fun to deal with. Just like plenty of things aren't fun, and that's just the way it is.

Me and Dolores, we're the only ones left around here. Most people have moved to the big city, I guess, but I prefer it right where I am. Dolores is the same. She's got a shoebox in her closet; it's crammed with postcards from someone called Mike or Mitch or something like that. *Dolly*, the postcards hiss, *I'm waiting for you. I've found a place for us and the rent's practically nothing. Let me know when you're on your way.* There are other ones with just a sentence or a few words scribbled on them. *Things are crazy here. Might be best if you stay with your folks for a while.* One has a kitten on the picture side and the words *love you* on the blank one. It's not signed, unlike the others—as if there was only one person in the world she'd expect to be loved by.

Dolores has never said a word about Mike or whatever his name is. She doesn't have to. She taught me to read when

I was five, and I knew right away that it was a useful skill. It lets me in on all the little secrets Dolores doesn't want me to know, as long as I cover my tracks. I enjoyed reading the newspaper, back when we still got it. I was too small to get through anything but the headlines, but that was enough. From them I gathered that Mike was right about the outside world. *Things are crazy here. Stay where you are.*

Dolores has saved some old newspapers and stacked them on top of the bookshelf. I don't think it's for sentimental reasons, because she's not that type. Maybe she likes to leaf through them and think that she dodged a bullet. That she's better off than Mike will ever be.

I sit at the kitchen table when she comes in after the chicken-feeding and shrugs her big coat off. I've tried it on— it's heavy, swallows me whole. Dolores enters the kitchen with her rubber boots still on and drops the chicken bucket in the corner. She's grim-faced and wiry, and I have a hard time comprehending that anyone has ever sent her love notes.

"We got us four eggs." She sets them down in front of me—they roll around on the table, shit-stained, a downy feather stuck to one of them. "You clean them up. I'm tired."

She leaves. I hear her move through the house, placing muddy footprints everywhere. It's been years since we bothered with cleaning. I watch the eggs, that one feather. If I had feathers I'd never want to part with them. I wouldn't fly away, but I'd like to be able to.

Holding an egg is a little like cupping a newborn chicken in your hand. One moves and squeaks and one is still, dormant, but they're equally fragile. Squeeze the egg too hard and it breaks, and you have goo everywhere. Squeeze the chicken...Well. I take my time polishing the eggs, because I don't have much else to do. They're the same muddy tea color as my hair, and I'm not sure if I like it or not. It's a stupid comparison, just as stupid as dreams of flying.

"Done yet?" Dolores barks from the innards of the house. "Damn roof's leaking."

She doesn't have to give me direct orders. I know what to do. After leaving the eggs on the counter I wrap the raincoat around me and head outside. This coat fits me better than Dolores' one does, but it clearly used to belong to someone older. There's a tag in it, with a dotted line where you're supposed to put your name, but nothing has been written. I've thought of jotting down my own name there, but it might make Dolores angry. I'm not scared of her, but it's just not worth it. It's not as if any other kid will come by and take the coat by mistake.

The ladder leans against the house like it's asleep or drunk. Its legs dig themselves deep into the soggy ground, down to where the furry things live. I climb fast, because I always do, because I don't trust the ladder and I certainly don't trust the house. Dolores once told me that it was built by her great-grandfather, which means it's ancient and should be dead, because everything else from that far back is. Up on the sagging roof, I slither with my belly pressed to the corrugated metal sheets, reaching for the hammer and nails that have been left up there since last time. It's not raining heavily, but the air is damp, icy needles stinging my hands. Dolores says winters used to be different. But when I ask her why, she refuses to answer.

The hole in the roof is tiny, but these things grow and spread. Before I get to work, I lower my face to the opening and peer down. Dolores lies on her mattress, face up but eyes shut. At first, I think she's sleeping, but then I see her facial muscles twitch. She makes an ugly sound, and I tear myself from the spy-hole. Dolores has no business crying. We are the lucky ones. I hammer for a while, but I only use one nail—I can push the scrap of metal aside and spy all I want. Not that I want to look at her right now, when she's all snot and tears. I want to store this moment at the back of my mind and forget about it.

When I come back inside a while later she's in the kitchen, knife in one hand and an apple in the other. She chops it in pieces, shoving them into her mouth and chewing soundlessly. The pale flesh is streaked with maggot trails, running here and there like scabs. The knife slices through a live maggot, and I look away. In front of the sink I spot that feather from before. It's crumpled—one of us must have stepped on it. Just another speck of dirt on a filthy floor.

"I didn't ask for this," Dolores says, apple kernels dropping from her mouth into her lap. "We're just surviving. That's all we've ever done."

I don't know what she wants me to say, so I stay quiet. In fact, I'm not sure she's talking to me at all.

***

The only time she lightens up is when Gabriel comes. Angel-faced Gabriel with the star on his chest and hair the color of night. His headlights slip into our corner of the world like a whisper, a quivering promise of something shiny. Dolores never talks about Gabriel when he's not around, but those headlights approaching is the one thing that can make her untangle her hair and splash icy water at her face and armpits. She waits out on the porch while his car coughs and wheezes its way from the main road up to our yard. I'm forced to wait with her, whether I like it or not.

Today, he drives slower than usual and it takes forever before he's even off the main road. I'm cold, and I'd rather be in the red nightlight glow in my room.

"Can I go inside?" It's not as if I think she'll agree to it. Dolores never agrees to anything.

"You stay right here where I can see you." She says that, but she only has eyes for the car.

"I don't like Gabriel," I lie. I do sort of like him. He's too stupid for his own good, or he wouldn't come here, but my chest tingles every time he smiles.

"Shut up," Dolores mutters. "Who the hell asked you, anyway?"

I think about that maggot, sliced in half. Death can be hard but it's sometimes easy, too. Like putting your shoes on or swinging a lantern.

Gabriel parks the car right below the porch and steps into the mud, shutting the car door with a creak. The car is the same rusty brown as all the other cars I've seen, but Gabriel's jacket is summer sky blue. He raises his hand in greeting, and Dolores does the same. Her fingertips are angry red from the cold.

"Hey there!" Gabriel grins, wiping the curls out of his face. "Nasty weather today."

Dolores shoves her hands into her coat pockets. "Always is, this time of year."

"You might be right about that." He gives me a quick look, the kind that is accidental and doesn't mean a thing. "Everything all right out here?"

Dolores nods. "How are things in town?"

I cling to her words, like I do whenever she mentions *town*. Every time I try and ask her about that place, she tells me to be quiet. But when Gabriel comes, Dolores is the curious one.

"Well, we had an outbreak of flu recently, and plenty of kids got sick—"

"Dead?" Dolores asks, cutting through his words like she did that maggot.

Gabriel's eyes ghost across my face, then back to her. "Yeah. Some of them. It's a good thing you're out here, on your own. There's not much that can hurt you here."

His lips remind me of blood when you wash your hands of it. Trails of bloody water, painting the world pink.

"There's plenty that can hurt you," Dolores says. "No matter where you are."

"I guess that's true." Gabriel runs a hand through his hair. "So, did you…Were there any cars passing by recently?"

Cars—that's the reason he comes here. It's all because of the road and that gap in it that outsiders have no clue about.

"No." Dolores seems to shrink a size, and her charcoal eyes sting me like a mosquito bite. "Not since last time."

She's telling the truth for once. It's not often that a car comes by. Usually it's just Gabriel, which is good because he knows not to drive past the bend. The people in town probably know it, too. Gabriel has put up signs by the main road, but they are invisible at night just like everything else. Outsiders drive past our house and past the bend, and wherever they were heading, they're not going to get there. And that's just the way it is.

"That's a relief," Gabriel says. "Let's hope people stay away from now on."

"Yep."

Liar, I want to tell her. *That's not what you're hoping for.*

"So, do you want to come inside?" Dolores looks like a bird, with her twig legs sticking out from under the coat. If I were older, I might have been able to snap her in two.

"I'm not sure if I…" Gabriel's eyes flicker. I want him to leave, and not come back until I'm all grown and Dolores is gone.

"Busy?" Dolores' voice hardens. "Sure."

"Someone needs to take care of things," he says, heading for the car. "You know how it is."

She mutters something. I hear her mutter all the time, and it's never interesting.

"Take care now." Gabriel opens the car door and it whines, because it's dying just like the rest of the world. One day that car will refuse to move, and then Gabriel won't be able to visit again.

Dolores waves before disappearing into the house and slamming the door. I watch Gabriel struggle for several minutes before the car roars and jumps forward. He's off, and there's no telling when he'll come by again. I'm not old, but I suppose that all things really do come to an end and that one day, Gabriel's visits will, too.

Dolores lies on her bed, coat still on. I peek through the doorway and she flings something at me. A postcard, squeezed into a ball. "Get out of here!"

I want to pick it up and see which card it is, but she's too angry. "He'll be here again soon enough."

She glares. "Shut up about things you don't understand."

So I do. I go to my own room and close the door and then I sit there, in the red glow, sorting my collection. There's the doll's head, the plastic car, the three stuffed bears. The pearl necklace and the picture book about wolves.

"I understand," I tell them. "I understand everything."

***

Dolores locks herself in her room the next day like a sulking child, and I climb up the ladder to spy at her. But she doesn't do anything, just lies on the bed with her arms hugging her legs. I watch her anyway, weighing the hammer in my hand. *Swing, swing.* If the hole was wider, the hammer might fall straight through.

"I hear you, Linda," Dolores says. "You really don't have anything better to do?"

I stay quiet, and she doesn't speak again. After a while I climb back down to the ground and wipe the grime from my jeans. Nothing has changed, really. I'm small and she's a grown-up, and I don't think Gabriel likes either of us. My thoughts skip up the ladder to where the hammer lies, sleeping. One day the roof is going to fall in on us and it won't matter a whole lot then what Gabriel thinks.

Dolores is up early the next morning. Her stomping boots force themselves into my dreams, and for a moment I feel like she's in my room, pacing the floor. The red glow is useless against her—but once I open my eyes there's nothing there. The doll's head lies on the nightstand, watching me with a glassy stare. It had a body when I found it, but it was too badly burnt. Just like the little girl in the backseat. I don't want ugly things, so I removed the head and left the rest where it was. The doll's hair is thick and golden, and when I wrap it around my index finger, the head hangs upside down, swinging.

I play with the doll until my stomach turns noisy, then pull the knitted sweater on over my pajamas and head to the kitchen to look for food. Dolores sits at the table, chewing her nails. They're thick, caked with dirt, and I can't look away though I want to.

"What do you want?" she says, still chewing.

"Eat." I open the cupboard. Once I saw a live rat in there, but not this time. There's not much else either, except for a carrot that I grab and gnaw a big chunk off before Dolores can stop me. She doesn't seem to mind, though, so I keep eating.

"He doesn't know what it's like out here," she mutters out of nowhere. I don't have to ask who she's talking about. "It's easy for him…them. They've still got shops, and there's gas if you can pay for it. What the hell do I have? He's got no right to come here and lecture me about the damn cars." She gives me a hard look, and I realize that she hates me. "People like that don't know shit. Life ain't a fairytale, and there's no happy ending. You going to cry now?" She laughs hoarsely, removing her hand from her mouth. The skin around her nails is raw and bloody. "Cry all you want. It won't change a thing."

I always expected her to go crazy eventually, but it would be inconvenient if it should happen now when I'm still a kid. "Is this about Mike?"

Dolores stops laughing. Her glares are like filthy fingertips scratching my face. "That's my business. Not yours."

"Just wondering." I tell myself that I'm not scared of her. "He sent you a lot of stuff. What happened? Did he die?"

She scoffs. "Of course he died. That's what people do."

I guess that's true. The chickens die, too, and the strangers who don't know about the gap in the road. Everyone who lived in this house before us have died. According to the newspaper headlines, there used to be cities with millions of people. Most of those people died as well.

"Anyway, I don't want to talk about it." She stands, swaying for a moment before regaining her balance. "It's in the past. It's over."

As if things in the past can't hurt you. I go back to my room and drop the doll's head to the floor. My naked feet push her around, here, there, and no matter what I do she keeps smiling.

***

There's a car that night. We both hear it, but Dolores reaches the front door first. She hides under her coat, shooting me a secretive look.

"I'll go out," she says. "See if they need help."

I don't like it when I have to stay inside. When she's been gone a while I sneak out on the porch and lean over the railing, listening for the crash. There's always a crash, because Gabriel's signs are useless in the dark. A crash, sometimes a blast, then nothing. It's not as if we want it to happen, it just does. And dead people don't need food or clothes or golden-haired dolls, so we might as well take what we need.

Dolores is gone a long while. I get bored and start playing with my hair, braiding and unbraiding it. The cold makes my fingers slow and clumsy. When Dolores comes I'm numb, but I don't let it show.

She puts the sack down in front of me and throws the shovel aside. I get down on my knees and rummage through the sack, weighing items in my hand. A tiny purse, sunglasses, three pairs of shoes. A pink dress, cool and silky against my dirty fingers.

"Merry Christmas," Dolores says. She grins, but her eyes are broken.

Later, in my room, I squeeze my pale limbs into the dress and twirl to imaginary music. The doll has no hands but she claps anyway, loud and clear, and the stuffed bears hum along. The floor is icy but the nightlight glows like fire.

Through the music I hear the crackling of flames lapping, licking, eating.

***

Gabriel pays us a visit a week later. He comes all the way up on the porch this time, the star on his chest blazing. His eyes jump from this to that, and to my sparkling pink dress more than once. I've worn it day and night ever since Christmas.

"There was this young family passing through town recently." He scratches his chin. His nails look soft and breakable, nothing like Dolores' claws. "Man, wife, a little girl. Looked like they had money. Wife was pretty, and that little girl was dolled up like a princess." He looks down at me again. Behind my back, Dolores tugs at my hair.

"We didn't see anything," she says. "Sorry you had to come all this way."

"Right." Gabriel glances toward his car. "Could I come in, maybe? Have a look around?"

Dolores makes a low sound in her throat, a growl that only I can hear. "Of course, officer. Do whatever you need to do." She pushes me out of the way. Her hands tell me to go straight to my room and hide away all my toys and pretty things. While I sit on the floor, shoving stuff under the bed, Gabriel follows Dolores through the other rooms. I listen to their voices, their noisy footsteps.

"It's messy," Dolores says. "Bet you've never seen a place as messy as this before."

"You have no idea what I've seen."

They reach her bedroom and the door clicks. She's shut it. I know she'll never tell me anything later, so I head outside and up the ladder, to the spy-hole. I'm quiet, ghost-like. I want to know.

Gabriel sits on the bed with the box of postcards in his lap. He's picking them up one by one, murmuring the words while Dolores stands, back turned to him.

"You could have had a different life," he says when there are no cards left unread. "Away from here."

Dolores' shoulders are shaking.

"The girl…Was he the father?" Gabriel's voice is as soft as a baby chicken. I'd like to snatch it out of his throat and store it in a jar.

"He came back," Dolores says. "He came to get me, but he didn't know what had happened to the road. The explosion woke me up. That's it. That's the story."

"I'm sorry." Gabriel stands. He's too tall for our house, he distorts the proportions. I wish he would leave. "That's a horrible thing to go through." He puts his arm around her shoulders, and she starts bawling. I grab the hammer. I squeeze it until my knuckles lose their color.

Dolores cries forever. I try to imagine the future, but I can't because there is none. Just me, just this house. I think about my mother and my father and about the fact that they are dead or soon will be. Then I climb back down with the hammer.

***

A car drives down the road some weeks later, when the smell has taken over the house and the pink dress has turned gray and filthy like everything else. I watch the headlights come closer, closer, past the warning signs. The night is dark and I'm a little scared and very hungry. I hope they've got food in the trunk and that they'll die quickly.

"Stay here," I tell the doll's head and the bears and Gabriel and Dolores. "I'll be back soon." I grab the sack, the lantern, and the hammer. The red glow sings, following me out into the night.

It's Christmas.

The Courthouse

Sea slipped off the bus and into the night. His boots and the hem of his jeans were quickly covered in mud, the same slimy muck he remembered from the Courthouse's yard. He didn't keep many memories, but one of them was playing in the rain and coming inside, leaving wet footprints on the stairs. It made his mother cry, which he had never understood. Other adults got angry, but all she ever did was cry.

The roadside was just a thin strip of slippery soil beneath defunct streetlights. No room for walkers, but people out here had never cared. Some carried torches, but most trudged on in darkness, too old and worn to fear cars. Most passing motorists probably never realized there were people out walking these roads at night. They were shadows, ghosts.

It was a five-minute walk to the Courthouse. Past shut-down cottages with years-old *For Sale* signs, past overgrown hedges and the rusty shells of cars. Sea didn't need light to know they were there, though he hadn't been back in this place for a decade. The village spreading like a dark stain around the Courthouse had been dead long before he moved to the city.

When he reached the dirt road and the collapsing heap of rotting wood that had once been the village wholesale store, a dog howled close by. Sharp, mad barks that filled the cool air before they were cut off. Not completely dead, then? It had always been hard to imagine neighbors here. His mother had never talked to any of the locals, and neither had he.

The Courthouse was always filled with people anyway.

Its garden lay in darkness, and there were no lights on inside the house. The white cedar hedge seemed well-trimmed, though, and the lawn was kept neat. Butler was a slob whose hair was as greasy as the peanut butter sandwiches he ate three times a day, but he'd always loved the garden. Sea wasn't sure he felt the same about the house.

He gave the main entrance with its bell and wide stairs a quick look before going around the back to try the kitchen door. Butler could have lived in the refurbished apartment upstairs or taken the fancy old office quarters on the other side of the house for himself, but he had always seemed content in his tiny room he'd had since the sixties, with the whirring minifridge and the sofa bed.

Sea knew even before he knocked that Butler wouldn't bother to open the door until after several minutes, and when he did, he'd be wearing the same knitted brown sweater and Birkenstocks that he'd had on the night Sea left the Courthouse behind all those years ago.

Now he was back. A sour taste filled his mouth as he rapped his knuckles against the green door. The sound echoed, multiplied. If a villager went by on the invisible road behind the hedge they'd hear, they'd know. Though he wasn't quite sure what they would know or why it would be bad if they did.

Seconds, minutes. His breath transformed into white mist in front of his face. Sea wasn't afraid of the dark, but he liked being indoors better at night. Didn't everyone? His sister Io certainly had.

A shadow fell over the frosted square of glass in the door before it was unlocked and opened. Butler's bulky frame filled the doorway.

"Oh," he said in his familiar, sandpaper voice. "It's you." Butler went back inside the house and Sea followed, locking the door behind him.

"It's been ten years," Sea said, dropping his bag to the floor next to a box brimming with emptied cans of Heinz Baked Beans. "I didn't want to, but I thought I should."

Butler bustled to an ancient computer and turned off the screen, but not before Sea caught a glimpse of heavy breasts and long, blond hair. "I can't offer you anything," Butler said, face averted, arms hanging. Gray tufts of hair stuck up on top of his head as if he'd been sleeping. "Well, there's tap water. Unless they've taken that, too."

"That's all right. I don't eat much. Or drink."

"No, I remember that." Butler coughed, his sunken face shifting. "Never were much like your mother, were you."

Sea studied the dented, liver-colored wallpaper and the ceiling lamp with no bulb. The room was lit by the fluorescent light over the kitchenette sink. There was a sour smell in the air, a blend of sweat and unwashed clothes and old garbage. It was as if Butler had been preserved in a jar for the last ten years—nothing about him had changed.

"Anyone living up there now?" Sea asked, even though he already knew the answer. Most people looking for a rental apartment would want something a little closer to civilization.

"I used to put ads in the paper, but I don't bother now." Butler glanced at the dark computer screen. "It's all on the internet these days. Young people don't read newspapers."

"I guess." Sea remembered his mother's stubborn refusal to learn how to work a computer. *I don't want any machine getting into my head.* "Can I take a look? At the flat?"

Butler was quiet for a spell, as if trying to come up with a reason to say no. Then he went over to the door next to the kitchenette—the door to the old courtroom. The keyring he removed from his pocket was just as massive as Sea remembered, with slender, rusty keys from another time. "Been a while since it was lived in," he muttered. "Don't expect too much."

They entered the courtroom. Sea had loved it back then, as had Io. It was a grand and spacious room, almost church-like, with windows that brushed the edge of the ceiling. The old wooden bench was still in place, as well; behind it sat the wide, semicircular table and its attendant chairs where the judge and jurists had sat, sentencing defendants to imprisonment or—sometimes—death.

What Sea and his sister had loved most about the courtroom, though, was that you could stand right behind the bench and get a glimpse of what went on in their apartment upstairs. A narrow hallway ran between the bedchambers and the other rooms, with only a railing separating it from the courtroom downstairs. They had leaned over that railing, pretending that a trial was in session, and they had hidden behind the bench and spied on their mother and her friends. Io had giggled once, Sea remembered, and he had put his hand over her warm mouth.

"Well," said Butler, his sandals tapping as he strode over the dark parquet floor. "Nothing's happened in here, as you can see."

"Yeah," Sea replied, running his hand over the bench's smooth mahogany. *Except plenty has happened*, he thought. *People were sentenced to death in this room.*

They reached the stairs, carpeted and turning, with its banister's intricate carvings. Butler moved in the gloom ahead, keys jangling. Sea didn't want to think about his mother, but her face and translucent eyes flashed through his mind.

It was strange to imagine a woman like her moving far away from society, with her tattoos and hippie hair, her pills hidden under the sink. All those parties she craved and her friends—all men—who'd stayed over for the night.

"Here we are." Butler pushed the door open and turned on the light. Dust swirled around them as they stepped inside. Io had danced through these rooms with the dust shimmering in the air around her, thin arms raised, pretending it was snowing.

Sea walked to the railing and gazed down into the empty courtroom.

"It's not so bad," Butler said, shambling over to the right and entering the first bedroom, Sea's and Io's. Sea followed and looked inside. There was nothing there: frayed wallpaper, some water stains in the ceiling...but not a single piece of furniture. It didn't matter to him—he didn't much care about this room or what it looked like.

Butler showed him his mother's chamber next. The walls had been painted white. There was no trace of her Lily of the Valley wallpaper, her Alphonse Mucha posters. Gone, just like her.

"She was colorful," Butler said. "More than you could say about the couple who had the place after she...after she left."

Sea stared at the wall where the posters had once hung. She would have wept if she knew someone had torn them down. *Darling, look. Just look what they've done.*

They went back to the hallway, Sea glancing back down into the courtroom. If he squinted, it was almost as if he saw the shape of someone small peering up at him from behind the bench, suppressing a giggle.

The kitchen was much the same as before, dusky and uninviting, which had never mattered because his mother never cooked. Past the kitchen was the corner room—the *parlor* as she had called it—where bearded men strummed acoustic guitars and downed cheap beer while the windowsills were packed with people smoking, letting the night air in. His mother claimed the rug in the parlor was Persian, a fancy heirloom from her grandparents, but most weekends it was sticky with either vomit or cat piss or both, and after a time, it wasn't fancy anymore.

He and Io had wanted to sit on the windowsill, too, but there had never been room. His mother knew too many people for there to be any room for them.

"And then there's the attic," Butler said, fidgeting with his keyring. They had reached the walk-in closet behind the parlor, an empty space save for the flight of stairs leading to the attic door. A short, steep walk up to the part of the Courthouse Io had feared the most. "Bet you don't want to take a look up there," Butler continued, eyes fixed on the low door above. "Not after what happened."

Her voice ran through his head. Flowed, echoed. "Did you…did you fix the floor?" he asked.

Butler shrugged, putting the keyring back in his pocket. "Would have liked to, but it cost too damn much. If I ever get any new tenants, they won't get the key to that door. The last ones didn't, and they understood all too well, when I explained why."

Sea wanted to walk up those stairs. Press his eye to the keyhole and see if he could get a glimpse of the place where his mother died. "They got…they got lots of space as it is," he said. "In the apartment, I mean. No need to bother with the attic."

"Exactly my meaning." Butler sighed, heading back into the parlor. "Sure, you might be able to use some of it, but I wouldn't take any chances with a rotten floor. What happened to Susanne made me swear not to ever go up there again."

Susanne. The name was like lightning, a blow to the head. Sea had forgotten her name because there's no need to call dead people anything. Besides, he never used that name and Io never did, either. It was only the bearded men, their drawling voices trailing after her wherever she went, through the hallway, down the turning stairs, into her bedroom. *Susanne, come on. Susanne, don't be mad.*

"Let's head back down." Butler moved heavily past the kitchen, like a bear, and into the hallway towards the apartment door. "I don't know what you came for," he said, "but if you didn't find it yet, then that's too bad."

Sea stopped by the railing in the hallway, staring up at the courtroom ceiling. Butler had mended that, at least. Covered it up, painted the new boards the same pastel green as the old ones. From beneath, no one could guess that a woman called Susanne had crashed through that ceiling and broken her neck on the spotless parquet. "Wait," he told Butler. "Just wait."

"There's nothing to wait for." Butler stayed by the door, a lumpy form in the shadows. "She's gone. There's nothing you can do to get her back, and neither can I."

"I don't want her back." The words slipped out harsh, too honest. "Who said...who said I'd ever want that?"

"Most kids would. That's all." Butler's voice was indifferent. He didn't care; he never had.

"You know what her parties were like. Her...her boyfriends." Sea thought of Io. Small, light as a feather, her long hair falling into her eyes. Io, the sister he was supposed to protect but never could.

Butler didn't reply. There was only a jangle as he twisted the keys in his hand.

"She lost control when she was drunk." Sea remembered his mother dancing, pulling her top off, her blond hair flowing over her breasts. He had yelled at her, hot with shame, and all those men had laughed at him. And she...she had laughed, too.

"Who doesn't?" Butler said.

"She didn't know what went on after she'd dozed off."
Io. Io.

"Susanne was the sensitive sort. She always came to me in the morning and apologized if things had gotten out of hand."

Sea stared into the courtroom. His mother was long gone. But he wished Io were here. "My sister," he whispered. "Mom invited all those people over and let them roam free, and she didn't care what they did to Io. I tried to push them out of her bed, but I was too small. I was just too small."

Butler drew a breath. Slowly he turned the key in the lock, and the door opened just a sliver. "Sea," he said, stepping out onto the landing. "You know...you know that you never had a sister. You were the only child who ever lived here."

Sea took no notice. He kept his eyes on the courtroom. Saw the dust swirl and shimmer as Io danced, danced, danced. "Mom should have taken better care of us," he said. "But I showed her." *I tricked you into the attic, Mom, didn't I? Told you Steve or Jim or Bob or whoever was waiting for you up there and you went, you fucking skipped up the stairs because Steve or Jim or Bob was all you ever could think about. And when I told you what he did when you weren't looking you cried and said I was a liar. Sometimes you have to pick sides, Mom, and you never picked mine. So why would I want you back?*

"You were just a kid back then." Butler was already halfway downstairs. "Well, you're still a kid. Come on, let's go down. You're heading back to town tonight, aren't you?"

Sea strained his eyes. Tried to look for Io, but all he could see was that floor where his mother had broken like a porcelain doll. Io, the sister, the little friend he had needed. The frail girl with his eyes, his face, his memories. So tiny and weak, she couldn't defend herself against the evil that came through her door at night.

"I don't want to go," he said. "There are no more buses tonight anyway. I want to stay here. You said you couldn't find tenants. Well, I can be your tenant." He spoke the words easily; they didn't mean anything. All he wanted was to stay for a little longer.

"You don't look like you've got any money," said Butler. "Just saying."

"But you'll like the company." Sea smiled to himself, until a tear ran down his face. His mother had cried, but never he; he wasn't going to start now.

"Not really," said Butler. "But I'm sure we can work something out. Your mother...your mother and I always could."

Steve or Jim or Bob or Steve or Jim or Bob or Steve or Jim or Bob

"Mm." Sea thought of rotten floorboards breaking. Tonight, he would walk through all these rooms, stand by every window, sit in every dark corner.

Tomorrow he would make the Courthouse his.

Uncle

Uncle says that it was for the best that Mother died. I didn't agree at first but I agree now. She was slow and clumsy, like a slug or cow or some other animal you don't have to be nice to. Her food tasted bland and she was always crying. *Boo-hoo*, Uncle said, then lifted one of her thin braids and spoke with his lips touching her ear. *Boo-fucking-hoo!* He doesn't want me using bad words but it's not the same when it's only in my head. I don't think it's the same.

Uncle is the only man I know. We don't need other men here. Svetlana does the cleaning and I answer the telephone and Uncle does everything else. Svetlana lives in town; she drives here in the morning and leaves at noon. She tried to smile at me in the beginning but smiles don't work on me. I don't despise her, really, but I don't care for her either. Uncle says she's sloppy and wears too much makeup. At least she never cries.

The motel is ours and when Uncle dies, it will be mine. I have a lot of responsibilities. I do as I'm told. The old woman in Room 12 says I'm very clever. She has a strange way of talking; the words come out all stretched and bent. She has stayed for one week already, which is good because there are no other guests. The VACANT sign blinks, blinks, blinks like a shock-pink constellation in the sky. The woman has a big head and a name I don't like, so I think of her as Head. Every day, Head drives off in her rusty white car with her canvas bag. I peeked into the bag on her first night here, when she forgot it in Reception, and saw an old camera and a book. I wonder if Head reads the same book every day or if she has lots of them to pick and choose from, lining the walls in Room 12. I have ten books but I haven't looked at them since Mother went into the tub. None of them have pictures, because Uncle says picture books are bad for children. Mother used to read the stories to me when she was around. I guess you could say it was the only thing she was good at.

I have a secret place of my own below the counter in Reception. I can sit there with my legs outstretched and Uncle doesn't notice, Svetlana doesn't notice, no one notices. It's a lockable hollow space inside the counter, dark and dusty, all empty because Uncle keeps everything important in his office down the hall. Sometimes I fall asleep in there. Other times I spy. I listen as Uncle asks guests for their names and hands out keys. I hear his voice ripple through the air. If the front door is open, which it is a lot because of the heat, I eavesdrop on the conversations on the porch. Those are what interest me the most. Uncle talks to all the guests. Only girls come here, and they are always alone. Their cars break down close to the motel in the middle of the night, or they come wandering from nowhere, barefoot, carrying nothing but their shoes. Hitchhiker girls, runaway girls, girls with pills in their pockets and china doll faces. Uncle tucks their long hair behind their ears and they laugh like a choir of broken toys, shrill and off-key. They ask him to fix their cars or make them coffee or let them stay the night. Uncle twirls their hair around his finger and they melt until the floor is a gooey mess.

There are no girls here now. Only Head. I like it when Uncle talks to her. Their talks are like cigarette smoke trailing through the air, beautiful but not beautiful at all. I don't understand what they talk about but I want to hear it and pretend I am grown like them. Uncle sips the peach-flavored iced tea you make from powder. He buys twenty bags of it every time he goes to town for supplies. Once, I tore open an empty package and lapped at the remaining powder inside. I imagine that real peaches taste just like that. An explosion of sweetness.

I sit under the counter tonight playing the spy game. Uncle is outside, and Head with her pale eyes and the usual scarf tied over her gray hair. I have made a hole in the counter with a nail. It's small, but if I press my eye against it, I see things. Right now, I see the rickety porch table with Uncle's glass of iced tea, his long thin legs and his hairy arm, reaching for the glass. Head sits at the other side of the table. She drinks from a hip flask. Sometimes it's a thermos, sometimes a water bottle. Uncle has never offered her anything from inside the house and she has never asked. Her bra is visible through her worn white t-shirt. Not like Uncle's girls would do it, to be sexy. Head doesn't know and if she did, she wouldn't care.

"Find anything today?" Uncle asks. His voice is cool as always but there's that sugary note to it that belongs to evenings on the porch. I know that his mouth would taste of peaches if I licked it.

"What's there to find?" Head's deep voice twists the words around slowly. "I won't go inside the place. I can't. The house looks just the same from a distance, though. All worn and sagging, like me." She makes a strange sound, some sort of laugh. "As long as I don't get too close, I can pretend I'm still living there and Bill's on his way home and Charlie's asleep in his room."

"Yeah." Uncle drinks. The hairs on his arm shimmer like gold in the ripe sunlight. "I've had places like that too. Before. I've found that it's best to stay the hell away from them. The past…it eats you."

Head runs her thumb along her cheekbone, as if she's brushing a tear away. "What if I want it to eat me?"

"Well, clearly you do." Uncle doesn't seem to notice her crying. Or maybe it's not a problem when Head does it. "I'm trying to help, that's all. You lost something, I lost something. We all lost something. But some of us don't like being eaten." He laughs. Uncle's laugh is smooth and warm as desert sand at the end of a hot day.

"I took a picture today." Head doesn't seem to want to talk more about eating. "I thought you should see it." She grabs her canvas bag from the floor and rummages inside, then picks up a photograph and shows it to him. Her eyes stay on his face the whole time. I want to know what's in the photo, but all I see is a dark and blurry, white-framed square.

"Not bad." Uncle doesn't grab the picture to take a closer look. It hangs between them, dangling from Head's wrinkly hand. After a while she puts it back in her bag.

"What happened?" she asks, her voice as cautious as a hand reaching into a lion's cage. "To her, I mean…your sister-in-law. I thought she'd be here, I thought she was working for you. Then today I saw that cross, in the middle of nowhere, and I—"

"Nothing happened." Uncle cuts her off without raising his voice. I wish he'd let her talk, so I could learn more about the cross. "She wasn't happy," he continues. "Some people aren't."

I know what you're doing, Mother whimpers in my head. *I know what you're doing to those girls.*

"It must be tough," Head says. "Bringing the boy up on your own."

My chest flares up with excitement. They're talking about me. It's the first time I've heard them talking about me.

"Not at all." Uncle's long fingers trace the rim of his glass. It must be cool and wet to the touch. "It's easier now, in fact."

Head shakes her head slowly. It reminds me of a turtle, or an old tree when a storm grabs hold of its branches. "Even for you, that's damn harsh."

"Blah, blah, blah." Uncle's hand opens and closes in the air like a nagging beak, a yapping dachshund. "You know, I do kind of enjoy your company. Don't ruin it."

"All right, I think we'll just call it a night." Head sighs and heaves herself out of the chair. "You know where I am if you want to apologize." She takes her bag and her hip flask and leaves the porch. The scarf around her head looks dirty, as if she's rubbed it into the soil. I've never noticed before.

"I'll be right here." Uncle's voice is laughy and light. He takes the glass and drinks. When he puts it back down, it's empty. "You can wait for an apology from me, Eleanor, but it won't come. Apologies are for normal people. Not us. You should know that."

He sits quiet and alone after she's gone. I sit quiet and alone too. I trace the inside of the counter with my fingers. Sometimes I get splinters when I do it, but not this time. With my eye to the peep hole, watching Uncle's unmoving form, I move my lips over the rough, uneven wood. *Hello, Head*, I mime. *Hello, Uncle*. I twist my mouth as if I was Head, imagining that I'm old and that I'll soon be dead and gone. I smile just like Uncle, baring my teeth.

***

When Svetlana arrives the next morning, Head has already driven off as she's done every day since she came here. I'm disappointed, because I wanted to have a look in her bag and see if maybe that photo she showed Uncle was still there. I stand on my stool behind the counter when Svetlana comes through the door. She heads straight for Uncle's office at the end of the hallway. Whenever she barges in there their voices turn loud and angry. It doesn't bother me, but she should learn to knock on doors. Even I know about knocking.

Sometimes when the telephone doesn't ring I play pretend and answer it anyway. I do it now to forget about Svetlana.

"You've reached the *Fading Sun*," I whisper, because I don't want Uncle to overhear. "How can I help?" The motel was called something else before. I like Uncle's name better. The other end of the line is silent, easy to fill with whatever words and voices I want.

Good morning, sweetheart, the silence says. It has a chipper voice that's both male and female, or neither. *I'd like a room for myself and my three children. We'll stay forever, me and my three boys around your age. They'll want to play with you every day.*

It could be just one boy, too. Maybe even a girl, as long as she's not too old. I put the receiver down and think about the games I could play with the three boys. Inside Uncle's office, Svetlana starts shouting.

"Hide-and-seek," I murmur to myself to drown out the office noises, and because I sometimes forget what my voice sounds like. "And I'll be spying on them, and they'll never-never-never find me."

Uncle's office door opens with a bang, and I start as if I've had my knuckles rapped. Svetlana storms out, mascara and eyeliner running down her cheeks. Her eyes pin me down, pin me to the space between the counter and the wall.

"Your uncle is an asshole," she hisses, but her voice shifts at the last word, goes high-pitched and desperate.

"Don't you use that kind of language in front of him," Uncle calls from his office. He protects me, and it makes me glow inside.

"Fuck you!" Svetlana cries before rushing out to her car. With her thin legs and feet that sway this way and that in the high heels, she looks like the spiders that make Uncle twist his face in disgust before he crushes them under his boot.

He comes out of the office, leisurely, taking his time. I watch as he flattens his hair, then puts his hands into his pockets. There's not a crease in his jeans, there's never a crease in anything Uncle wears. "She asked for a raise, the greedy bitch," he says, smiling. Uncle's low voice is much nicer than Svetlana's. "We're better off without her. Isn't that right?"

I nod. For a second I think about Mother, but I shut that part of my brain down until it remembers. Remembers that we had no more use of Mother and that holding on to useless things is wrong.

"I think you're old enough," Uncle says, "to start cleaning."

***

The girls stay away this week. I wish they'd never come back. Uncle forgets about me when there are girls around and leaves me alone after the house has gone dark and the desert starts its night whispering. But now he is home, teaching me to play chess and to flay rats. Not for eating, only for practice.

"You've got to know how to do things," he tells me when the kitchen table is stained red and the matte gray fur has gone dark and sticky. "It's a bad world out there. That's why we stay here, you and me. But sometimes you've got to go into town whether you like or not."

"Will I be able to drive a car?" I ask. "Will I sit out on the porch just like you?"

"Yes." Uncle puts his bloody hand on my head. "You will do everything that I do."

***

That evening, Uncle takes his iced tea out to the porch and tells me to clean his office, before I've had time to slip into my hiding place under the counter. I don't mind.

"Just dusting, hoovering," Uncle says. "No touching any of my stuff, all right?"

I promise. Uncle nods and puts his glass down and the shades on, before he tells me to leave. His cowboy boots are the only part of him that's visible from inside the house. I go to the cleaning cupboard and take out what I need, a cloth and the old hoover. When I was small, Mother used to call it the Roaring Monster and chase me with it, both of us laughing. It doesn't look like a monster now.

Uncle's office is the coolest room in our house. The blinds are always closed in there. The office has shelves and folders and a desk with only his computer on it. On TV, I've heard that other children play games on computers, but the one Uncle has is different. It's for work and I'm not allowed to touch it.

I wipe the dust off the shelves and desk first before I get on with the hoovering. The hoover is heavy to drag around, and the noise hurts my head, but it doesn't take long. When I'm done I stand on the other side of Uncle's desk, next to his swivel chair. I push the button on the hoover and it turns off, the house going quiet. I should put everything back in its place and return the hoover and cloth to the cupboard, but I've never seen Uncle's desk from this angle before. There are so many drawers, the slim one at the top and then three drawers on either side of where you should put your legs. The shelves are filled with folders and books, too, but not the kind of books you read for fun. I can tell just by looking at them.

What does Uncle keep in all his drawers? I guess that his gun is in one of them, because he doesn't have it on him most of the time. But that's only one drawer, and he's got seven.

From the porch comes voices. Head has returned from wherever she's been all day. I can't imagine Uncle has apologized to her like she asked him last time, because Uncle doesn't apologize. Head must have decided to forget about it, which is what Mother should have done.

"I'm not doing anything bad," I whisper to myself as I open the top left drawer to peek inside. "Uncle won't be angry because I'm not doing anything bad and I'd never-never-never take the gun."

The drawer is empty. So is the next one, and the bottom one, and the slim one at the top won't budge. Locked. It must be where the gun is, so I ignore it and move over to the drawers on the right instead. Empty. Empty. The final drawer looks empty at first, too, but then I notice something catching the light in there. Hair. Long strands of hair, blond and brown and black, tied together with ribbons in bright colors. One of them is braided, a thin colorless braid curled like a snake on a bed of human hair.

I close the drawer. It doesn't make a sound. The voices from the porch guide me out of the office, back into the real world. I put the hoover away. The Roaring Monster. I think of Mother in the tub and Uncle's strong hand on my neck. *She made it happen herself.* Uncle smelled of peaches and Mother of rot. *She didn't want to be with us so we had to let her go.*

"Where's the kid?" Head asks from the porch. "He doesn't go off on his own, does he?"

"He's cleaning," Uncle says, Uncle with his smiley voice and a drawer full of girl hair. Mother hair. "Should be done by now. Hey," he calls, and I know he's turned his head toward the doorway. "You finished yet?"

I step out on the porch. The sunlight blinds me, and I put my hand over my eyes. Uncle is like a river in his chair, all fluid and calm, long limbs dropping to the floor like water. He's removed his shades as if the sun can't get to him, as if nothing can get to him. Head holds her thermos to her chapped lips as she watches me. Her jeans are baggy on her. Everything she wears is coated with dust, as if she spends her days somewhere where the sand whirls up around her and the desert clings to her skin.

"Uncle," I say. He frowns, so I quickly add, "I'm done now."

"Good." Uncle doesn't ask any questions. He doesn't suspect anything. "You should sort out Eleanor's room tomorrow."

Head gives me a smile, or something like it. "Oh, you don't have to do that." Looking back to Uncle she says, "He's too young to work. You know as well as I do that he should be in school." Her voice is bitey. I'm surprised she dares to talk to Uncle this way. School—Mother used to talk about school. I would like to go there, because all the children on TV do, but Uncle says that if I went to school, bad people would take me and I could never see him again.

"He's being homeschooled." Uncle slurps up the last of his iced tea without looking at either of us. "End of goddamn story. You mind your own business, Eleanor, all right? We're living a good life here. He helps out and I teach him everything he needs to know." His voice is cool even when he's angry. I can sense his anger, I can see it in the way his jaw is set, but I can't hear it. "To be honest," he continues, "I'm surprised you're telling me how to raise a kid...you of all people. Bet Charlie would've had some complaints about you, if you'd let him live long enough."

Head jumps out of her chair and drops the thermos to the floor. There's nothing running out of it, no liquid, just the clang of metal crashing into the floorboards. "Don't you dare." Her face is drained of color. "You promised you'd never judge. You promised!"

Uncle shrugs. "Be nice to me, Eleanor, and I'll be nice to you. I'll let you stay for free while you're chasing your ghosts, and I won't ask for a thing in return. But cross me, and things can get pretty fucking unpleasant for you."

I watch them like I watch the news, eyes wide open. This is much better than spying from inside the counter. I hear and see everything.

"Yes," Head says, sinking back into her chair. Her arms fall to her sides. "I know that. It's why I'm here, isn't it? The real world has spit me out and I have to stay among…my kin." She starts fidgeting with the scarf around her head, rewrapping it, tucking her hair in. Her fingers look ashen, as if they were made out of clay. "Bill used to say that if I ever got into trouble, I should go see you. Well, he wasn't wrong, I guess." She stares into her lap.

"Good old Bill!" Uncle winks at me. "He sure wasn't wrong. I said you could stay here, and I don't go back on my word. I'm not a liar."

"All those girls," Head murmurs. "It's different. It's not like the things Bill did, and not like…like what I did."

I think about the drawer. The hair. I'd like to cover my ears now. I'd like to go inside the counter and be invisible.

"You did something unforgivable, Eleanor. Poor Bill. Poor Charlie."

Head sniffles. Tears and snot drip from her face.

"No one out there wants anything to do with us," Uncle continues. "We're cursed. Or blessed, rather, because we have our freedom." He claps his hands together and starts singing some song I don't recognize, which has no other lyrics in it but the word *freedom*. Uncle has a good voice, but I don't want him to sing now.

"You could stop." Head looks at him. Her eyes are raw, everything about her is raw as if her skull and bones are shining through her skin. "Stop what you're doing and I...I won't tell anyone. Ever."

Uncle puts his hands over his knees. His fingertips are tapping, drumming madly under the table. "Eleanor," he says. "That's the one thing I told you never to ask of me, and now you have. What a shame."

Head's sunken cheeks are wet. When she opens her mouth, snot runs from her nose and down between her lips, and I want Uncle to stop it. "No," she says. "You don't mean that. Please, you know I have to be close to—I have to be where Charlie—"

"You'll be leaving in the morning," Uncle says. "That's final." He stands and she does the same, shaking just like Mother did before she went into the tub.

"But I—" Head used to be interesting but now she bores me. "But I—"

Uncle takes his empty glass and hands it to me. It's damp and sticky and almost slips out of my grip. "But I," he mimics in a silly voice. "But I, but I, but I."

Head skulks away from the porch like a wild animal, a raccoon or stray dog. She presses her bag to her flat chest as if it was a child. As soon as she's entered Room 12 and closed the door, Uncle looks down at me. He smiles.

"Eleanor is old and sick," he says. "I really don't think she should be driving around anymore. It could be dangerous."

Uncle should know, because Uncle is good with cars. He can fix cars and he can break them, and then the girls can't get away from him.

"How old was Charlie?" I ask, thinking that there was another boy living in the desert, and he could have been my friend.

"Oh, I don't know. About your age." Uncle puts his shades back on. "Would have been all grown-up by now, though, if she hadn't done what she did."

I nod. Maybe Charlie is a ghost now, and he can be my friend anyway. Maybe next time I pretend there is a telephone call, Charlie will answer.

"All right, we should get to work." Uncle walks past me, through the hallway and into his office. When he comes back he's got the gun swaying in his hand. I think about Head's gray hair and wonder if he'll bother to put it in the drawer.

She'll cry, I think as we leave the porch. The sun shines in Uncle's hair and makes my cheeks burn. *She'll cry and beg just like Mother did.*

But Uncle knows how to stop the crying. And then it will be just me and him on the porch, and our mouths will taste like peaches.

Snow White

The hallway seems larger with the mirror in place. I can hardly recall this room from the past—it was just a darkness, the space in between. There was outside and the kitchen and the stairs leading upwards, stairs leading to the basement, but in the hallway, there was nothing but the cold, seeping into your toes. Large mud-colored roses overflowed the wallpaper then, but I'm unsure if they are still there. It might be that they don't annoy me anymore.

The floorboards were chipped and worn down when I grew up. There were a pair of blue socks I loved as a child, and the floor tore the soles to shreds, one bursting thread at a time. One day they were gone, but specks of blue peered up at me from the garbage can. There is carpet from wall to wall now. It was a simple procedure that didn't cost much. All I had to do was move my shoes into the kitchen until the work was finished. I don't know why my parents never thought of it. I don't think that they realized how easily such things can be managed.

I'm not pointing fingers, though. You mustn't think that I do. I give the matter a lot of thought these days. I love them very much.

The mirror was in Mother's room originally. That was where she put her makeup on, her creamy lipstick and mascara. Perfumed herself with the heavy scent of roses. Mother does not need the mirror anymore. I have allowed all of her other things to remain—the embroidered duvet, the faux silver hairbrush. I have no use for them. When I took the mirror down from the wall, I noticed the dark red square of wallpaper underneath. The one single spot of order in a room that had been damaged by sun. I realized then that the home care women had ignored my mother's wishes and let the sun in as soon as they arrived each morning, and she was too frail to get out of bed and close the curtains once they had left. The curtains were heavy, velveteen; they made it dark, shut the world out. That was how she wanted it.

It's the street—that's what she used to say. *I can't stand it.* She was talking about the empty houses. People died on our street. Not while we lived there, but before, and the once-pretty bungalows and terrace houses lined the road like broken shells. I don't think my parents noticed it at first. The desolation. Our house is a good one—two stories high, with a large basement and an attic. We even have a porch. But no matter in which direction you look, there are untamed gardens and weeds that have wormed their way through cracks and blocked doors. Our dead neighbors' windows are black eyes staring into nothing, and a few tiles slide off the roof of the house next door every time there's stormy weather. Many of the houses have been demolished, of course, leaving only foundations behind bushy hawthorn hedges. Every time I go grocery shopping I have to walk past them—the remnants, the reminders. The asphalt is rough and the pavement is lined with the very same bricks I used to pretend I was tightrope-walking on when I was a child. A deserted land, and I am the only one here.

Of course, there's Father, too—but he hardly ever leaves the house anymore. I think it is for the best, because he gets upset very easily and the chair is heavy. They tell me that there is help available; they've given me many telephone numbers to call. I have put the note on the refrigerator door, like you do. Father doesn't like strangers. He believes that he can hear cars rolling by, and that they all belong to the municipality or to this or that demolition company. I allow him to indulge in his delusions because it is easiest that way.

Before, when he worked at the factory and read five books a week, he regularly sent letters to the editor. They were, mostly, aimed at a single civil servant at the planning office. It happened, occasionally, that the local paper published them. Father was against the downfall of our neighborhood and said it was a scandal to let an entire area go to waste when there were homeless people in the world. I never understood it and I didn't care much. I knew there was something that had made people die, or leave, or both. But I would not have been a popular girl even if I lived somewhere else, and I enjoyed being alone. Mother did not like Father's writing much, but she tolerated it. Once, a house across the street was demolished in the middle of the night and Father rushed out to give the men working there a piece of his mind. When he came back inside, he said that he wouldn't be surprised if we woke up to them destroying *our* house next. He's still saying that, several times a day. Now, there is terror and suspicion in his eyes. Father has become too old for reading, and he believes that the authorities will tear the house down while he's sleeping. He has made it his truth.

Father—dear Father. They are strange, all the little changes. There's a fragility to him now, a childishness or *regression*, as they have told me that it's called. The final stage. I can hear him now, the thin slivers of his voice from the living room. The name. And fear is in it already, his endless grasping for me though I've only left the room for a couple of minutes. The jar is on the sideboard so I take it, watching the smooth movement of my hand in the mirror. He hasn't eaten anything else for years.

Darling Father. Tomorrow I'll take him to go look at the rabbits. He will like very much to feed them.

***

Snow White and I had known each other for two months, a week, and four days when she died. It was during that time, that one summer, that the Mansion was inhabited. I was going to have company on my way to school when autumn came— that was what my parents said, as though it was all that mattered. I didn't spare a thought for school then, or the girls there, and I didn't like being reminded. School-thoughts were irrelevant in June.

Mother noticed the moving van first. Dread ran along her face; she whitened. Mother never did like changes. She had learned not to expect anything good from our street. Father was still consumed by the newspaper, invisible behind it. It was an everyday morning, and I ate my toast and did not think of school at all.

"My God," said Mother, and it was all that needed saying. After that, we sat there, silent, watching the Mansion as lamps, cushions, and beds flowed into its innards. It was located right on the other side of the hedge—the Mansion, as we always called it. I never mentioned the name to Snow White. All of the other houses were small, as insignificant as our own, with flowerbeds and flagstones and straight lines. The Mansion was different. It had a tower—an oblong, protruding stretch of wood and glass—that ended in a spire. I don't think they ever had the chance to start renovating up there—perhaps the decay had gone too far. The entire house was large, bold, with gingerbread work ornamenting the porch and shutters covering every window. It had a huge garden and gooseberry bushes and even a larch, which hung low over the pavement outside and littered the asphalt with cones. I never liked the street, but I loved the Mansion. The other houses were ugly, and I couldn't care less if the authorities wished to get rid of them. But the Mansion—the Mansion was the one beautiful thing we had.

Snow White and her family moved in on a Monday. We became friends on Tuesday. Mother made me go over to them with a sponge cake, and I was angry and afraid. There was no reason for me to go talk to them. I can't remember now, but I suppose there was the promise of money and that I let myself get bribed. Snow White was the one who opened the door, after I had rung the bell, standing there with the cake. Snow White with her blood-red lips, her hair.

"You must be the neighbor. Come in."

That was what it was like—neither of us bothered with introductions out there on the porch. She closed the door and darkness fell over us, since they hadn't had time to put up the lamps. Snow White said we could go to the kitchen and took me there, with her skirt brushing against her thighs. She still hadn't told me her name.

I got to meet her parents after that, and the little brothers. They sat there on the couch and there were boxes everywhere, and the mother looked at me like a nervous little girl when she asked questions about me and my parents. None of us mentioned the fact that we were surrounded by deserted houses. The twins were beautiful—curly-haired angels. Snow White sat next to me, and when everyone had had a piece of sponge cake, she turned to me. Her eyes were blue and very big.

"Come, Anna. I'll show you my room."

It was after that that I told her that my name, my real name, was Anna Lynn. Anna was for school, for Mother and Father. I had never liked it. It was gray autumn skies, it was mist and rain. They called for Anna and in my head I added *Lynn*, Lynn which was a name for pretty girls with dimples and long hair. I can't recall when I first made it up, but I was Anna Lynn—not Anna.

"Pretty," said Snow White. I already knew that was what I should call her—she had whispered it to me while we were cutting the cake in the kitchen. "That's a pretty name you have, Anna Lynn." I enjoyed hearing her say it in her low, soft voice. And I told her hers was prettier, and she laughed.

I showed her foundations and ruins. Trees with twisted branches, forgotten toolsheds where the wood had gone sick with mold. Snow White whirled through weeds and brushwood and made me follow; she took my hand and pulled me with her into the spiderwebbed hollows of the playhouses. Sat there in front of me with her naked legs swinging, as she chewed on a straw of grass. I tried it too but had to spit mine out immediately; I couldn't stand the foul taste. Snow White laughed. The bow in her hair was just as red as her lips, and it shone against her black curls. I had never, even as a child, been bold enough to wear bows.

She asked me to take her to the cemetery. It's not far away, and as desolate as the street. I showed it to her, just as I showed everything, even though I had hardly visited it myself before that. It was the atmosphere, she said, the people, their stories hiding in names and dates. She loved all such things, and she loved our cemetery. The very first time there, we just walked among the graves, read the names out loud and climbed up on the stone wall: she did, and I watched. She held her long arms outstretched like birdwings. And she was the one who discovered the rabbits.

"Look at that!" She jumped down from the wall and pointed. Placed her hand on my shoulder. "That's the strangest thing I ever saw."

We tiptoed closer without making a sound. The animals saw us, but they didn't move—ten or so rabbits, a few grown ones but most of them babies. There was a large tomb slab right there, and Snow White started to giggle when we realized where the rabbits had made themselves a burrow.

"Oh my God," she said, hand covering her mouth. I was reminded of Mother. "They're too cute to live like that, Anna Lynn. Don't you think it's ghastly?"

Ghastly was one of her favorite words. *Macabre* was another. She threw them around like confetti, the words and songs and poems she had claimed. Just a week after her arrival, she had already named almost every single house on the street and inhabited some of them with imaginary ghosts. She stated that the house across from ours was haunted by an entire family, the youngest child barely three years old. I don't know where she got such things from.

We came close enough to frighten the rabbits away and saw them escape into their hole, barely visible under the slab. Down, down to the dead. I was still watching the hole where they had vanished, but Snow White had turned her eyes to the grave instead and started reading out loud. Names, strange and distant. Unknown people who had died a hundred years ago. I was more interested in rabbits.

"*Beloved Daughter*," Snow White read. "Oh, the poor girl, they couldn't even be bothered to write her name. What do you think it was that killed her?"

Beloved Daughter. I knew that a story was forming in her head. We sat down in the grass and she kept talking about the dead girl, said that she had been lonely, she just knew it, and had probably died horribly at a very young age.

"She might have been my soul mate," she said. "But I was born a hundred years too late."

We had known each other for two weeks then. I wished that she would talk about something else.

It became her favorite ghost. A ghost made out of nothing, because the nameless girl was just bones and dust deep in the ground, but Snow White's mind made her come to life again. She wanted us to sit there, in the warm grass by the grave, where we could talk, watch the rabbits, and leave flowers. She said she felt safe there. I sat next to her, felt her bare calves brush against mine every time she moved. I did not speak much, but I listened.

Snow White visited us rarely. She didn't fit in our kitchen, with its ceiling stains and heaps of dead flies on the sill. Mother couldn't handle the cleaning, she said; she was too exhausted from work. As soon as she came home, she put her bathrobe on, painted her nails. Rubbed her back and shoulders to ease the pain. Snow White's mother didn't need hair curlers, and she wore high heels every time I came to the Mansion. I don't know if Mother ever met her.

We hid away in Snow White's room. She had lace curtains and a floral duvet cover, a white chest of drawers, earrings and bracelets. A skull figurine with gleaming eyes on top of the bedside table. If you stood by the window and looked out, the larch's soft shadow fell over the nothingness and made it beautiful. The view from my room was weeds and broken toys.

"They're always fighting." She was talking about her brothers. She opened her tube of lipstick, made her lips pouty in front of the mirror. "When you're not here."

The twins were playing quietly whenever I saw them. I can't remember if I ever heard them talk.

"Mirror, mirror on the wall…" She smeared her lips with red, then laughed. I sat on her bed, clawing at the duvet flowers.

"Who's the fairest of them all," I said. I know that she did not hear me.

***

Nature takes over. That's something that Father used to say. In the gardens we passed, roots ran like snakes through the grass, and lupines, lilacs, and berry bushes had grown grotesque. The moss had turned to velvet over forgotten flagstones and we lay there often, watching the clouds. Talking.

"Why do you think they moved away from here?" Snow White said. "All of them, just like that."

"They died. That's obvious, isn't it?"

She turned her head to look at me. I wondered if the moss felt tickly against her cheek.

"Don't say things like that." A wrinkle appeared between her eyebrows, like a thread tying them together.

It was hot and sunny, and her hair was black and mine wasn't. But when I looked at her I noticed a streak right where her hair parted, the color identical to her mother's light brown curls.

"I was joking."

She sat up, smoothing the creases in her dress with both hands. "I know."

Snow White. Her hair was back to black again the next day—but I would always know.

***

Warm weather, heat. Other girls rode their bikes to the beach, but we went to our cemetery. She had her arms full of peonies and lilies from the flowerbeds of the dead, and I had nothing. We sat by the grave, and Snow White's imagination ran wilder and stronger than ever. I thought that it was stupid, but I could never have told her so.

"It's really sweet," she said. "The rabbits, I mean. Don't you think it's romantic, that they chose this grave over all the others?"

I didn't think so. "Just imagine all the human meat they feed on," I said. "All their tunnels under the cemetery, where there's chewed-off fingers lying around."

Snow White stared at me. "Stop that." She seemed angry. "Rabbits are herbivores, in case you didn't know."

Not these ones, I wanted to say—but there was no use teasing her.

She had put up star stickers in the ceiling of her room. They lit up at night like a tiny starry sky that was just hers. I told her that it was impossible, but Snow White said that the stickers could glow in the dark. I never saw them—in daylight, they were invisible against the white ceiling. There was nothing special about them.

"You can borrow this one, if you want." She held up one of her dresses. One I had seen her wear.

"I don't need it." I had clothes of my own. And maybe she was relieved by my answer, because she put the dress back on its hanger. There was a knock on the door—the mother with her loud heels. Snow White went out to her in the corridor. She pushed the door shut, but there was a gap.

"You know we don't mind that you have Anna over, dear, but you need to learn to clean up after yourself in the kitchen. Not even the boys…"

The bed was soft underneath me. Even if I had stretched out on it, I wouldn't have been able to see her stars.

"I'll do it later! Could you stop bothering us?"

I didn't have to watch her to know that she had that usual, angry wrinkle between her eyebrows.

"Sarah!"

The conversation went on, and when Snow White came back in she was annoyed and told me that I'd better go. At home, in my own room, I smiled. She had never told me her real name.

There was nothing special about her. *Sarah.* And I never saw her stars.

***

Two months, a week, and four days. They had an unlocked toolshed, the family in the Mansion. There was little more than the lawnmower in there. The garden was large and grass grows fast in summer—unnaturally fast, Mother always said. I had been in the toolshed with Snow White. I had seen the gas cans. They hardly had time to tend to their lawn anyway, and the cans were just standing there. Waiting.

It was after that that they sent me away. Anna. Anna Lynn. They sent me away.

The shovel was for the flowers. She had talked about it forever, she never stopped, and I had to say that rosebushes were pretty and that pink roses would look nice against the slab. We had a bucket with us to keep the plant in. I think it came from our garden, that bucket, not that it matters now.

"It'll be wonderful," she said, "so wonderful."

If I had protested, she would have refused to listen. The grass was soft against my ankles, the soil black and a little wet. Most of the rabbits vanished as soon as we came, but there were a few tiny ones that peered at us with velvet eyes. Snow White dug a hole in front of the slab. It was hot, and a sweat stain appeared under her armpit. She wore the same dress that she had once told me I could borrow.

She cooed at the rabbits, giving them a little wave. "I'd love to take one home and keep it as a pet."

I had not mentioned chewed-off fingers again since that time when I made her angry. I suppose she had forgotten about it.

"It's so heavy. Take over for a while, will you?" She handed me the shovel. Sank down in the grass, her face turned away. Skin white as snow, hair black as ebony.

It was the next morning that they sent me away. They came in a car between the rows of houses—three strangers. Mother and Father stayed in the kitchen the entire time.

Lips, red as blood.

At the institution, they asked me why I wanted to see the Mansion burn. I always told them the same thing: I didn't. The Mansion was the one beautiful thing we had.

And the Mansion was taken from us.

Snow White's family moved away after that night. They made it out in time, the mother and the father and the curly-haired brothers. Nothing remained of the bedrooms afterwards. *She died in her sleep*, they said. *Why didn't you realize that someone would get hurt?* They searched for darkness in my eyes. *She was your friend*, they said. They didn't know anything about the shovel, the tomb slab, or the deep hole in the ground. They didn't know anything about the rabbits.

***

Father smiles when I enter the room. It's the usual, distant smile—the one that might as well be directed at Mother, Grandmother, or the white-dressed nurses in the care home where he'll end up soon. Me, I got sent away. It's a long time ago. He doesn't remember it anymore.

"I'm waiting," he says. I'm not fond of the tone in his voice. I open the jar and hand it to him. I watch as the trembling hand breaks through the moldy layer on top. He's such a pig when he's eating. Sticky red stains cover his chin, the front of his shirt.

"Jam is the best, isn't it?" Half-chewed berries fall from his mouth as he speaks. "Anna mustn't forget to buy more."

I don't want him to say that name, and I have tried to teach him to stop. But Father is so old now.

"She won't," I say and drape the blanket over his scrawny legs. *Anna*. Sweet, sweet Father, who hasn't got any memories left. I care so much for him.

They always said that I behaved well. One of the women was in charge of my money and she bought the color for me, rubbed it into my scalp. They said that I looked good wearing lipstick.

They said that I was kind-hearted when I went home to look after Father.

"Who's the fairest of them all," I murmur. Father watches me. His eyes are as round as an animal's, and there's jam all over his face.

"Snow White," he says in a monotonous voice. I wonder if he's returned to some childhood memory, a bedtime story from a forgotten time. Slowly, I brush my hair, as black as ebony, back behind my ear, and press my lips to his smudgy cheek.

"Good boy."

He's still staring at me when I leave, clutching the jar in his hands. Yes, I care so much for him now, when his brain has gone red and sticky and no roaring flames can get in. I care so much for him. From the kitchen window, I see untamed hawthorn hedges and overgrown house foundations, one of them taller than the rest.

I am alone, fairest of them all. I am Snow White.

Honey, Silk, Gold

At night, he is back in those tender first months with her. His daughter, his only daughter when she was still tiny enough to fit in his hand. They called her angel and princess and any endearment they could think of that meant love. He turned old nursery rhymes into lullabies and as he sang them to her she fell asleep, slipping into her baby-dreams. *Oh honey-child, golden-hair, I'll do anything for you. I'll give you the stars and the moon and the entire galaxy. I'll hand you the sun on a silver platter and watch as it squirms and struggles, trying in vain to match your beauty.* He would hold the sleeping infant in his arms and wait for each sighing breath she made. He would stand over her crib and watch the rise and fall of her baby blanket and the frail chest underneath. When the servants started perishing, he barely noticed. When his wife died, he was sad. But most of all, he took precautions, letting no one into the nursery but himself.

They had baptized her. He loathed the name because it was nothing like her, nowhere near her honey and gold. His wife was from the South, though, and both she and her mother believed in old folk magic and superstition. *You curse a beautiful child by giving it a beautiful name*, his mother-in-law told him over the phone, her voice coughy and weak. His wife was already ill by then—his wife who had a name that was much too pretty for her but who had never been much to look at. The child got her looks from his side of the family, his still-blond mother (alive) and doe-eyed sisters (dead). His wife was buried on Honey's second birthday, a mass burial, no plaque or stone. A month later, his scientists discovered the cure.

***

The vaccination campaign starts one year and a day after his wife's death. He sits in front of the TV and watches people crying on the news, masks covering their mouths and noses. *It's too late for my kids*, they say. *It's too late for my wife husband parents brothers sisters friends*. His daughter sits on the floor in front of him, playing, oblivious to the ugly world outside. Her hair falls down her back, golden, shiny, a pink ribbon holding it in place.

"Don't do that!" she yaps in her doll-voice, struggling with the consonants but doing so well, being so advanced for her age. Her dolls are strewn around her, a leg here, a grinning head there. "You should be quiet. I decide who gets to talk, and you should be quiet."

He turns aching eyes back to the screen. A young reporter rolls up his sleeve and gets a shot from a headless nurse while he looks into the camera with his mouth opening and closing.

"There are plenty of rumors circulating at this time. Most of them are likely untrue, but there could—"

No, there couldn't. He mutes the TV. *I decide who gets to talk.*

Honey grabs a half-naked doll with her chubby hand and shakes it.

"You're being naughty! You're going away and not coming back, like Mama." She throws the doll away with all her force. It lands with a thud in the other room.

"Darling," he says, his heart thumping out of sync for an instant. "Mama lives in Heaven now, remember? She's not gone."

The girl doesn't turn around. On the screen, a doctor is interviewed in a crowded hospital ward. At the back of the room, a woman lies motionless on a bed. Her arm has fallen to the floor at an unnatural angle.

Honey murmurs something. He strains his ears but can't hear what she's saying.

"There may be a cure now," the doctor on the screen says. He is wrinkled and gray, and his left eye twitches. "But for those already affected, it won't make any difference. This epidemic has had a large impact on our society, and it will continue to do so for months, maybe years to come." He jerks his head to the side at the sound of a strangled wail, then hurries off-camera. The frame goes black before a news presenter appears, someone who doesn't explain why the interview from the hospital was cut off. Did someone die? Was that guttural, ugly sound someone's final cry of pain, or anguish, or relief?

He tries to remember his wife's final days, but he fails. Was she sent to hospital, or did she stay at home until the end? It troubles him that he can't remember. But a look at Honey, brushing a doll's long hair with a pink plastic brush, unties that particular worry. Of course his wife was in hospital. He would never have allowed all that misery and pain anywhere near his child. And his wife would have received proper care, she would have had all the painkillers she asked for.

That wail he just heard on TV was an anomaly, a mishap. Death is nothing like that. Death is like sleep, and it's not his fault that the vaccine wasn't ready earlier. Nothing is his fault.

"Don't worry about Mama," he tells Honey, though she seems too absorbed in her playing to hear. "Don't worry about anything." The image of that crowded, chaotic hospital ward fills him and he pushes it away. The world out there is ugly. His daughter's world, however, is beautiful. He will make sure that it is always beautiful.

"Boring," Honey says suddenly, sticking her tongue out at the TV. "It's boring, Daddy."

He snaps out of his thoughts, staring at the news presenter in his dark suit, handsome face blank as he talks about death, death, death.

"Oh, I'm sorry!" He gets to his feet, grabbing the remote and turning the TV off. "You're right, darling. It's very boring."

Honey looks up at him with her round, hazel eyes. She keeps brushing, mechanically, untangling the white-blond doll hair. "That lady was asleep," she says. "But I don't think she'll wake up again."

That woman at the back of the hospital ward. He hadn't realized his little girl had watched. Understood.

"She doesn't matter." He walks up to her and pets her head. When he smiles she does the same, like a reflection in a tiny mirror. "None of the people on TV matter. No one outside this house matters. What's important is you, darling. Your happiness. And Daddy will always give you what you want."

Her smile widens, and she shows all her pretty little teeth. Impossibly small, just like her nails. When she was a newborn, he couldn't stop putting his big hand next to hers just to compare. Make it even clearer how flawless she was, how wonderful.

"I want a lot of things, Daddy."

"Yes, I know." He scoops her up and holds her, only because it won't be long until she's too old for hugs and caresses. She fits perfectly in his arms, as if she was always meant to be there. "And I will give you whatever you ask for."

***

Three years later, people have stopped getting the disease. It's a distant threat now, one that has moved on to other continents and disappeared from the news. No more mass-burials, no mask-wearing people on the streets. Hospitals are back on their feet, schools have reopened.

Honey is old enough, but he's put the school letters away in a drawer and the school thoughts at the back of his mind. It's too soon. Whenever he pictures his daughter among other children, they're all loud, big-boned boys with meaty fingers and cruel eyes. They'd take one look at her headband and clean white stockings, and they'd crush her to dust. The images are so vivid that his breath hitches. His daughter is too precious, too special. He won't allow the world outside, the ugly, hopeless world, to contaminate her.

He rarely leaves the house these days. Business goes well, the vaccine is still being distributed worldwide—he can afford the very best managers and assistants, scientists, PR people. Only rarely is his presence required at the office downtown. Most days he spends in his study at home, laptop balanced on his knee, this or that online meeting going on in front of him. The study is his favorite room in the house—all dark, polished wooden surfaces and crimson velvet armchairs. The windows are tall, letting in glum light and offering a view of the autumnal oaks in front of the house, stripped of leaves. Sometimes, when he stands at the window looking out, someone walks down the sleepy street on the other side of the hedge. It doesn't happen often. Their street is far from the city center, and most of their neighbors were old and died quickly after the flu started spreading. Every time he spots someone passing by, he's torn between curiosity and contempt. Who is it? How dare they come so close, and what if Honey notices them?

So far, she never has. Honey spends her days on the ground floor, happily playing with all the toys he's ordered for her from the most expensive department stores. When she spends time in the garden, she stays at the back of the house, and he's always right there with her. No one will put their hands on her. No one will even see her.

When he comes downstairs in the afternoon, once a long meeting has finally ended, he hears her singing to herself. Her squeaky, childish voice trails through the rooms, and he swallows hard to keep from crying. Without recognizing the melody or any of the words, he walks through the hall, the kitchen, the dining room, and the parlor. Her song leads the way as if it were a twinkling star in the sky.

"Darling?" he calls. "Where are you?"

"A ghost," Honey sings. She's much closer now, her words as clear as glass. "My mama is a ghost…I want to see what Mama looks like now." She giggles before repeating the words. He hurries, entering her play room and finding her cross-legged on the floor, hands folded neatly in her lap. She's not playing, just singing those eerie lyrics with a sweet, innocent look on her face. Her round cheeks are glowing pink, the same shade as her dress. When he barges in she stops singing, blinking up at him.

"Hello, Daddy. I made a song."

He nods, trying to shrug off his unease. This is what children do. She's testing out words; she's still processing her mother's death. He mustn't let her know how it affects him. "So I heard, sweetheart. What an amazing songwriter you are."

Her face lights up with a grin. She's lost a few milk teeth recently but her smile is pretty, so pretty. "I know, Daddy! Mama likes it, too."

"Mama?" His voice wavers, and he resists the instinct to spin around and check that the doorway behind him is empty. "Oh, of course..." *Kids. Nothing to worry about.* "You're a very good girl to make a song about her."

Honey nods one time, two, three. "Yes, I am." She grins again with those missing teeth. "I'll make one about you too, Daddy. When you die."

***

The meetings blend into one long, eternal wake of flickering blue light and naked branches tapping the window. Downstairs Honey plays by herself in the empty rooms filled with cushions, curtains, and furniture that her dead mother once picked out. He comes down in the evenings to find her in front of the TV, sullen and sweet, dolls and teddy bears and tiny plastic shoes and handbags littering the floors. One night, her favorite soft toy, a pink and purple bunny with bead-like eyes, lies at her little feet with all the stuffing torn out of him, leaving only a hollow, sagging carcass.

"Daddy," she says without taking her eyes off the cartoon she's watching. "I don't have any toys."

The bunny's floppy ears look obscenely big when there's barely a body attached to them. "Darling, what happened?" He remembers buying the bunny for her second birthday. She hugged it to her chest the moment she got the gift box open. "Don't you like Bunny anymore?"

Honey gives him a sharp look and huffs, the way she used to when she was throwing tantrums thirty times a day. There's no tantrum now, though, but her glowering look makes it all too clear that there might be one if he's not careful. "Daddy, don't talk about Bunny! Don't! I said I don't have any toys, and I'm bored. You're never here to play with me, and neither is Mama. I have no one."

Every word pricks his heart like a needle. *I have no one.* He's a useless father, just as he's always suspected. She didn't want to hurt her bunny but he let her down and made her angry. He's allowed his work to eat at him, eat at his hours and days. He's allowed the world outside to come between him and the one he loves. "No, darling..." He's faint when he kneels in front of her, patting awkwardly at her arm. She's in one of her countless princess dresses, the fabric stiff and sparkly against his fingers. "You have me, always. I'm sorry I've been preoccupied, I should have thought more about you."

"Yeah, Daddy." She keeps her eyes on the singing ponies on TV. "You should think about others and not just about yourself."

He nods in defeat. She sits in front of him in the corner of the sofa like a queen—there's even a lopsided crown on her head.

"I want other toys," she states. "I want you to give me something I don't have."

He goes through the inventory of her play room in his head. He thinks back to all the orders he's made, all the shipments of doll houses and fancy costumes that have arrived. Boxes stacked on top of each other, shelves and drawers filled to the brim. She's got it all. He's made sure she can't ask for anything more, but now she has.

"But darling, you have everything." His mouth is dry. There's a stale taste on his tongue, and he thinks that his breath must reek of coffee and all those empty nights in front of the computer. "I can't...I can't think of anything that I haven't given you already."

Honey twists her head and looks at him. He knows immediately—here comes the tantrum. She cries, she screams, she kicks her feet into his chest. He stays crouched in front of her, takes it. Allows her to tear at his hair and target his heart with her Dorothy shoes.

"I hate you, Daddy! I hate you, I hate you, I hate you!"

Tears stream down his face. His eyes sting when he looks at her. After a hundred *I hate yous* he caves—he can't take it anymore. "We'll go to the department store," he says, his voice thick and strained. "We'll go to the department store tomorrow and you can pick anything you want." *Don't hate me, honey-child, silk-hair. Anything but that.*

She stops her screaming. Her body goes still. "The department store? What's that, Daddy?"

"It's a very large shop down in the city." He sniffles. Is it over? "They have all the toys you can dream of."

Honey's eyes turn wide and shiny. Her face is light now, angelic, sweet. "We'll go to the city, Daddy? Do you promise?"

Something cold claws at his insides. He's tried to keep the world away from her. Now it has tricked him into handing her over.

"Yes," he says, focusing on her missing-teeth smile. Just this once. One trip only, and she'll keep loving him. "Yes, darling. Of course. I promise."

***

The cab pulls in outside the gate early the next day. Maybe if they go there in the morning, the department store won't be full of people. The less contact she has with the world, the better.

The cab driver is young, skinny, all stretched-out limbs and baggy uniform. He frowns when he spots Honey in her mask and white gloves, but he doesn't bother to ask. In the car's backseat, she turns her little face here and there, taking everything in: the leather seat, the belt strapped across her chest, the radio playing at a low volume.

"Daddy," she whispers as the car starts moving. "Is it supposed to sound like this?"

He smiles reassuringly at her. He's happy, despite everything. Seeing her this excited warms him, calms him down. They'll go into the department store while the cab waits outside. She'll get to browse, pick whatever she wants, and once she's fed up, they'll return home. Simple. The mask and gloves are unnecessary, he should know that more than anyone, but better safe than sorry. His little girl is so delicate, such a fragile child. He will do everything in his power to protect her.

She keeps her head turned away from him, eyes drinking in the sights of the world outside. The graying fronts of abandoned buildings, overgrown gardens, pavements strewn with litter. People here and there, walking by themselves, feet shuffling slowly. Too few people for the wide streets and the skyscrapers pointing at the sky. The cab driver is quiet, the radio is quiet, and Honey's gloved hands are still in her lap. *Once upon a time*, he could tell her, *there were millions living in this city. Your mother was one of them.*

The entrance to the department store is a frame of glass and gold, inviting them in. Honey walks stiffly by his side, the clicking of her Mary Janes muffled by the red plush carpet. Sunlight follows in their tracks, turns the dark wool of his coat unbearably hot. He discreetly opens up his scarf a little but removes nothing, not even his leather gloves. He has to be a good example to his daughter, even though his back is damp with sweat.

He hasn't visited the store for years. When his wife first found out that she was pregnant, they came here together, giggly like teenagers as they chose the nursery wallpaper, the sky-blue baby blanket, the teddy bear that would be her first toy. Back then, the aisles and sections were crowded with toddlers and school kids and parents pushing strollers. Now, the store looks abandoned, much like the estates they passed on their way here. Everything is neat and shiny, the floors scrubbed clean, the dolls and plushies staring out of plastic packaging. But there are only a couple of customers in, aimlessly browsing the shelves. They are all adults.

"Daddy—" Honey begins, her voice small, but then a plump woman in a yellow blouse swoops in and flashes a too-bright grin at them. She wears a name tag with the store logo on it.

"Oh, hello!" Her voice is too loud, her eyes too eager, and Honey takes a step away from her. "What did you have in mind today, dear? Is it your birthday?"

He clears his throat, and the woman looks from Honey to him without losing the manic smile.

"Very welcome, sir. How lovely that you've decided to shop at—"

"We'd like to browse," he says, struggling to keep his voice free from venom. "Undisturbed."

"Of course." She steps aside, clutching at her name tag. Her nails are painted white as bone. "Don't hesitate to ask if you need anything."

He puts his hand on Honey's back to bring her with him into the store. She peers up at him and it's unnerving, as if she can see too much about him here in the outside world.

"Daddy, who was that lady?"

"She works at the store." He recalls what the employees here used to be like. You'd be lucky if you spotted one, let alone found someone who'd agree to give any assistance. How long was it since that woman had seen a child in here? "We don't need her help. You just look around, sweetheart, see what you want. Would you like a doll? They've got all the dolls right over there." He points to the left, to the rows of life-size baby dolls, fashion dolls, doll houses. Honey loves dolls. With luck, she'll find something she adores within minutes and then they can be out of here. His back is still sweating and he regrets this trip, this foolish whim. The world has nothing to offer his child. It is ugly but she is beautiful, and she must stay beautiful. He won't allow reality to tarnish her.

Aisle after aisle they walk, she first and he after, her head turning right and left. She is as quiet as a ghost.

"How about this one?" he tries, randomly pointing at this or that pink furniture set or massive doll house. "You can have anything you want. I promise."

Honey mutters. She trots faster, her toes kicking the ground, while he follows like a tall, looming shadow. Out of the corner of his eye he notices the woman from before watching them, and sweat breaks out on his forehead.

"Darling." He sweetens his voice. Keeps himself from gripping her shoulder. "You're not even looking properly. Isn't there anything in here that you—"

"No!" She spins around, fair curls dancing around her face. The fury in her eyes shocks him. "I've got everything in here and I hate it and I want to go."

"But we only just came." He brushes his fingers against his brow. He wishes she'd remove the mask, only because it distorts her features, makes her alien. "Honey, they've got all the toys in the world here."

"I've got all the toys in the world!" She's shouting. The next step is screaming, kicking. It's seconds away, the scream already growing in her little lungs. "You said I could have anything I want but I don't want any of this!" Angry tears wet the white fabric of the mask as she snatches a staring doll from the shelf beside her and throws it to the floor. It lands face-down, then says something in a tinny voice.

I love you, Mama.

As the female employee rushes over he grabs his daughter and holds her squirming, thrashing body against his chest. "Calm down," he whispers as she scratches at his hands, his wrists. "We'll go somewhere else. A much better place."

"I hate you," she cries, his honey-child, his angel. "I hate you, Daddy."

"Oh dear." The female employee is there, head tilted, eyes wide with compassion as she puts the doll back in its place. "They can be a bit of a handful, can't they?"

He leaves without a word, Honey howling and kicking, her nails piercing his skin like claws. The cab driver opens the car door without talking, without showing any reaction to her tantrum. She's red-faced and snotty now, out of breath in-between her crying.

He, her father, sits down beside her. His head throbs as if he's been bludgeoned. He longs for his study, for the view of the oaks outside his window. "Darling," he says, his voice raspy though he's not the one who's been screaming. "We'll go somewhere else now, all right? A much better store, and if you don't like it, we'll leave right away." He can only think of one other toy store, but he's not sure it's still in business. So many places have closed down, after all. Dead people don't do much shopping.

"Where to, sir?" the cab driver says.

He has to jog his memory for a while before the address comes to him. It's several blocks away. The more he thinks about it, the more he knows that Honey won't find anything there either. It will be all the same brands and products, the same pink plastic and princess costumes. Nothing she doesn't already have.

She leans her head against the window, sulking, but at least not crying. He wants desperately to caress her head, brush the tears from her cheek. Her silence eats at him.

Then, as they're stopping at a red light, she jerks her head up and puts her little palm against the glass. "There, Daddy! Look! Is that where we're going?"

He cranes his neck to see past her. It takes him a moment to focus, see what she sees. At the street corner is an antiques shop, with a faded wooden sign above the entrance. He has never seen the place before. There are toys on display in one of the windows—a rocking horse that must be at least a hundred years old, a child-size piano, and porcelain dolls with ringlets framing their pale faces.

"Oh, please Daddy, can we go there? I want to look inside." Her pleading voice turns sharp at the end, commanding, not taking no for an answer. As if he'd ever tell her no.

"Of course, sweetheart." He tells the driver to make a turn, and soon, they're out of the cab again, Honey holding his hand as they walk into the store.

"Daddy," she says once they're inside the crammed room, where the ceiling is so low he has to stoop. "Why does it smell funny in here?"

He shies away from his reflection in a tall, gold-framed mirror. There are clocks everywhere, ticking out of sync. "Old things smell different," he says. "It's nothing to worry about."

But it is, isn't it? How many of the old carpets and sofas in here come from homes where someone died of the flu? The thought has him closing his mouth, putting his hand on Honey's head as if that might protect her. "Darling, I don't think you want anything in here. Isn't that right?"

"No! It's not!" And just like that, he's failed once more, and she runs away from him. He glimpses her thin legs behind a chest of drawers, before she's swallowed up by the murky room with its nooks and crannies and its smell of dust. He stares after her. His hand falls to his side.

"Can I help you?" The shopkeeper appears just as Honey vanishes, emerging from some unseen counter or staff room at the back. He's small and wrinkly, with gray hair sticking up in tufts behind his ears. "Looking for anything in particular, sir?" His strong voice makes it obvious that he's not quite as old as he looks.

"No, no." Where did she go? How could he let her slip away? "Sorry, my daughter…" His eyes search the room, darting over and under the furniture. "Darling? Come back here!"

The shopkeeper gives him a pitying look. "Parenting isn't simple, is it?"

He's just about to put an end to that pity with a harsh retort, when Honey's shrill voice comes from the back of the room.

"Daddy! Daddy, I found the toy I want."

He rushes through the shop, guided by the sound of her voice. She hasn't touched anything, has she? She hasn't removed her mask, surely?

He finds her by a small, filthy window next to a counter cluttered with papers and ancient candlesticks. She's pressing her face to the window, and he has to crouch beside her to see what it is that has caught her attention.

It's a workroom. Nothing more. Broken chairs, clothes with rips and stains, shelves filled with books that need rebinding. In the middle of the room is a child, hunched over some sewing. A skinny, miserable child with long, matted hair and a college sweater so large it must have originally belonged to an adult. The face is obscured by hair and there's no way of knowing either gender or age. The working child unnerves him and he wants to turn away, leave the store, but Honey seems oddly captivated.

"It's a doll," she says, in a monotonous voice as if she's back home absorbed in one of her games. "It's a doll and it's the one I want."

The child doesn't look up or show any reaction to her voice. It keeps bringing the needle up, down, making invisible stitches.

"Darling…" He's sweating again. He regrets ever leaving the house. "It's not—"

"May I interest you in this fine old piece?" The proprietor shows up from out of nowhere, holding a gilded candelabra that looks much too heavy for him to carry in one hand. "18th century, but just look how well it's been taken care of!"

"Daddy," Honey declares without taking any notice of the shopkeeper. "You said you'd buy me anything I want."

Why is it so damn hot? "Look, I really have no interest in any candelabra. Thank you." He turns his head only to find her staring through the window just like before. Perhaps it's not so strange. She's never met any other children, never played together with others. His gifted, beautiful girl, all she wants is a friend.

The shopkeeper peers at him as if expecting him to change his mind about the candelabra at any moment. "My prices are very agreeable."

"Daddy has money," Honey says. "Daddy has all the money in the world."

"I..." He dabs his forehead, flattens his hair. She's pushing him, little by little. She's getting her will because neither of them can imagine a world where she doesn't. Lowering his voice, he looks to the shopkeeper. "That...that child in there, is that...I mean, my daughter..."

"Oh!" The shopkeeper chuckles, as if the conversation is completely light and normal. "She's been here a few months. Doesn't do much difference, but I didn't have the heart to turn her away when she showed up outside. Deaf, poor child, and both parents dead in the flu. It's like having a shy cat around, really."

He nods, blinks, wets his lips. "I see. Would...would, um, maybe...My daughter has taken a shine to her, and she has no one to play with at home. I'd pay, of course. The girl would get a good home, and, well. Name your price and you shall have it."

The shopkeeper is quiet for a moment, but his face is calm. As if there is nothing mad about the proposal. "You'll take her?" he asks. "Well, I can't say I'd mind. I can tell from the look of you that you've got money in your pockets, so she'll be better off with you than in this dump. I'll go talk to her. You just wait here." He puts the candelabra down on the floor before heading for the workroom.

"Sweetie, come here. I've spoken to the man now. You'll have what you wish for."

Honey rushes into his arms, tiny and warm, smelling of apples and powdered sugar. Her gloved hands pet his hair as if he were a puppy. "Oh, thank you Daddy! Thank you!"

He rocks her in his arms, and her golden curls tickle his ear. "I'll give you anything. You know that." When the shopkeeper comes back out the girl trails after him, eyes cast down. Her arms hang, the long sleeves covering her hands.

"I've told her," the shopkeeper says. "Well, I wrote a note. I said she should think of this as a wonderful opportunity, and I'm sure she does."

"And payment?"

"No, no!" The shopkeeper waves with both hands. "That wouldn't be right. But if you'd care to buy any of my items, that wouldn't hurt."

He reaches the cab ten minutes later, with the gilded candelabra in his grip and two little girls to keep in check—one who blabbers excitedly, and one who doesn't say a word. He gestures for the deaf child to sit in front, next to the driver. She obeys without fussing. Her dirty hair bothers him—everything about her bothers him. Does she have lice? Or worse, does she carry the virus that killed her parents? Honey has been vaccinated, of course, but what if—

"You're the best daddy in the world," Honey says as the car starts moving. "I love you." And just like that, he forgets about his worries.

***

As soon as they come home, he orders Honey to have a bath and a change of clothes. While she's in the bathroom he shows the deaf girl into the kitchen and gestures for her to sit down. The kitchen chairs are the least expensive ones in the house—still, he'll have to scrub everything clean later.

Grabbing a notepad and a pen he tries to come up with the right words. At first, he thinks he should ask her name, but then he decides against it. He's not sure why. Instead he writes a note, hoping her reading skills are good.

You'll be my daughter's friend and play with her as much as she likes. You won't complain. You won't do anything bad. And you'll always let my daughter have her way. Nod if you understand.

The child nods without looking at him.

You'll have a bedroom to yourself downstairs. There are security cameras and alarms everywhere. I'll know immediately if you try to steal or run away.

Another nod. Then he stands there, watching her hunched form until Honey comes running out of the bathroom in a heart-patterned onesie.

"Daddy, can I play with it now? Can I?"

"No." He watches that filthy sweater, the dull, brown hair. "It has to take a bath first. That's very important." He scribbles quickly, another note, then shows her to the downstairs bathroom with its pastel tiles and scented candles. After finding a clean towel and some of Honey's old clothes he leaves her there, hoping she knows how to manage everything.

"It's a doll that can walk and run and sew and everything." Honey dances around him, elated, lively. "But it can't talk, Daddy. Only I get to talk."

"Yes, darling. That's right." When the deaf girl emerges from the bathroom she's in a blue dress Honey never liked anyway. It's baggy on her and shows too much of her thin calves and knobby knees. Honey frowns before a grin spreads on her face.

"Come on! Come!" She grabs the girl's arm, dragging her toward the play room.

"She can't hear, sweetie," he calls, as an after-thought. As if it's not important. "You'll have to point and show things with your hands, or she won't understand."

"It, Daddy! And I know dolls can't hear." She sounds far away, though she was there just a moment ago. A worry comes over him, a gnawing unease. Then he hears her speaking in her softest voice, her doll-voice, and there's nothing at all to worry about. He hangs up the wet towels, cleans the tub. Takes out the deaf girl's discarded clothes and puts them in the trash. Then he heads upstairs, to his study and his view of trees. The world outside tried to destroy everything, tried to hurt his angel-child. But there is nothing that can harm her. Nothing.

***

Days go by. He immerses himself in work, as the wind blows outside and the branches pat his window. Downstairs? He has nothing to worry about. Every time he comes down, Honey is playing sweetly with her friend. They're dressing up as princesses, brushing doll hair and painting their nails. If he only watches them for a moment everything seems normal—two little girls playing together. Not one girl telling the other what to do, pinching her arm every time she does something wrong. He only comes into the play room a few times a day. He never stays long.

"You're ruining it, Daddy," Honey says. "We're playing!" The deaf girl slouches on the floor beside her. She never looks at him.

Every once in a while, he tries to talk to his daughter. Half-heartedly, giving up before he's even started. "Honey, she's a little girl just like you. We have to be nice to her."

The worst thing is when she doesn't even scream, or kick, or cry. When she just looks at him as if she detests him more than anything. So, he tries to have the talk less and less often. In the end, he leaves things as they are. She'll tire. She's tired of every single toy he's given her. And as soon as she does he'll find the deaf child a home somewhere else and be rid of her.

One evening he comes downstairs and hears crying. His little angel, crying. She comes running at the sound of his voice, face wet, eyes glittering with tears.

"Daddy, the doll is mean! I hate it!"

He strides into the play room with her in his arms. The deaf girl stands by the window, still in that same blue dress. Her cheek is stark red as if she's been slapped. "What happened?" he asks, heart racing. "What did she do?"

"It's supposed to do as I want." Honey leans her little head against his. "Isn't it, Daddy?"

He puts her down on the floor and caresses her hair. "Yes, she is. But I'm sure she's very sorry."

Honey nods. She walks gingerly up to the deaf girl, tilting her head. "Oh, yes. It is sorry, and it cries."

***

That night, a note is slipped under the door to his study.

Please let me leave. I'm scared. My name is—

He tears the note into pieces. He has no desire to know her name.

***

He wakes while it's still dark. The house is quiet. He makes coffee—makes it strong. Brings it to his study and opens the computer. Documents, calculations, meetings. He works, thinking of that torn-up note in the trash can. He stares at the naked branches outside his window.

The day flies by, pale sunlight fading before he's even noticed it. He keeps working. He doesn't want to see her. He doesn't want her to have a name.

When he hears the scream, he puts the laptop away and stands as if he's been expecting it all along. Honey bursts into his study like she's never done before and blood drips from her chubby fingers to the carpet. There's a muffled clang, a thud, as one of the kitchen knives falls to the floor. She cries, wails like a baby, and there's blood in her hair, too. Specks of red that remind him of the past, of flu, of dying. But she's not dead. His child, she's not dead.

"The doll!" She wipes her hands on her dress. Red fingerprints all over the pink velvet. "Daddy, it talked. It talked!"

He walks up to her and scoops her up in his arms. Covers her, shields her, protects her from the ugly world that tries to take her from him. *Oh honey-child, angel-eyes, what have you done?*

"It couldn't do that." She bangs her fists against his chest, but he can't feel it. "I didn't want it to do that."

He doesn't know what awaits him downstairs—but in a way, he knows all too well. That child without a name, without a voice, trying to communicate. Breaking the rules.

"There, there." He cradles her. Kisses her temple, her blood-stained hair. "Everything's all right. Daddy loves you."

"And I love you, Daddy."

He nudges the knife with his foot. It slides under the carpet without making a sound, as if it was never there. As if it's far away, in the past, and can't hurt them anymore.

Mother Spook

When my brother Paulie was born, he was limp as a hay-stuffed doll and had a twisted spine, and that's why he was brought to Mother Spook. Mama cried and said he would be fine, but Father had no use for cripples. He stepped into his boots, so big that they left footprints like a werewolf's in the snow, and Paulie hung over his shoulder like an old rag, thin and sour-smelling and unloved by everyone but Mama. If Paulie had been a kitten or a calf, Father would have crushed his skull with the hammer as soon as he was born, but it was different when it was people. You couldn't drown sickly babies or throw them away, but if you dared, you could seek out Mother Spook. She was the meanest old witch who ever lived, but the brews bubbling in her cauldron could cure children of anything that ailed them.

"Don't go," Mama said as Father pushed open the door, letting the cold wind inside. Mama leaned against the doorpost, her face as white as the sheepskin around her shoulders. She loved babies, but having them wore her down until there was no fat in her cheeks and no color in her hair. A week after Paulie's birth, she was practically see-through, and the wedding ring kept slipping off her finger. "She'll want..." Mama coughed. "She'll want to trade."

Mother Spook never did a thing for free. The stories said that there was no negotiating, no exchange of gold and silver. No one knew what Mother Spook would take in return until the trade had been made. Sometimes, a cow went missing in the woods, or a red silk shawl disappeared from inside a chest as if it had never existed. Then, there were the darker tales—of burned-down cottages, maids falling into wells, and men strangling their wives. But the children who had been treated by Mother Spook lived long and healthy lives.

Father put his wide-brimmed hat on and huffed. "Trade? Well, there's plenty in here for her to take if she's got any use for it." His dagger-sharp blue eyes stung each of us in turn, four scrawny girls who were his but still not. "This ain't the son and heir I asked for, woman. But the old hag might know how to reshape him." He lifted Paulie's floppy arm, and it fell back against his chest as if there was no life in it.

"Joe," Mama pleaded. "At least wrap him in something warm." She pulled the sheepskin from herself and handed it to Father with trembling hands. There were dried bloodstains on the front of her shift.

"My boy ain't a weakling," Father spat, dropping the sheepskin to the floor. "He'll come back here strong as a bull." The moment he stepped out into the night, Mama fell as if he'd hit her.

I sat by her side because I was the oldest, and my sisters gathered behind my back.

"Mama, don't worry," we said. "It's too dark out for Father to find Mother Spook's cottage. He'll come back with Paulie, and everything will be all right." Nothing was all right when Father was home, but that was one of those things she had warned us we must never talk about.

Mama didn't say anything until she was back in bed, swallowed by covers and lumpy pillows. Her round, brown eyes were wet as a cow's, and I wondered if Paulie might have been better off as a dead calf than a living baby. "Your father will have his way," Mama said. "We must believe in him and have faith."

In the gloomy light of dawn, Father returned to the cottage with the bundle in his arms. Paulie's back curved as it should, and his arms waved in the air as if he was dancing. Three weeks later, Mama died, and we found out what Mother Spook had wanted in return.

***

Paulie grew up fast, and he grew big. Between them, he and Father ate and drank like ten strong men, and there was little left for us girls. Mama was dead, but her shadows lived, and our eight hands never stilled. There were sheep and a cow, and cats that came and went, and our little fingers were calloused and rough. In Father's wizened, pea-sized heart, there was no room for anyone but Paulie. *I have one child*, he used to say, though there were five of us with his thin, dark hair and lanky frame. My eyes were the color of cloudy winter skies, and so were his. Paulie's eyes were strange—sometimes, I wasn't sure they had any color at all, sometimes they shimmered like polished copper. My sister Mary claimed he had been born blue-eyed like me, but I couldn't remember much of those first few days of his life.

Mary liked Paulie until he bit her. Not playfully, as babies do—Paulie didn't pull back when her hand started bleeding. Father came inside at the sound of her screams and Paulie turned to him, cooing, mouth smeared red. Mary doubled over next to the hearth. She buried her fist in her apron, blood spreading over the white linen. Father laughed, and Mary stared at him with wild eyes.

"I wish she'd kept him! I wish Mother Spook had taken Paulie and let Mama stay."

After that night, Mary was deaf in one ear. She never talked to Father about Mother Spook again.

***

The one good thing about Paulie was that none of the other village children dared to play tricks on us when he was around. Paulie had tricks of his own, though, and they were meaner than anything the other boys could come up with. Once, he told some little kids to stuff their mouths with manure, or he'd break their bones, and the poor things were too scared to defy him. When their outraged mother came knocking on our door, Father scolded her. She should take better care of her children until they were old enough to defend themselves. Once the woman had left, Father closed the door and turned to us. His face was as tense as a clenched fist. I was right next to the hearth, on the other side of the room, but my skin prickled when I saw his dead eyes.

"Never," he said. Paulie sat at the table in front of us girls, head resting in his big hands. He was munching on some bread, and his loud chewing didn't stop as Father spoke. "Never bother folk like that again, you hear?" Father's eyes were locked on Paulie, only Paulie. "In here, in our home, we do as we please. We mind ourselves and what is ours. But out there, we don't make trouble for no one, or trouble will come to us. Understand? You understand me, boy?"

Paulie didn't answer. He only lifted his head, slowly, and looked at Father. I couldn't see Paulie's face from where I stood. But there was a glimpse of something in Father's eyes, something new and terrible. Fear. He murmured something before leaving, and I exchanged a look with Mary. Seeing him scared was good because it meant he had weak points. And it was bad because it meant there were things even he couldn't handle.

"Boring," Paulie said. He spun around in his chair, grinning at us as if he was thinking of a joke. There were crumbs on his shirt, in the corners of his mouth. "And you're boring, too, little sisters." He leaped at us, fingers curled into claws, and Mary shrieked. Paulie snickered before wandering off as if nothing had happened. Neither he nor Father ever mentioned again what had occurred that day, but my sisters and I remembered. And the other girls woke up time and again from nightmares where Paulie chased them through the woods with claw-like hands and eyes that shone in the dark.

***

Paulie grew, and so did we. I turned into a maiden, and I danced at the fairs, my braids whirling around me. I started loving a village boy, and at nights, we met in a glade close to my home, whispering and touching and weaving dreams about the future. His parents would never accept me because I was poor, and Father would refuse to let me marry just out of spite. But the boy's hair was soft, and his skin warm as the ground on a sunny day, and in my dreams, many things were different.

Winter comes early in our parts and the long nights with it. But I was in love, and I stole out into the darkness as before, treading over moss and rocks, foolishly hiding a kitchen knife in my hand in case I came across a bear or wolf. I reached the glade and the boy, who was just as warm and sweet as he had been in summer. Every time we met, he whistled a signal to let me know he was there, and I learned to long for that whistling almost as much as I longed for him. Nights came and went, and in between them, I lived as I had before, never breathing a word to anyone about my secret. Father didn't seem to suspect a thing—if he had, he would have locked me up.

One snowy night, I came to the glade and found no one there. No whistling and no warm embrace. It confused me since Tom was always the first one to arrive. For a long while, I waited, the wind tearing at my apron and braids. My freezing hands were stark red against the snow on my cuffs. I was about to give up and go home when something moved below the pines in front of me. Here he was at last. But there was something strange about the figure heading toward me— it was too small to be Tom, surely, and it was shrouded all in black…

Then, I heard a voice. The voice of an old woman, frail and broken but clearly audible. "You'll come looking for me," she said. "Soon enough, little girl, you'll come looking for me."

I didn't stay to hear more. I ran from her, from the one whose name I had known and feared since childhood. When I reached our yard, I forced my feet to slow down, but I couldn't relax my breathing. She was out there. Mother Spook was out there.

I was just about to sneak into the cottage when I heard a sound—a low, melodious whistling. It was his signal. Forgetting all about Mother Spook, I hurried past the cottage and toward the toolshed. The whistling turned louder, and my heart hammered along with it. It was foolish of him to come anywhere near my home, I knew, but that didn't matter as long as I could see him.

I pushed open the door to the shed. It was pitch-dark in there, and I carried no light with me. "Tom?" I called, trying to keep my voice steady. "I don't much like this game."

Whistling was heard from inside the darkness again, then his gentle voice. "I'm right here, sweetheart. Come now, don't be scared. Give me a kiss."

I couldn't help smiling as I stepped inside, tracing the walls with my hands. It wasn't like Tom to be this playful. I took slow, tiny steps—we used to hide from Father in the toolshed when we were small, so I knew it well, but there were rusty nails here and there on the floor, and I didn't want to step on one. Now and again, Tom whistled, encouraging me, and I giggled. To think that we were right next to the cottage where Father slept!

"How wicked you are," I said, reaching my hand out. There was only one corner left where I hadn't been. Soon Tom would be in my arms.

"More wicked than you think," Tom said. Then, I felt something. My fingers traced the lapels of his coat, but the coat was sticky, and when I touched his face—

I fell back against the floor, screaming. The smell of blood hit me like a blow, and I stared, stared into the darkness as he whistled again, and his eyes glowed like fire.

"That's what he gets for bedding my sister." Tom's voice—no. It was Paulie. He lit a torch, and I shut my eyes. I couldn't bear to see what he had done.

"Look," Paulie commanded me. "Not so handsome anymore, is he?" He dragged me off the ground. His meaty fingers forced my eye open. Tom was there, propped up in the corner like a scarecrow, staring back at me as if he were still alive. Cuts, slashes. Blood bubbling from his slack mouth that would never smile again.

Paulie leaned against me and whistled in my ear. The sour, unwashed smell of his body mingled with the stench of blood, and I threw up. "That's what he gets," Paulie sang in Tom's voice. "That's what the wicked boy gets."

I couldn't remember what happened after that. When I woke up the next day, Mary sat on the bedside and held my hand. She wept and said she would never forgive that horrible boy for assaulting me, but it was fortunate that Paulie had come to my rescue. "I don't like Paulie much," she murmured, "but now at least he's done one good deed in his life."

Father believed Paulie's tale, too. They all did. I wanted to tell the truth, clear Tom's name—but if I did, I'd be lucky to be thrown out of the house. So, I said nothing. I stopped visiting fairs, I stopped dancing. I sat at home with my sisters and fed the men. I prayed that nothing would come out of all those nights I'd spent with Tom. Then, one morning when I was by myself in the byre feeding the sheep, Paulie entered. I looked away, pretending I didn't notice. He came right up to me. His big hand pressed against my belly, and he whistled Tom's signal.

"What's this?" There was something odd about his voice—it was rough and croaky as if it belonged to someone much older. "No husband in sight, and a little one on the way."

"That's not true!" I snapped, freeing myself from his hands before I rushed outside. But a few weeks later, all the signs were there, as if Paulie's words had made it happen.

***

Springs were floods and never-ending rain. Our hems stuck to our feet, wet and heavy, and there was always at least one of us coming down with a fever. Father was angry at everything, but that wasn't new, and we were skilled at staying out of his way. We girls stuck together like we always had, but there was something inside me now that I couldn't let my sisters know about. Something that grew and hurt and gnawed at my innards. That spring, I tried everything—I worked hard and ate little, I struck at my bulging belly with curled fists, and I jumped over and over from the table. I picked strange-looking weeds and mushrooms, but the ones I dared to try only made me ill. Nothing could make the thing inside go away. It was as if it were clinging to me with claws and fangs—Tom's child, but I had no good memories left of Tom. Whenever I closed my eyes at night, I saw his ruined face in front of me. His hands, dripping with blood. Sometimes, out in the byre, I thought I heard his voice calling my name—then I saw a flash of Paulie's leering face in the window, and I hated myself because of that split second where I had been fooled.

Mary was the first one to notice. We shared a bed, and one night as we undressed, her gaze ran over me before stopping at the rounded shape of my stomach, visible under my shift. I turned away, but I was too late.

"When?" she asked once we had slipped under the covers and turned out the light.

"I don't know. In the fall, maybe." I remembered how protracted Mama's pregnancies had been. How big and clumsy she had become each time.

"Father—" Mary didn't need to say more. "What will you do?"

I imagined getting away with it. Hiding my sin under layers of linen, walking with a hunched back. Giving birth alone and leaving the child for the woods to take. But I knew Father. There were many months left, many days when a tiny mistake might turn him suspicious. And Paulie knew my secret. So far, he hadn't told anyone, but that didn't calm me. Father was a mean, old drunk and that was it, but what Paulie was I didn't know for sure. Sometimes, when his eyes gleamed at me in the dusk, I wondered what it was that Mother Spook had done to him when he was a baby.

You'll come looking for me, she had said. As if she knew all along. I held out for another fortnight—then, my youngest sisters noticed my belly, too, and I realized I must be rid of it.

There was only one way. I didn't want to go to her, but what else could I do? And I thought to myself, as I sneaked out of the window and into the rainfall, that if Mother Spook wanted to trade, she could have my father or my brother, and I wouldn't care in the least. She could have them both.

The rain whipped at me from all sides: cold, furious rain. I slunk past the shed, trying not to think of that snowy night when I found Tom's bloody corpse in there. It was dark now, too, always dark, as if we didn't deserve sunlight. Inside me, the baby kicked and thrashed. I had a lantern with me, but I didn't light it until I was at the edge of the woods. It made the pines and firs ahead look even taller and gloomier than before, but at least I saw the ground in front of me. I walked fast. My thin shoes were soaked through, my braids stuck to my wet face. Rain streamed into my eyes, and I pressed my hand to my brow, squinting as I tried to keep track of where I was. I didn't know how to find Mother Spook's cottage—all I could do was walk on and pray I'd come across it. Then, somehow, I'd have to find my way back again.

The further into the woods I went, the soggier the ground became. Murky water lapped at my calves, and I clung to branches and twigs to keep from falling into the dark pools. The pines tore at my hands, scratched my wrists. Rainwater washed down my back. When the lantern went out, I began to cry, sinking to my knees in the mud.

"Curse you," I told the one growing under my heart. "Curse you, curse you, curse you!"

I heard something, then. A sharp noise from far away, a noise that had me scrambling to my feet. I pushed on, I don't know for how long. Then, in a clearing, I saw a cottage. A small, gray cottage much like our own, but there was no smoke rising from the chimney and no sheds or outhouses. There was water everywhere, flowing, streaming down. A slope next to the cottage rose above the waterline, though, and I made for it. When I was just about there, I heard that sharp noise again, closer this time. It sounded almost like whistling.

Shivering in my damp clothes, I climbed to the top of the slope. The door to Mother Spook's cottage was in front of me, below the slope, below the waterline. I imagined her sitting in there, wrapped in her dark veils. Waiting.

I took one step toward her door and then another. I had almost reached the waterline when the ground collapsed under my feet. Lumps of grass and soil washed away around me. And I saw bones, human bones, bursting out of the ground. Corpses, the tiny corpses of children.

"No," I whispered. "No!" Then, I stumbled on something. Something small and twisted—Paulie's spine. The deformed spine of the baby Father had carried into the woods.

Behind me, I heard it again. The whistling.

"Oh, dear," Paulie said—or the thing that had stolen Paulie's face. "Old Mother won't like that you've seen her children."

With a creak, the door to the cottage opened. Water flooded in, then out. It was pitch dark in there as if there was nothing inside. No bubbling cauldron, no witch. Only that brittle voice trailing from inside like a serpent, thin and slippery.

"Come inside, my child," she said. "Mother Spook will free you from what ails you."

"Go," Paulie said with Tom's voice, soft as honey. "Go to her."

When I took the first step, my foot landed on the curving spine in front of me. It broke with a crack, and Paulie laughed in a voice that was neither his own nor Tom's.

"Come, come, child," Mother Spook sang from inside the darkness. "We must free you."

When I took the second step, the baby started kicking wildly. I bit my lip against the pain.

"Soon," Paulie growled in that strange new voice. "Old Mother makes all children better."

When I took the third step, Mother Spook appeared in the doorway with her face unveiled. And I saw in her eyes that I was not the child she wanted to free.

Teeth

When I was twelve, my mother told me I was different. Five years later, my cheeks were still as round and rosy as a doll's, and there were no lumps growing on my chest. Mother was long dead by then, so I couldn't ask her why. Not that I needed anyone to tell me I wasn't like other people. The evenings were long and slow in the house on the hill and I sat in my quiet room, letting my tongue run over the two rows of uneven teeth. Whenever I stung myself on those four pointy canines, I giggled, lifting my head to pretend that blood was trickling down my throat. It was a game, and my tongue was fine afterwards. No marks, no pain to speak of. Pain was not for me.

Mother had raised me on her own, working endless shifts at the nursing home to keep us off the streets. I can only remember bits and pieces of my earliest childhood. Loneliness, that's the main thing. The birthday parties I didn't have and the friends who never visited, because of the color of my eyes and my habit of biting. Mother slept at daytime, so I did the same. I never enjoyed the sun much anyway.

She never told me who my father was. Her words about him were harsh and few, but her eyes told me what he was really like. Handsome, exciting. Different, like me. Whenever she was working nights I stood on the porch, wind tearing at my hair as I whispered for him to come and get me.

"I'm like you," I said, murmuring awkward, twisted spells and prayers that I'd made up and hoped were magic. "Not like them."

I was golden-haired and gray-eyed while Mother's colors were dark, and that was how I knew how to recognize him. If a stranger came up to the gate and had my eyes, I would know he was my father. He never came. I made up tales where he was travelling the world, a prince or wizard doing heroic deeds. If he wasn't so busy, he would return to me. And we would fly away.

"You need to go to school," Mother told me whenever she was home. She was never out of her ugly, sick-green healthcare tunic, and her face was shadowed by backache and sleep deprivation. "I got another letter from your teacher."

I knew about the letters. I tore most of them to shreds and threw them in the trash, but she sometimes found them before I did.

"I'm tired," she said. "I don't know what you want me to do."

I didn't want her to do anything. She was there, she paid the bills, but that was the only relationship we had. I watched the night sky, hoping that a star would fall so I'd get a wish. A wish, gray-eyed like me.

The girls in school called me Witchy. I liked the name, but not their dagger stares. The boys never called me anything. I had my revenge by giving them all nicknames that I never spoke out loud. Sailor was tall and freckled and once wore a marinière shirt. Kitten and Pup were even shorter than the girls, and Benito was a boy I couldn't stand. Shelley was the prettiest of them all, with silky black hair and model-thick lashes. Whenever I didn't dream about my father, I fantasized about Shelley. Sometimes he was the reason I went to school, sometimes the reason I stayed away. I never told Mother about my dreams. She slept all the time, but I was sure she never dreamt.

I wasn't surprised when she died. Death had been in her eyes all along, bloodshot and weary. I had a ceremony in the backyard and wrote a letter of resignation to the nursing home. When I carved the cross, I realized that I didn't know her first name. The carving was too time-consuming, anyway, so in the end I went with *MOTHER*. After I'd gone inside after the burial, the crows gathered around the freshly dug grave. They stayed with Mother during her first cold night in the ground, and that made me happy.

I didn't go to school after Mother went away. Next to the other girls, I looked like a preschooler, and I began avoiding mirrors. While the other kids went to parties and got drunk or high, I sat at home reading Russian classics. Social services called every now and then. I pretended to be Mother and after some months, they stopped calling.

I kept making my wishes and late-night offerings, hoping Father would come. I sat by Mother's grave, lighting black candles and singing in high-pitched Latin. There was something wrong with me, a piece missing. I didn't know what it was, only that he could mend it.

On the night before my seventeenth birthday there was a full moon. The garden was quiet, no crows out when I went into the backyard in my best velvet dress. I stood in front of Mother's grave, not because it was hers but because it was a resting place for the dead. With a kitchen knife, I slit my palm open, and blood spilled over the lawn.

"Father," I said. "I offer you blood. Help me. Help me out of childhood."

I slept through my birthday. No one knew about it but me, and it had been many years since I craved sweets or gifts. When I woke up in the evening it was dark. And there was a pounding on the front door.

I knew it was he as soon as the door fell open. Shoulder-long golden hair, alabaster skin, and those eyes that I'd inherited. As beautiful as a god, as shining Apollo or mighty Zeus. He didn't ask about Mother. He grabbed my chin with his snow-cold fingers and forced my mouth open.

"Child," he said. His voice was melodic and just a little raspy, like a song played on a gramophone. "Did no one feed you?"

I shook my head. My father, he was finally here.

"You have to eat." He ushered me inside and came after, putting his long black coat on a hanger. "You'll never become strong and healthy otherwise."

I sat on the living room sofa and watched him with my doll-eyes. "But Daddy, I don't like food. It tastes yucky."

"I know, darling. Food isn't what you need. Say, is there any human that you…like?"

"Oh, yes. There's this boy." I still had those fantasies from time to time. Once or twice, I had gone to the house where Shelley lived and peeked inside. He had been sweet at twelve, but at seventeen he was the handsomest boy I'd ever seen. When he slept, his lashes fluttered against his tanned skin. I was certain that he was the sort of boy who had dreams.

"Then we should bring him here," Father said. He came up to me and sat by my side, grabbing my chubby little hand. "Picture him in your mind. Focus as hard as you can."

It was easy for me to think about Shelley. Father closed his eyes and murmured words I couldn't understand, still squeezing my fingers. He didn't let go until the door opened a long while later.

"Now, let's see." He gave me a secretive smile. "Come along, child, there's nothing to be scared of."

Shelley was in the hall. He seemed to have left home at a hurry, because he was barefoot and without a jacket. He frowned first at Father, then at me. "I know her," he said. "She's that strange little kid from school."

Father patted my shoulder before walking up to Shelley and grabbing the back of his head. I didn't think Shelley would like that, but Father stared into his face for several seconds, muttering something. After that Shelley's eyes glazed over, and his arms fell to his sides.

"All ready," Father said, leading Shelley into the living room. "Well? Won't you tell me his name?"

"Shelley."

"What a coincidence." Father grinned. "I'm Byron." He let go of Shelley and took my hand, bringing it to his lips. "And you're Mary."

He sat on the end of the sofa, pulling Shelley into his lap. Shelley was limp, relaxed, and his hair looked darker than ever against Father's white shirt. Father hummed a tune I'd never heard as he tore Shelley's t-shirt open and exposed his skin. He pushed Shelley's head to the side, then guided my eager little fingers to the pumping jugular. "Feel that?" he said. "Think you can manage on your own?"

I wasn't sure. But I curled up next to Shelley and put my hands on his hot skin, and my jaw twitched. A snarl emerged from my throat, and Father chuckled.

"They're growing. You're growing."

My mouth on Shelley's neck, sucking, lapping. Father leaned back, telling me I was doing well. I cried as my teeth ached, as my canines morphed into fangs.

"You like him, don't you?" Father said, and his fingers combed through Shelley's hair. "Then eat."

So I ate. My teeth pierced Shelley's skin as if it were a tender piece of meat, and his blood sprayed into my mouth. I pressed myself against him, burying my fangs in deeper, and Father locked him in a firm grip when the glamour wore off.

I don't know how long it took him to die—if I killed him, or if he was still alive when I was full and Father took over, feasting on my leftovers until the sofa was soaked with blood and our faces were glistening red. We buried Shelley next to Mother, and I made another cross. I carved a heart into it because I had sort of loved Shelley, though I loved Father more.

"You'll be a woman soon," he told me as we bowed our heads in silent, ungodly prayer by the new grave. The crows swarmed above us, circling around Father and I as if they knew what we were.

"Will you stay?" I asked. I knew the answer already, but I wanted him to feel bad.

"No. But I won't leave tonight."

I ran my tongue slowly over my teeth. Blood burst forth, mixing with Shelley's. I winced, then cried for a split second at the thought of being alone again. And then I laughed, because all my wishes had come true and I would live forever.

Chalk

It was night before he found the house. Dirty big-city rain washed over his glasses, blurring and distorting the quiet suburban street. He had to stoop low to read on the letterbox. The name was written in minuscule, cursive, old-lady handwriting on baby blue paper. He thought again of the notebook he had dropped somewhere, most likely in the backseat of that cigarette-stinking car. The lady's name and address had been in there, along with everything else he needed to remember. But thinking about the notebook only made him anxious, so he forced his eyes toward the house instead. It was a gloom-gray, two-story building at the far end of the street, away from lights and traffic. The garden was overgrown with weeds and the untrimmed hedge rose high above his head, though people often told him he was tall. He didn't look forward to spending the night in a place like this, but he hadn't looked forward to anything in a long while. Pressing one arm to his forehead to keep the whipping rain out of his face, he opened the gate and slipped inside.

His knocks were loud and rude, but his windbreaker was too thin for rainy late-fall nights and he had never liked being wet. There were no lights on inside, not even the blue glow from a TV. He knocked again, then wiped the glasses with his dripping sleeve.

No sounds but the drumming rain, no footsteps or voices. Nothing until the door was unlocked, hurriedly, and that woman stood there. Her eyes reminded him of the snarling Rottweiler that had bitten him as a child. They were small and inky and brimming with accusations of this kind or that. He was much taller than she but she was firm and fat and seemed carved out of alabaster. While her face was round and moon-like, the top of her head was oddly small and pointy, her scalp covered with sparse, coffee-colored hair pulled into a knot the size of a baby's fist.

"Yes?" Something about her deep voice unnerved him.

"It's about the room." He reached into his soggy front pocket, then remembered the loss of the notebook. "I wrote to you...Sorry, I should have come earlier but the man in the car took the wrong turn."

"I see." Her mouth twisted as if she had a cherry-stone in there. "You have money?"

He let the words roll around in his head a few times until he realized that she had a foreign accent. That explained the name. "Yes, I do."

"All right." When she moved away from the doorway, the house sighed. "Room is in the basement. Breakfast between six and eight. No guests."

"Understood." He tipped his head backwards to look for damp stains, but there was nothing to see except the bleary ceiling fixture and a pair of drowsy flies circling it. The image was as depressing as the woman in front of him. "Do you live alone?"

"No." She turned her head, barking out a monosyllable name. Her booming voice made the flies scatter. "The girl is upstairs." Lower, she added, "She's sick."

He didn't have anything in particular to say to that information. He wished he still had the notebook.

A door opened and closed somewhere on the second floor. Soft, slow footsteps tickled the skin inside his ear.

"Sick," the woman said again. "Don't mind her."

The sounds from the stairs made him wonder what the girl looked like—her legs in particular, if they were bent or broken, or if she was extremely obese like some of those people on TV. Heavy thuds filled the house as if there was a fight. The beginning of the stairs was at the far end of the hall, in a windowless corner. The woman kept watching him, as if the unsettling sounds were everyday occurrences to her. *Thud-drag-thud.* Part of him would enjoy it if the girl turned out to be plagued by some rare, disfiguring illness. But when she showed, emerging from the shadows by the stairs, she was a short and scrawny thing with no visible faults. As pale as the mother, with the same dark hair, but her face might almost have been pretty. If it weren't for her slack, open mouth and the vacant stare in her blue eyes. The hanging arms and slow, strained walk.

"Sleepwalker," the woman said sharply. The girl stopped dragging her feet forward at the sound of her voice. She blinked, once, before her head slumped forward. "Disease. Called something, can't remember what. Now you know. Don't disturb, don't talk to her. Makes her upset."

"She can hear you," he said. It troubled him how the girl's flat, unwashed hair hid her face. "How?"

The woman shrugged. The movement seemed to pass through her body like slow, dark water. "Go back upstairs," she commanded, then scratched at a large red mark on her neck as the girl turned around. "Is sad," she muttered over the sound of arduous walking. "She used to be like you and me."

He nodded. "I should go see the room."

She pointed to a closed door with her alabaster hand. "Basement stairs. There's a bathroom down there, towels, linen. Goodnight."

Rubbing a droplet of water from the tip of his nose, he thought of asking her how old the girl was. But her eyes barked at him, tired of questions. He went down the steep basement stairs and found a square, brick-walled room lit by a naked bulb. The bed was narrow and there was a crack in the bathroom mirror. It was perfect.

***

Whiny house sounds tore up his dreams. Sounds he wasn't used to and didn't like, but he didn't like his dreams either. They made him sweat. He sat, eyes shut as he inhaled his own stink. There was an air vent somewhere, making a noise like a choir of insects screeching. Maybe he could talk to the woman about that in the morning.

It took him a while to discern the other noise. The *creak-pause-creak*. Opening his eyes, he felt for his glasses on the nightstand. The room wasn't completely dark—there were two narrow windows high up on the wall, twin slits allowing the moon-glow inside. He pushed the glasses against the point between his eyes, counting quietly. *Creak, pause, creak.* Someone was walking through the hall upstairs. Someone was coming.

The insect noise sank to the floor and died when the basement door opened. The stairs were concrete; they swallowed the footsteps without chewing. He watched the end of the stairs, expecting the alabaster woman—but it was the sleepwalking girl. Except she was awake.

"Mister, you have to help me!" She pattered over to the bed, barefoot, polka dot pajama sleeves covering her hands. "She's sleeping now. Finally."

He pulled his knees up as she sat down on the edge of the bed. Her eyes were like marbles, too pale for real life. "I thought you couldn't talk," he said.

"It's only because…" She sighed. "You are not her friend, are you?"

"No." He liked how small the girl was. Her voice was small too, breaking here and there as if she didn't trust it. She was like one of those tiny glass animals his grandmother had collected, the cats and does and velvet-eyed horses. Kept high up on a shelf where he couldn't reach.

"You can't become her friend," the girl said. "She's evil."

"Then I won't."

She gnawed at her bottom lip, wine-colored like his mother's roses. Her skin made him think of chalk. "Why did you come?" she asked, her fingertips slipping out of the long sleeves to press against each other.

"I had to go somewhere."

"I suppose." She didn't sound interested. He didn't mind. Her fingers moved like earthworms writhing on a wet road. "But you can't stay here long. It's a bad house. It steals your dreams." Her milky eyes prodded his own, as loud as her voice was quiet. Her eyes screamed.

"It can have mine." He laughed at the image of a house with a sour, sagging face. The girl gasped, motioning for him to be quiet.

"You don't understand! She…she doesn't like laughing. That was why she started punishing me in the first place."

He remembered what she was like in the hall. A broken toy. "How does she punish you?"

"You know." She shook her head with unnaturally large movements. "I'm only myself at night…like in a fairy tale. It's horrible. She's horrible."

"Is she your mother?"

The girl started crying. She didn't bother to wipe the tears away. "You have to help me. Please. You have to do something."

He lifted his arm but wasn't sure what he wanted to do. When he woke up in the morning he couldn't remember more than that. His lifted hand, and her distorted face stitching itself into his memory.

***

Breakfast was bitter tea and a hard-boiled egg with toast. He ate fast as usual, alone at the kitchen table while the woman stood with her back to him, doing dishes. She looked the same as the night before. Sturdy black dress, dark slippers. As if she hadn't gone to bed at all. He hadn't seen the girl, and the woman hadn't mentioned her. She had only spoken to him to ask how he preferred his egg.

"It's a good house," he said, trying not to think about what the girl had told him last night. "I slept well."

"No talking." She didn't turn to him. "Is unnecessary."

Her back was a square of resentment and stiff muscles. Had she fed the girl some drug? She looked like a poisoner, though he'd never met one before. She had those dog-bite eyes he didn't like. When he was done eating he went downstairs, wishing he still had his notebook. There were plenty of empty pages left when he lost it. White as chalk.

***

The girl returned to him that night. He woke from one of the angel dreams and she stood there by the bed, hand waving. He sat up, thinking about poison.

"I had to see you," the girl said. "It's the only thing that makes me happy." Her pajamas had changed color: they were pink with tear-shaped buttons down the front. She was so small, a doe made of glass. A velvet-eyed creature. "I like you," she said. "I like your stories."

He nodded, absent-minded. That noise from the air vent was back, stronger now. He had to speak with the woman about it.

"Tell me something then." The girl giggled, her mouth full of teeth. "You haven't told me anything yet, remember? About you. I want to know about you."

The pink stung his eyes. "There's nothing special about me. I needed somewhere to stay, that's all."

"But you have to have a name. A family. Something."

The family question seemed less dangerous. "I've got a family. My father is away a lot, but he always brings back treats. My mother loves flowers. Grandma does, too, though she likes anything pretty."

The girl's eyes seemed to have grown a size. "I love pretty things too. Don't you?"

"Yes." He winced. The air vent whispered around their conversation like a broken echo. "Then there's Cassie as well. She's the prettiest girl you've ever seen."

The girl huffed. "Prettier than me?" Then she shrugged, smiling. "It's nice that you love her so much. You're a great older brother."

"Thank you."

"I don't have any brothers." Her smile was gone. The shadows stuck to her face like dirt. "There's no one who cares for me. There's no one who can help me get away from her."

He reached out to pat the back of her hand. It was as cool as glass. "I care. I'll help you."

"And then we'll be together forever," she said, and the whispers grew until the world was wrapped in pink cotton.

***

He slept late the next day, missing breakfast. When he came upstairs, the woman was gone, and there was a note to him on the basement door. *Gone shopping. Back soon.* He didn't know when she had left or where the nearest grocery store was. He didn't care. The one thing on his mind was the girl.

The stairs to the second floor whined, every inch of wood slippery as ice. There were three doors upstairs, all closed. He opened the first, the second, the third. She was in the third room. On her back, fully clothed, empty eyes open. Matte hair spilled over the pillow like dead leaves.

"Oh, no." It pained him to see her like that. He didn't want to. "How can she do this to you?" He sat down on the bedside, the way she used to do at night. He touched the back of her hand, and it was warm. "I'll put an end to this," he said. "I'll make her pay for what she's done."

The girl blinked, but there was no other reaction. Nothing but a girl on a bed in a dark room, her eyes going *blink-blink-blink* like a sparrow's heart. He wanted her to smile but she didn't, so he left her there and closed the door. Went back to his basement whispers, imagining that he filled his notebook with thick black strokes.

***

When she came to him that night, she was crying. "I don't want you to see me like that," she said. "Like how I am when her poison has taken me." She wiped her cheeks with her sleeves, refusing to look at him. "That's not who I am."

"I know." The whispers prickled his skin but he pushed them back. "You're a pretty girl. You deserve to be free."

"Do you really think so?" She sniffled. The sound tugged at a memory somewhere, and he pushed that away too. "But I'm nothing special. Not even my own mother thinks so."

"Spread your wings," he said, drawing in the air. White shapes, white strokes all around her. "Angel."

***

He was up in time for breakfast the next morning. The woman boiled the eggs, put the kettle on. No talking, because that was how she wanted it. No air vent whispering. Bitterness slipped down his throat, egg yolk painted the inside of his mouth. He cut one slice of bread, two, three. The woman stood by the counter sipping her tea, back turned. She didn't notice when he rammed the bread knife into her throat. But she made a sound, a gurgling scream that shot into that stinking dark corner of his mind and tugged at his hideaway things. The things no one could know. Her cup crashed into the floor a moment before she did. It was ugly, nothing like that other time. It was sticky tiles and broken china, it was limbs going in the wrong directions. The blood clawed its way toward him but he stepped aside, dropping the knife. No more need for it. He was done.

When he turned to the doorway, the girl was there.

"Angel," he said, and for the first time since that day when they took him away, he felt calm. He had put things right now. Even without the notebook he was fine. Doctor Stein would never have believed it, but he would never ever meet Doctor Stein again.

The girl made a noise. It wasn't words, it wasn't anything like their nighttime conversations. She shook, hands fidgeting while her mouth hung open and all that came from it were those raw, strained sounds. Her eyes stayed glazed over as if she wasn't there. As if she had never been there.

See now what you've done, his mother said. *She's distraught, poor thing.*

"Not now, Mother."

It's like I've always said, Grandma cut in. *He can't be trusted.*

"Oh, shut up."

He closed the door in the girl's face, that pasty, lifeless face he couldn't bear to see. The noises wormed themselves through the keyhole, animal noises, noises almost like the ones Cass had made. Cass in her pink cotton pajamas, playing hopscotch by herself out on the street despite the autumn chill. Chalk lines around her. Chalk wings spreading from her body, and sirens howling like wolves in the distance.

Cassie. Angel eyes.

Don't look at me like that, freak, said—no, that was a false memory, one of those that Doctor Stein had put into his brain with his pills and his electric shocks. "You wouldn't," he said as Cassie jumped from square to square, too focused on her game to notice him. "Never."

"I loved her just like she was," he told the door. "That's why I didn't want her to grow anymore." The girl on the other side grunted. The woman was dead and the blood clung to her legs like a demanding toddler. He went over to the phone on the wall and it rang, one sharp signal before he lifted the receiver.

The call came from far away, a sea of static and a male voice drowning in it. "Is this Mrs.—?" The phone line chewed up bits and pieces of his voice. "I'm sorry to disturb this early in the morning. I'm Chief Inspector—and I—" There was a wind howling, tossing the man's words here and there. "Your name and address were found in a notebook that we believe—and it's of the utmost importance that—"

Notebook, he thought.

"This man is a highly disturbed individual and—ran away from a mental institution on November 10th."

The wind tore through again. The thin line of waves and wires between the policeman's voice and his own auditory canal swayed and shivered like a skipping-rope slapping the asphalt, *thud-thud-thud*.

"He is very dangerous. I don't want to scare you, but—his own little sister—"

The girl had stopped with her noises, but there was a different sound now. Slow, unsteady knocks on the door. *Bang, bang, little fists*.

"Keep your door locked, and don't invite any strangers inside," the Chief Inspector continued. "And if you notice anything out of the ordinary, don't hesitate to give me a call. My number—"

"Thank you." He pressed the receiver to his mouth, blowing hot, stale air into the transmitter. "It was nice of you to call, Chief Inspector." He saw Cassie in front of him, her wings glowing in the sun. She was smiling. The banging on the door continued, but it wasn't important. He would take care of it in a while.

The Chief Inspector shouted something, but that wasn't important, either. The girl made a sound like that of a dog drowning.

"I've got something to attend to now, if you excuse me. When you're done with my notebook, can I have it back?"

Laurent

I was all alone in the woods until Laura came. Well, my parents were there, though I preferred not to think about them. They were still married back then, but the cracks had started to show. They cut through my dad's gaunt face, my mom's eyes. The house was either quiet or filled with sounds that made me hide outside. I had several hideaways—or nests, as I thought of them, as if I were my own pet bird. Most of them were at the bottom of a pine-tree, where the heavy, thorny branches shielded me from view. One nest scared me, but I had to go there sometimes anyway. It was in a crevice between some rocks, and I hated standing there in the dark with spiders and who-knows-what crawling over me. I only went to the crevice when my parents were out looking for me. It was the one place where they would never find me, because they knew I was scared of the dark. I stood there with that sliver of sunlight showing me the way out, and the crawlies ran over my bare arms as I heard my name being called over and over. The dream I had was that my parents would stay out all night, refusing to stop looking until I had been found. I thought that if they only searched everywhere, then finally I would be rescued from the dark and I wouldn't have to go there again. But my parents only searched for an hour or two, and after that, they went home. As if they were now childless, and that was something they could live with.

I didn't know about Laura at first. I guess no one did. There was only one house further up the dirt road that ran by our home, and I'd been told by some kids at school that a witch lived there. An old, mean witch who was many hundred years old and ate innocent little babies whenever she could get hold of them. I never went anywhere near the witch's house, because I wasn't stupid—I might not be a baby, but I was shorter and scrawnier than any other kid in school, and witches might not be too picky with their food. The woods were large and I knew my way around, though, so I figured I was safe. As long as I stuck to my nests and my Good Places, which were places where I could play without being found out. The brook was one, and the ditch by the bus stop was another. I was in the ditch one morning, studying the frogs I secretly thought of as mine, when Laura showed up and asked what I was doing. Naturally, I didn't know then that Laura was her name—I saw a pale girl with hair like a raven's plumage, and I figured that her name was probably a lot nicer than mine. And it was.

"Is this where the school bus stops?" she asked after we had both introduced ourselves. "Sorry, I just moved in and I don't know a thing."

I nodded, proud to be able to help her. She wore a baby blue coat and shiny lace-up shoes, a type of clothing I had never before seen on a child.

"You see," Laura continued, "I live with my grandmother and it's no good asking her anything. Granny has too many worries already."

I couldn't imagine living with any of my grandparents. My parents didn't have a good relationship with them, so neither did I.

"You can sit with me on the bus," I offered. "If you want."

"Oh, yes." Laura's eyes were a weird, washed-out color. They were the only thing about her that I didn't instantly like. "How is school? Are the teachers kind?"

She didn't ask about the other kids. I suppose she knew enough about the world not to ask.

We spent the entirety of Laura's first day in school together. I used to sit by myself, and it was a nice change to have someone to talk to. Laura liked talking, about books and cartoons and the apartment she had used to live in before.

"But the air was bad there. It made Laurent sick."

I hadn't heard that name before. "Who's Laurence?"

"*Laurent.*" She gave me a strict look, like the ones I received from my parents whenever I did something wrong. "He's my twin brother. We look exactly alike, except he's a boy."

"You have a twin?" I struggled to comprehend this. I had always wanted a twin—someone I could switch places with. Someone who could hide away in the crevice instead of me.

"I do." Laura grinned. It was the first time I saw her teeth. Of course they were perfect, like a string of pearls. "But Laurent isn't well, so he can't come to school yet. Granny is treating him. That's why we had to move here."

When the school day was over, we took the bus home and got off at the stop I had never shared with anyone before. Laura was going in the same direction as me, so we went up the dirt road together. It wasn't until we reached my gate that I realized she was living further ahead. In the direction of the witch-house.

"Have you seen her?" I asked. I lowered my voice just in case, because witches might have excellent hearing. "Be careful when you walk past her house, or she might cook you for dinner."

Laura laughed. A bird-laugh, brittle like glass. "You're a strange one. I'll see you tomorrow."

***

She caught up with me on the way to the bus the next morning, and we spent the day together as if we always had. Laura showed me her sticker album, which was all sparkly on the outside, and I told her the names of my favorite frogs.

"Laurent would love that," she said. "He's mad about pets. We couldn't have any in the apartment, though, and he can't look after a pet of his own now that he's sick."

"What kind of sickness is it?" I asked. I wondered whether it was smallpox, or dengue fever, or maybe the plague.

Laura sighed. "I don't want to talk about it. Granny is very talented, and she'll cure Laurent in no time. You know, he told me yesterday that he's feeling better."

She smiled, so I did the same.

"I think it was because I told him about you. When he's well enough, we can all play together."

I didn't know what to think about that. Being friends with Laura was really all I needed, but I felt sorry for her brother who had to lie in bed all day.

When we were walking home from the bus stop that afternoon, I heard car sounds and saw a flash of my parents' red Volvo up ahead, where the road made a turn.

"Hide!" I hissed at Laura, and we dashed into the woods. I thought of deer and darkness and fire-eyed wolves, and I grabbed Laura's hand. The car went past us—both my parents were in it, staring at the road in front of them, seeing nothing.

"Who was that?" Laura said. There were fresh mud stains all over her shoes, but she didn't seem to notice.

"Monsters," I told her. "We can't let them find us."

We looked at each other. For a moment, I thought she was going to laugh at me. Then she shrieked, and so did I, and we ran. Away into the woods, away, away, with the books in our backpacks thumping against each other. When we were out of breath, I showed her to one of my nests, and we sat there under the pine-tree with needles in our hair and listened to the silence.

"I've got lots of places. Hideaway places." I said it casually, as if it wasn't important. "You can use them too, if you want."

Laura watched as an ant walked across her hand. A big one, the kind that stings. I wanted to slap it away, but she just studied it. "I'm not good at hiding," she said. "But thank you."

***

I was too small to reach the spare key above the front door, and so was Laura.

"Don't cry," she said, though I wasn't going to. "You can come back to mine until your parents are back."

I liked that. I was curious about her grandmother and the sick twin brother. We continued up the dirt road together, and even though I was scared of the witch I didn't say anything about it. Laura might think it was childish, and that was the last thing I wanted.

The first thing I noticed about the house was the rumbling. It sounded a little like a running car, but the only car I saw was standing in the driveway with the lights off.

"Does it always sound like that?" I asked, and Laura frowned before laughing.

"Oh, that's just the generator. Granny says it's a good thing there are no neighbors who can complain about it."

I didn't know what a generator was. "Is your grandmother home?"

"She's always home." Laura opened the gate and skipped across the yard, and I followed. The house looked old and somehow tired—the sagging roof reminded me of a drooping eyelid. The hood of the car was all rust, no color, and one look at the garden told me that Laura's grandmother didn't own a lawnmower.

"Come in." Laura opened the door and ushered me inside. The first thing I noticed was the chill. It was September, early autumn, but the days were warm and I still wore my thin pink jacket. In Laura's home, it seemed to be winter.

"It's cold," I said. Laura shrugged, before putting her coat on a hanger and pulling a knitted sweater over her head.

"Old houses," she said. "We've got tons of sweaters. Here." She handed me one, and I put it on. It made the cold easier to bear, but not by much.

"Granny?" Laura called. "I brought a friend home."

We went into the kitchen. It was cluttered with things—plants, books, pans, dirty dishes. There was music coming from an old radio in the corner, but it didn't sound right. After a while I realized that it was the generator-hum that distorted it. There was a trace of something in the air, a faint smell of rotting food. The trashcan probably needed emptying.

"How nice." An old woman entered the kitchen from another room. She had long, gray hair and a woolen cardigan wrapped around herself. Her eyes had dark smudges around them, which made her look like an Ancient Egyptian. "Do you girls want some lemonade?"

"Yes." Laura sat down at the table, and I did the same. When a fluffy cat jumped into my lap and peered at me I yelped, then started stroking its long fur.

"Oh, look. Maya likes you." Laura smiled at me with her pearl-teeth. "Just don't stick out your finger, or she'll bite."

"Or your toe," said her grandmother with a chuckle. "That's how I usually wake up in the mornings—with a tooth or a claw piercing my big toe."

Maya cozied up in my lap and purred. I couldn't imagine her attacking anything, not even a toy. "I bet Laurent likes having a cat around," I said.

Laura exchanged a look with her grandmother.

"I mean, since he likes animals. You told me." My voice turned pleading. I wished it hadn't.

"Yes." Laura nodded enthusiastically, as if she had forgotten until I reminded her. "He really does. Doesn't he, Granny?"

"Our Laurent is an animal lover for sure." Laura's grandmother handed us the lemonade not in glasses, but in coffee cups. "Here you are. There's more in the fridge if you want."

The lemonade made my mouth itch, in a good way, but I would rather have had something warm. I felt sorry for Laura who had to live in such a drafty old house.

Maybe she noticed me shivering, because she looked a little sad. "There might be some cinnamon buns left," she said, as if that would cheer us both up. "Granny? Are there any buns?"

"No," her grandmother called from the other room. "Only in the freezer."

"Oh." Laura's eyes darted to a green door next to the fridge. "Never mind, then."

"It's all right. I'm not hungry."

She sighed. "No, it's just that Laurent is asleep, and I don't want to disturb him."

I tried to look as if I understood, but I didn't. "He must be very sick."

"Yes." Laura stood, emptying the last of her lemonade. "But Granny knows how to fix things, so she will fix Laurent, too."

Back then, I didn't know what she meant. I wish I still didn't.

When I came home a while later, my parents had returned. They didn't ask where I had been or apologize for locking me out. At the dinner table I told them anyway, because the silence was eating at me. I missed Maya's weight on my lap.

"I have a new friend," I said. "Her name is Laura."

"The one you were running around with before," my dad said. "Playing your silly games."

"She lives with her grandmother. I went to see her today."

My mom raised her thin eyebrows. "Mrs. Grey? And here I thought you were scared of her."

"I'm not scared. She's a nice old lady."

My dad cleared his throat. "Then I suggest you stop calling her a witch."

I stared at him. His face seemed to stretch out, melt, the way it always did if I looked at him for too long. "What?"

"It's a very bad word." My mom cut her turkey in tiny cubes, until it barely resembled food at all. "You should know better."

I ran then. To my nests, my hiding places. I sat in the dark with the pine needles raining down on me, and I wished Laura had been there to keep me company. My parents stood on the porch, calling my name. They didn't even bother to leave the house.

***

Sometimes the other kids teased Laura and me. There was rarely any reason—schoolyard logics, that's all. For some to be on top, others have to be at the bottom. The boys could never leave Laura's hair alone, especially when it was braided. She didn't even look up from her book, just slapped their chubby hands away. I told her they were stupid and disgusting, but in reality, I envied her. When they were targeting me, they would just push me into a puddle and run off laughing. No one had ever touched my hair.

I always liked it better once we had jumped off the bus and were back in the woods. Laura was all mine then, and I came up with endless games just to make the way home as long as possible. On rainy days, we would save earthworms from the road and place them in the ditch where they couldn't be run over. Or I'd pretend to be Mary Poppins with a flying umbrella, and we'd let the wind push us here and there as if we were weightless.

One afternoon we were in the woods, immersed in a game where we were fairies who could talk to animals, when we fell silent at the sound of nearby voices. Two men, older—there were men in the woods sometimes, during hunting season, which was only weeks away. I hated hunting season and wanted the men gone.

"They're bad," I told Laura in my fairy voice. "They're bad men who want to kill everything."

Laura grabbed my arm. Her nails were sharp, like tiny teeth sawing through my jacket. "They can't."

"We have to hide." I knew where my nests were. I knew that there was only one where the hunters would never find us.

Something shifted in Laura's pale eyes when she saw the crevice. "What's in there?" she asked.

"Death," I said. I don't know where it came from, and it made me shudder.

"Don't be stupid." She stuck her tongue out at me and went inside. I followed, wishing I hadn't said that word. The darkness swallowed me. I couldn't see Laura.

"Here." She took my hand. Hers was cool and soft. I wondered if the crawlies were nearby, but I wasn't scared. Not when Laura was with me.

"Is your grandmother a witch?" I asked. I had never dared to bring up the subject before. It had been lurking at the back of my mind, showing itself at times—usually when I was about to go to sleep.

"I'm not sure," Laura said. Her answer surprised me. I had thought she'd be angry, and was relieved that she wasn't. "Would it be strange if I wanted her to be?"

I thought about it. "Only a little."

Laura squeezed my hand. "People tell stories about her. I've heard them. None of what they say is true. But Granny knows things, and she can make Laurent better. That's why I want her to be a witch. For Laurent's sake."

"I'm sure Laurent will be better soon," I said, though I had no idea how his health was. I didn't even know what he looked like, though Laura had said he was like a male version of her. I had tried, but I couldn't picture it. There was only one Laura.

"Thank you," she said and pressed her dry lips to my cheek. She smelled like lemonade.

***

Hunting season came. We weren't allowed to go into the woods anymore, so we stayed on the road or in the ditch by the bus stop. There were plenty of little animals to rescue, and we sang to the worms and beetles and told them stories. Sometimes Laura said I could follow her home, so I did. She never asked why we couldn't go to mine—maybe she understood anyway. I liked it in Laura's house, despite the cold. Maya was always snuggling up to me, as soon as I sat down, and Laura's grandmother told me cats could tell if people were good or bad.

"Not that I'd have my doubts about you if it weren't for Maya." She talked about me but she watched Laura, who sat across from me sipping tea. "I'm glad my Laura has a friend. Come by anytime, dear."

Later that same week, when we came inside singing loudly to drown out the generator noise, Mrs. Grey came through that green door in the kitchen. She was in a fur coat that made her look like she was part of a polar expedition.

"Girls, girls!" She held her hands up—they were blueish, with chunky silver rings on all fingers. "You have to be quiet. Laurent is sleeping."

"Oh, sorry." Laura bit her lip. "Poor Laurent."

I had been to her house many times by now, but I had never met Laurent. I didn't even know where his bedroom was. Laura's room was at the back of the house, so was her grandmother's, but neither of them had ever mentioned where Laurent slept. I was curious, but I didn't want to pry.

"Do you think he's any better, Granny?" Laura's voice was tiny, like a shivering animal I could hide in my pocket.

"A little better. The treatment is just what he needs."
Mrs. Grey smiled, but only with her mouth. She ran her hands
down the dark fur of her coat, then caught my eye.

"The chill is bad for my joints, that's all. I bet your
house is much warmer and cozier, isn't it?"

I didn't know what to tell her. It had been a long while
since I ever thought of that house as mine.

***

I had never heard the word *separation* until that night some
weeks later, when my mom woke me up before dawn and told
me to pack my things.

"Your father has decided that he wants a new family."
She opened my closet wide and threw socks and panties in a
suitcase as big as my bed. "We're going. Be quick, if you want
to take your stuff with you."

I was so scared that I couldn't move. I don't know why.

"Hello?" She glared at me. Her angry hands were
moving, tearing at everything I owned as if it were trash. My
stuffed animals were snatched from the bed one by one and
swallowed by the suitcase.

"I want to stay," I said. My voice was as small as Laura's
had been that time. A dying animal.

"Well, you can't." Her tone was triumphant, as if my
reaction delighted her. "We're putting it on the market. The
whole thing's decided."

I tried to imagine a world without nests. I couldn't.

And I could never imagine a world without Laura.

"I have to say goodbye." I thought about Maya and
Mrs. Grey. I thought about lemonade.

"Oh, yes." My mom curled her lip the way she used to
when I was younger and asked for a pet. "Your friend."

"I have to say goodbye," I repeated.

"Go there after breakfast, then," my mom said as her thin hands ripped my childhood apart, toy by toy. She turned to me and sneered. "To the witch-house."

***

My dad was gone once I was let out of the room that wasn't mine anymore. I didn't mind, but I wondered what it meant to get a *new family*. If he had other children, would he stop being my father? Was it the same with my mom? I sat in the kitchen eating cereal while she hissed to someone on the phone, and I wished that they would both have new children who could live with them instead of me.

Once I was done eating, I slipped outside. The woods were cold now, almost down to the red line on the thermometer. I thought about visiting all of my nests to say goodbye to them, too, but there was no time. Laura was more important.

I ran the whole way. When I reached the gate and heard the generator-hum, I wondered what my mom would say about Mrs. Grey's cluttered yard. She'd say nothing, probably, just curl her lip. I opened the gate soundlessly, like Laura had taught me, and went over to the porch. No one opened when I knocked, so I went inside.

"Laura?" I said in the tiny-voice. "Laura, it's me."

The kitchen was empty. Not even Maya was there. Maybe they were still asleep—when I had had some time to think, I realized that it was Saturday. I didn't want to wake them, so I waited. It was comforting to be in their kitchen, even though it was cold. And the garbage-smell was worse than usual—I couldn't tell what it was, but I didn't like it. It made me think of some meat my mom had thrown away once

117

since it had gone foul, and I had to breathe through my mouth even though it was just a whiff. The kitchen was messy, sure, but it wasn't like Mrs. Grey to let food go to waste.

I looked around to see where the smell was coming from, and that's when I noticed that the green door next to the fridge was ajar. I went up to it. The smell was clearly coming from inside. I knew I shouldn't peek, but curiosity got the best of me. I opened the door, brazing myself for the smell. It was pitch dark in front of me, and my breath hitched when I thought of the crevice. The spiders and the things that crawl. My hand found a light switch, though, and with a popping sound a fluorescent light came to life and showed me a narrow flight of stairs. So this was the basement. It was freezing; I understood why Mrs. Grey had worn that fur coat. I went down the first step, wishing that the switch would have been connected to some lights away from the stairs, too— now, I couldn't see what was down there. Only darkness.

When a loud noise broke the silence, I yelped, then relaxed once I realized what it was. A cat.

"Maya!" I said. "Did you open the door?"

The meowing continued. I'd rarely heard her make any noises at all, and I wished she would stop.

"Is there another light switch?" I asked, as if the cat would tell me. My fingertips touched the stone wall, searching—it was so cold that I would have needed mittens. Finally, I found what I was looking for. Standing on the final step, I turned on the light.

It was just one naked bulb in the ceiling, and it blinked at me like a spying eye. I saw shelves lined with jars and bottles, neatly labeled, and a whirring freezer in the corner. I saw Maya, pacing the floor, her meowing growing louder when she spotted me.

And I saw him. Laurent. There was a bed, a little boy's bed with blue sheets, in the middle of the room. In it was a boy who looked just like Laura, with shiny black hair and those pale eyes that I had never really liked. Those eyes that stared at me, wide open, even though he was asleep.

Maya ran up to me, screeching. When I reached down for her, she bit me before dashing up the stairs. Blood gushed from my hand as I followed her, with the stench clinging to my skin. I shut the green door. I wished I had a key to turn in that lock and throw away.

Mrs. Grey and Laura sat at the table. They were in their nightgowns, and their hair flowed free.

"There, there." Mrs. Grey's voice was monotonous. Her face looked strange without makeup, as if a skin layer had been peeled off. "It looks worse than it is."

"You shouldn't have gone into his room," Laura said. "He's afraid of strangers."

Mrs. Grey reached for her hand and started stroking it. "Laurent won't mind. Soon he's well again, and all three of you can play together."

"Yes." Laura smiled at me. It was the prettiest smile I had ever seen, and it made me terrified. "Laurent talks about you all the time. He can't wait to be your friend."

I don't remember what I said to them. All I know is that I never told Laura about the move. I left that house with my bleeding hand wrapped in my sleeve, and when I came home I was scolded for ruining my shirt. I barely noticed. My mom shoved me into the car, and I left my woods and my hideaways. I never went back. Life took me places; I grew older. I had no need to hide anymore.

But whenever I'm in a dark room, I see Laurent in front of me. And chills run down my arms, like the crawlies in the nest I left behind.

Razor, Knife

She calls me Twiggy, and I call her Bell. We're cousins, but everyone thinks we're twins. We share a birthday, but her mom's in jail and mine's dead. That's all you need to know about us.

Bell's thoughts are toxic green, they twist around mine like phantom limbs. My thoughts, she says, are violet. Like stormy skies or a bruised wrist. We sit on the porch as the moving van drives by, neither of us speaking. We don't have to. Rex scuttles between us and the gate, tail beating. He's Aunt Gin's favorite, the one dog allowed inside the house. Big and dumb, but I let him into my bed sometimes. After Bell has gone to sleep and won't notice.

"Shut up that damn dog!" Aunt Gin calls from the backyard. She's burning trash, there's that nauseating smell in the air of charred plastic. Bell picks up a pebble and aims it at Rex, but the lawn swallows it.

"Be quiet, stupid." Her voice is flat, she hardly ever uses it in school. I've heard people call her the Mute.

"He's not ours," I say. "Let her deal with him herself." We lean our chins in our bloodless hands, hair like sand and ashes falling into our eyes. Bell is as flat-chested as I am, I'm short like her. If it weren't for our clothes, no one would guess one of us was a girl and the other a boy. Another car drives past, a white sedan, three people in it. Aunt Gin has told us that the priest moving into the vicarage is married, but we haven't heard anything about children. Bell's eyes sting my face and I bury my violet thoughts out of her sight. We don't care about other people. We don't need them.

Still, we sneak to the vicarage that evening and crouch in our old hiding place by the hedge. The moving van has left but there are boxes piled up on the porch. All the windows are open, there's classical music coming from inside. We know Wagner, because Aunt Gin likes him. We don't know these silky piano whispers.

I bet he's a freak, Bell thinks. *Priests are always freaks.*

I pinch her bony little hand, and she pinches back. Her nails are scissor-sharp.

We should do a pagan ritual in their garden. Sacrifice something tiny.

Sometimes I don't know if the words coursing through my mind are hers or mine. Sometimes I know all too well.

"Let's go to the altar," I hiss. "This is boring."

A boy comes out of the house. He's in shorts and a tank top, barefoot, tan. He scans the garden before grabbing two boxes. They hide his chest, neck, face, but not his hands. They're veiny like a man's. I glance down at my child-fingers, then look away.

"Jock," Bell says once the boy has gone inside. "I smell it from a mile away." Me and Bell, we don't approve of jocks. They're high up on our list.

I force his hands from my brain. "Come on, let's go."

Bell stands, brushing grass and imaginary beetles from her skirt. The cotton has been washed so many times that there's barely any pattern left, but I remember when it was strewn with lilies. Most of our clothes are like that. Tattered and torn, with memories attached.

The altar is our home. It's where we come to be ourselves. No one walks as far into the woods as we do— most places around here are uninhabited, and all the neighbors are Aunt Gin's age or older. They stagger to the mailbox and then back inside. They don't see the paths we make at the back of their gardens. They don't notice the sparkles we leave behind.

We built the altar out of stones, in a clearing halfway up the hill behind the cow field. The deer skull came later—we found the deer close by the clearing, long dead, and we went home to get the wood-axe and Aunt Gin's hunting knife. Flies swarmed up when we sawed the head off, crawling around our ears and nostrils. Bell yelped when the head rolled away and maggots spilled out on the moss. She'd never admit it, but she did.

The skull is beautiful now, clean and raw with no flesh clinging to it. The antlers spread out like the wings of an eagle. In a way, I'd like it if someone came by and discovered this place. I'd like them to fear us and wonder. But then they might discover the list, and we can't have that. The list is for me and Bell only.

It's hidden under a stone in front of the altar, wrapped in a plastic bag. We hold our breaths as we lift the stone and seize it.

THE DEATH LIST

Blood on lined notepad paper. I've got a Swiss army knife in my pocket, Bell has a pink razor. It gets messy, every time we add someone to the list, but we don't mind a mess.

PONYTAILS

Ponytails are the popular girls in school. Most of them are called Jessica, but our name is better. I don't hate them like Bell does. I just don't care whether they live or not.

JOCKS

Some things don't need an explanation. My thoughts brush against tan skin, veiny hands, and I slice through them until they're dripping.

MRS. LINDEN

The English teacher with her cow eyes and tilted head, her too many questions. Once, she asked me whether I wanted to "talk to someone."

~~REX~~

Bell's written it, I've scratched it out. That's the difference between me and her. I believe death lists are for people.

MOMS

Because they left us. Because if Mom hadn't died, I'd still be living with her in the city, and I'd be a different person.

"We should put him on there," Bell says. She stands so close that I can smell her—that familiar blend of dog stink and cheap fabric softener. "The boy in the vicarage."

"We don't even know his name." People like him could be called anything. Anything would suit them.

"We'll find out." Bell fidgets with something in her skirt pocket. The razor. "And then we'll write it down right here." She taps the paper twice.

"Right here," I echo, only to camouflage the violet stirrings in my head.

Can he die and still be my friend?

***

We return to the house with the night chill and the shadows. Aunt Gin doesn't care what time we get home, as long as we do our chores. Rex knows she'll be mad if he barks, so he trots into the hall and whimpers quietly.

"Whatever you want, you're not getting it," Bell mutters. She slinks up the stairs, her long legs white as milk. They remind me of a pair of blindworms we saw once in the woods, thin and lightning-fast. Bell is always quicker than I am.

"Tommy, you remember the door?" Aunt Gin shouts over the TV noise.

"Yeah," I call as I reach out to lock it. This is how our conversations go—she tells us to do something, and we do it. The only reason Aunt Gin isn't on the death list is because she's better than foster care. For now.

Bell has shut her door when I come upstairs. Whenever she's alone, she writes in her diary, a book I've never seen and have no idea where she keeps. *Some things are just for me*, she said that one time when she told me about it. *And if you peek, I won't like you anymore.*

I don't want to read her scribbles. I know Bell inside and out, her green wires. I've seen her dig the razor into her skin, and the look on her face when she does it.

There are other things I want to know. His name, his age. If he's going to stay, and what his hands would feel like on top of my own. I used to be the only boy in the world, but now there's two of us, one broken and one brand new. I have no book to put my wishes in, no hiding place safe enough. Only a short while at the end of the day, when my thoughts are all mine.

***

We have no tombs to visit at the graveyard, but we go there anyway. It's our favorite place besides the altar. Bell balances on the stone wall, arms spread out like birdwings. I hum funeral psalm fragments as I scan the inscriptions. Most of them are boring, old couples who lived forever and died in peace. We want the young. The deaths wrapped in velvet, laced with heartbreak. The ones with tragedy and crushed dreams mixed into the soil.

"*Her golden curls turned to hay*," Bell chants in her graveyard voice, like a girl-priest in a faded sundress. "*Her blue eyes dead, hollows gaping in their place*." She curses as an old woman walks through the gates carrying a bunch of roses. "Don't people have anything better to do?"

"She should leave soon." Our eyes follow the woman as she grabs a vase, fills it with water and finds her grave. We watch her arrange the flowers and clean away some withered lilies. She knows we're there, the knowledge is in her jerky movements and downcast eyes. Our stares don't leave her until she's gone back to her little car and driven away.

Bell jumps off the wall, cat-smooth and quiet. Her barrette has slid to the side, and she pushes it in place. It's plastic, bright red, cheap like everything we own. She's worn it since we were six. Her thoughts swirl like December snow; I can barely catch them. They are dead girls with grinning skulls and green ribbons in their hair, but I don't know what they're saying.

"To the new ones," she says, skipping along the path, waving for me to follow. There's a corner of the graveyard that's only been in use for five years, with plenty of space left between the rows of stones. We like the graves there because the stories require no digging. A thirty-year-old, dead two years ago—we can find out what he looked like and what he was like and what he died of. I think the old graves are more romantic, but Bell craves family photos and Facebook profiles. I once saw her print a photo of a dead boy from one of the school computers.

We've almost reached the wall separating the old cemetery from the new one, when she stops with a hiss. I notice him a moment after she does. The new vicar's son. He's perched up on the wall, shadowed by the oak-trees on the other side. Crouching at an awkward angle, face turned upwards, which makes no sense until I spot the camera in his hand.

Come, Bell shoots at me. The command drives through my mind like a syringe. *We don't want to go near him.*

"Hey!" He's noticed us. He hangs the camera over his shoulder, then jumps to the ground. Bell was a cat but he is a tiger, all power and flexing muscles. "Do you live around here?"

Don't answer. He's everything we don't like. His grin tells stories of Mom's apple pie and soccer games with Dad. His sneakers are stark white, they lap up the sunlight. And he's in clothes that fit him, not outdated hand-me-downs left by his dead mother.

He's so beautiful that my black heart twitches.

"You do, right?" A crease appears between his eyebrows. I'd like to smooth it with my thumb. "I saw you come through the gate before. Figured you live close by."

Bell takes a step toward me. Her fingertips brush my forearm, cool and damp. Bell, the Mute.

"What if we do?" I say. "We've got as much right to be here as you do."

"Yeah, of course!" He fidgets with his camera, strokes the controls and shiny buttons. It looks new and complicated, just like him. "I just meant that, you know, it's nice to see some people my own age. Hadn't expected that when we moved here."

I wonder where he's come from. Where he's been up until now.

"I'm Martin," he says, holding his hand out. I'm a moth, glued to those long fingers. I want to reach out, clasp, touch, but there's Bell and Bell's eyes and her toxic warnings in my head.

"Tommy." Technically, I'm not telling him it's my name. Bell is mad at me, I feel her wrath like wasp stings under my skin. "She's Bell."

"Nice to meet you." He drops his hand. There's a pause in which anything might happen but doesn't. "Um, I…I couldn't get a picture of the two of you? Sorry if it's a weird question, it's just that it would make such a cool photo. Twins in the graveyard. You guys are twins, right?"

"Sure." I smile at him for the first time. My skin stretches awkwardly around chapped lips. I want to tell him that I wasn't always like this. If only Mom hadn't died, I would have lived in the city and I wouldn't have been stuck with Bell.

"So, can I snap a photo? Just one?" He grabs the camera, removing the lens cap. The lens is like a huge all-seeing eye, eager to expose our secrets.

"No," I say, staring at myself through that hungry eyeball, seeing nothing. Nothing anyone like him could want. "We have to get home."

"Oh, okay. Some other time, then."

Bell starts walking before I do, her red ballerinas hitting the ground. I don't catch up with her until we're at the edge of the cemetery.

"What an idiot," I say, making my voice light as air. "Right?"

Her shoulders are drawn up, sharp-angled and tense. The green oozes out of her. She doesn't speak until we're past the hill and Aunt Gin's house closes in on us.

"Now we know his name," Bell says, her whisper-voice like dripping icicles. "Now he goes on the list."

Altar, razor, knife. Martin's name bleeds onto the paper, finger-thick letters crossing the lines. Bell hums something, I don't know what. I have no music in me.

"Because we don't like him," Bell says once the list has gone back in its hiding place. "Because he thinks we're freaks." She drags her fingertip across the deer skull, blood streaming toward the eye sockets. War paint. "No one can think that. No one but us."

I recall the first time I met her, by Mom's hospital bed. Bell came with Aunt Gin and a social worker. *Here's your cousin Isabella. Won't it be nice to have someone to play with?* Bell said nothing. She was weird and tiny, and her milk teeth left angry red marks on my skin. I knew that Mom would die. And I'd have no one but Bell for the rest of my life.

***

Aunt Gin's booming voice comes to find us the next morning, while we're on cleaning duty in the kennel. The dogs tumble around us, all German shepherds, starving for attention and warmth and whatever dogs need. Bell hates their long hanging tongues and tells them as much. When Aunt Gin calls, the dogs stop moving, eyes fixed on the open backdoor, and Bell smothers her skirt with a grimace.

"Kids, come here! You've got a visitor."

It's Martin. He's on the porch, petting Rex, who skips this way and that with his tail wagging. Aunt Gin has gone back to the TV.

"Oh, hi." Martin grins, scratching Rex behind his ear. "Sorry to barge in like this, I hope you guys weren't busy?"

We shrug, my scrawny shoulders mimicking hers, Bell mirroring me.

"Just thought I'd come by, see if this was where you lived. Didn't know you had a dog. What's his name?"

Bell writing Rex's name on the list. Me, cutting myself just to be able to undo it.

"Rex," I say, knowing I'm breaking the rules one by one. Bell doesn't want Martin here, so I shouldn't want him here, but I do. His t-shirt clings to him in the way t-shirts are supposed to, not because he's outgrown it. The print on it says *BE PROUD* in violet letters.

"Invite him in, for God's sake," Aunt Gin shouts. "Show him your rooms or something."

We walk the stairs, Rex tagging along. Bell's door is closed and stays closed. I open mine and let Martin into my room, which is really just a closet with a slanted ceiling. Rex darts to the bed and lies down by my pillow, but Bell stays in the doorway. Her thoughts are too quiet for me to hear, or perhaps too loud.

"Very cozy," Martin says, and I know he's lying and I regret taking him here. The ceiling lamp is broken in my room and there's a sour smell seeping out of the walls. Martin probably has new furniture and an expensive computer and a phone that wasn't stolen. His brain isn't twisted like mine and he's got parents. I watch his symmetric face, all straight lines and glowing skin, and I want to stroke it and tear it to pieces.

"Tommy, right?" He looks at me, his scissors coming for the stitches that hold me together. "Your name?"

Before I answer, Bell steps into the room, shaking her head. "He's called Twiggy. *A little boy with twigs for legs, and a girl with a bell around her neck.*" She laughs, and I hate her.

"Is that from a song or something?" Martin asks me, not Bell. Because he likes me? Because I'm the least freaky one?

"Oh, yeah," I lie. I want to be alone with him. I want to scratch his name off the list and carve it into my chest.

"Well, I should head back home. Promised Mom to help unpack a few more boxes." He makes a face. A face as pretty as the rest of them. "But we can hang out sometime, yeah? I don't know anything about this place. Would be great if you wanted to show me around."

As if there's anything to see except cows and dung and dirt roads. As if someone like him will want anything to do with us once school starts in September and he gets to know other people.

"Sure," Bell says. There's that laugh again, and I remember her smearing the deer skull with blood. "We want that very much. Let's be friends." Once he's left, she sneaks up behind me and forces her bony hand into mine.

You don't need any other friends, little Twiggy. You have me.

***

Martin with his suntan and chestnut hair, his two living parents. I've locked him in a drawer inside my head and I only take him out at night, when Bell is busy with her diary. We never spy outside the vicarage, we never do anything to seek him out. He comes looking for us, always with that camera over his shoulder, always smiling.

"What do you guys do in the summer?" he asks in the backyard, while the dogs push themselves against the kennel fence and howl at him. Rex is circling around us, licking Martin's hands whenever he gets close enough. Martin's fingers glisten and he laughs, and I exchange looks with Bell that I hope he doesn't notice.

"There's nothing to do here," I say, shooing Rex away. "Obviously."

"But there has to be a lake nearby, right? We could go swimming. Do you have bikes?"

Bell scoffs, but doesn't say anything. Her dress is too short, the scar high up on her thigh shows. Not that Bell cares about things showing.

"No. No." I tilt my head as if Martin is the pathetic one. "Swimming is for kids. But if you really want to do something with us…" I pause. My brain reaches out for Bell, but all it finds is anticipation buzzing in the air around her. She leaves this decision up to me. She wants to see what I will do.

"Let's meet up at the graveyard at midnight. If you've got what it takes, that is."

"Oh. Okay, sure. Might be able to get some good pictures." His voice is light—I don't know if he's scared or not. He's too shiny for me to read. "See you tonight, then."

The kennel racket doesn't die down until he's left the backyard. Rex slips into the house, dragging his tail behind him. If I were a dog, I'd do the same.

"What's going to happen to Martin at midnight?" Bell murmurs, toying with the razor in her pocket.

"Who knows?" I say, pushing my whole weight against that drawer. Turning the key.

***

We get there first, our four feet tiptoeing past the parking lot, through the open gate. Martin comes five minutes later, carrying a chunky flashlight that stings our eyes.

"So," he says, too chipper for midnight, too sensibly dressed in a hoodie and jeans. We're in the same clothes as always, bare-legged, cold. Neither of us has ever had a tan, and mosquitoes don't bite us. Mrs. Linden once told me I need to go out more and get some sun. It's one of many reasons she's on the list.

"So," Martin says again, lower now. There's a glint of something in his eyes. Something newborn and vulnerable. "What are we doing?"

Bell murmurs in my ear, but the only word I can make out is *him*.

"We spend some time with the dead." I can't look into his face so I watch the curve of his shoulder instead. It's big and broad and everything else that I'm not. "If you dare."

"Yeah. I'm not scared of ghosts." His smile underlines the words, shows he's not lying. "Are you?"

I shake my head. Bell's thoughts worm themselves into my head, uninvited but always there. *We're not scared of anything. We're scary.*

"Let's go." For a moment, I'm in an alternate universe where it's just me and Martin in the middle of the night. But even in that universe, Bell is there, right outside the frame, watching. Waiting. She's quiet when he's around, none of the usual chanting. But I hear her sad-girl poetry in my head, eerie whispers about blood-specked handkerchiefs and hangings. Martin snaps pictures here, there. The flash perches on top of the camera like a gargoyle, spewing light. His day-world seeps into ours, brightening the gloom with flares and talking.

"This is really cool. Thanks for bringing me here." He talks about developing the photos; he'd been using the darkroom at his old school, but his dad is going to help him set one up in the basement. "It's a bit old-fashioned, I know, but I like it. You've got no idea what anything's going to look like until you're in the darkroom. You don't even know if you'll have any decent shots at all." He runs the flashlight over the graves we pass, murmuring the names to himself before crouching to snap a photo. Bell brings her arms out, swaying ahead of us like a tightrope walker. The shadows swallow her whenever the flashlight isn't pointed forward.

I want to climb the tower, she hisses without sound, and her hands reach into the star-heavy sky. *I want to be up there and look down at everyone*. The church tower reaches for the stars just like her, never-sleeping, lit up by spotlights in the dark hours. I imagine Bell up there, but I don't know if she's the locked-up princess, or the witch.

Not now. I glance at Martin, at his shifting light. My thoughts sink back into the fairytale and he's the prince pulling himself up, his hands running through golden hair. Gripping hard.

Bell spins around, a ghostly shape splitting the darkness, rearranging the pieces. Her head is crammed with singing and her fist slips into the razor pocket.

"Can't I get one of you two? You didn't let me that other time." Martin stops, flashlight hanging from his wrist, camera ready. "Please. It would make a really nice picture."

We don't want it. But Bell's eyes can't do much talking in the dark and I'm held back by fingers that aren't there, fingers grabbing my hair. I step forward and she flutters back and the flash blinds us.

"Perfect," Martin says. "Thanks."

I know it's not perfect, and nothing to be grateful for. That sliver of us locked in the camera, dark where we are supposed to be light, light where we are supposed to be dark. Two broken, twisted shadows leaning toward each other in an endless white night.

***

The storm comes in the dead hours, after Bell has put away her diary and I've slipped from Martin-thoughts to sticky

Martin-dreams. Our sleep is shadowless and heavy, and we never see the monstrous clouds or hear their roaring. When we come down in the morning, the air is clear and thin as if something has died and been born again, and Aunt Gin barks from the TV room.

"Damn weather last night. Neighbor came by, said the church was struck by lightning."

Bell shows her teeth, laughs without sound. But her giggles fill my head, *hee-hee-hee*, sharp and sweet like rotting fruit. Her eyes pin mine down and when Rex trots into the kitchen, I don't reach out to pet him. Bell stirs her muddy tea, wormwood-bitter and scorching. Shameful secrets whirl and waltz in her stare.

"God is a poor little girl," she says, the spoon whining against the cup's brim. "God is a boy made out of sticks."

We slink away from our chores once Aunt Gin has dozed off, following the road up the hill and past the vicarage. The church parking lot is packed, cars blocking each other, old men grouped together like wrinkly children on the first day of school. Bell hisses a string of curses, sliding in behind a toolshed, squeezing herself past a hedge while I follow, dog-like. Her mind glows, flares.

Fucking idiots. Just because this is the first exciting thing that's ever happened around here.

We move like water, trickling, away from people. Our eyes seek the church, the gaping hole in the tower. A tear in bone-colored silk, a missing tooth in an angel's mouth.

I want to get closer, we think, green and violet, violet and green. *I want to see everything.*

"Hey, wait up!" Martin. He comes jogging after us, tousled hair, pet eyes. "I thought you might be here. Can you believe this happened? Dad is freaking out."

Something twirls in my chest so I have to strangle it and make my voice mean. "Why? 'Cause he thinks it's divine punishment?"

He laughs. Whatever it was that I just killed stirs to life again. "Yeah, right! He's starting to realize what the repairs will cost, more like."

Bell lurks behind me, anemic, writhing. Her anger scratches my neck like nails, like the blade of a razor.

"Listen," I tell Martin, gathering broken green wires, hoping to mend them. "You wouldn't happen to know where the tower key is, would you?"

"The church tower?" He watches me warily, tension sharpening the lines of his face. "Why?"

"*Two little boys went out to play,*" Bell sings, voice distorted by a childish lisp. "*Snip, snap, snow hid the corpses away.*"

"Don't you want to see what it's like up there?" *Grab my hair and pull.* "Come on, bring the key and meet us at the gate by midnight. You might get some good photos."

It's forever until he nods. His smile has faded. I'm not sure if I'm going to see it again. "Okay. As long as no one finds out."

Oh, Martin. We'll be sure to leave no traces.

***

He's at the gate when we get there. Camera in one hand, key in the other.

"Don't touch anything," he says once we're past the church porch and the entrance door. "You'd better not get me in trouble."

Bell's thoughts dance around mine, electric. Magnified.

The church air is stale and heavy, paper-dry. Martin has left the flashlight at home and none of us have brought our phones. Bell skips up the tower stairs first, weightless, humming. I go after her, and Martin last, shutting the whiny door. The darkness eats at us, swallowing our limbs and clothing until we're invisible. Step after step after creaking step, the walls brushing against us from both sides. Bell sings, but I can't make out the words over the wailing in my head.

The tower isn't fit for neither princesses nor witches. Murky walls, heaping dust, and nothing to see except for the bell. We press our backs to the walls to get past it, around it. Bell's giggles crawl under my skin like maggots. Martin stands by the lightning-hole, his breaths hard and shallow. I picture myself beside him and our hands touching, merging. I picture many things, violet-laced, pure.

Not for you, Bell whispers, teeth sinking into my hesitation. *Not for us, Twiggy.*

Would it make you feel better if I cried? If I didn't just walk up to him and tap his back?

"Martin. What's your favorite flower?"

He spins around. The world shifts, turns as sweet and minty as his toothpaste-breath. I know what's about to happen, and that's the only reason I dare to place my hands on his chest. He's warm, with a drumming heart and blood rushing in all directions under my fingertips.

"Flower?" The spotlights from outside wash over me, blinding, slicing through. I can't see him. Only a shadowed hole where his face used to be. "Carnations, but why are you—"

Push. Easy and not easy at all. His scream is a yelp, a distant cry. Bell stands by my side when he hits the asphalt. Her fingers curl around mine, cold, burning.

"And we leave," she says, her voice a songbird's. "We depart this world and become angels."

Outside the church he lies, skull crushed, a game of jack straws. His hand rests against his chest, still warm, veins rising. I swallow and swallow while Bell looks for the camera. It's landed by a nearby tomb, cracked apart just like Martin's head. Bell grabs the film roll with the picture of us, the one picture. When we reach our altar, we dig with our little hands, dig a tiny grave in front of the deer skull. The film roll slides into the ground and dies, and our inverted shadows die with it.

Bell forces her thoughts at me as we walk back home. *He sleeps. He would have left us but now he's ours forever.*

I lock my own thoughts away from her. *Carnations, but why are you—*

Push.

***

There's a bus going to town once a day. Aunt Gin doesn't know about the money I take from her purse, and she doesn't see me leave. I come back in the evening with flowers wrapped in hissing paper. At midnight, I head to the graveyard.

His grave is the newest, strewn with lights and flowers. No one thinks his death was anything but an accident. We've heard that his mom is in a home somewhere, and his dad doesn't leave the house. But Martin is right here. I lay the carnations down—I'm the only one who's brought him carnations, because I'm the only one who really knew him.

I lie down on the night soil, in a sea of flowers. My fingers dig down, bury, bury deeper. I reach my hand out for him, fist sinking into the ground, wrist, forearm.

Grab me and pull.

And he does.

Swan Song

The road signs stick out of the ground like trampled weeds. They are the mark: *Go No Further*. Scilla doesn't know the myriad of symbols that have been sprayed on them in angry red, at some point after the Accident, but she knows the meaning of the grinning skull lying like a forgotten toy below the signs. *Run. Danger. Death*. She turns, rushing toward the woods. The top of the hill calls to her with its throaty wind-whispering. The firs are withered, stretched out like skeletal arms reaching for the sky, begging for something they can never have. The ground is covered in gray, viscous lichen, gnawing away at the tree roots. Swan calls it deathgrow. It's because of the deathgrow that she's trudging around in the gigantic boots—Swan's old pair. Once, she ran barefoot from the cottage all the way to the edge of the woods before she realized her mistake. The black marks are still visible in daylight.

The tune keeps the loneliness away. She has no idea where it's from—it's as if it lives inside her head. Most of the time, it curls up in a dark corner and sleeps, out of her reach. Sometimes it's nice. Allows her to hum it out loud, pour it over the woods like the rains of the old world.

Swan doesn't like the woods. "Dead," he says when she asks why he hates the trees. "They are all dead."

The branches creak and cry when she touches them. The trees aren't alive, but without them she would have nothing to cling to when she trips. The deathgrow can't climb far up their naked trunks, but it devours anything that falls. Slowly, like shadows creeping after the sun.

Eat. The hunger is like the imprint of clawing fingers in her belly. Swan never talks about hunger and only craves the dark liquid Cain brings. Scilla saves the emptied bottles and fills them with cold brook water, from the fresh stream up by the butchers' house. When Cain demands them back, she pretends not to know where they are. She guards her water like a dragon its gold.

Swan gets them meat from the butchers and Cain comes with heavy loaves of bread and sour cream. Cain has a boat and ferries people between the isles, and Swan pays for the meat with his sewing and mending. Scilla is in training, but every garment that leaves her hands has gaps and visible threads. It will be long until anyone will want to trade with her. Swan sometimes says that she has to hurry. Take whatever knowledge he can pass on to her. Scilla doesn't like how his voice and hands shiver whenever that topic comes up.

She's almost reached the brook when something small and filthy blocks her path. One of the butcher boys—half-grown and ugly, with the same coarse hair that all the butchers have.

"That scared you!" He laughs in her face. The sound echoes throughout the woods.

"You're supposed to leave me alone." Swan has told her not to have anything to do with the butchers. The kids shout and throw tiny rocks at her every time she goes with him to their dwelling, but she tries her best to ignore them.

"Leave me alone," the boy says in a bad imitation of her. His talk is fast and sloppy—the words are like mush. "Going to our brook, are you? Steal our water?"

"Why would I?" Scilla raises her chin. The boy is shorter than her and can easily be looked down upon. "We live by the lake, Swan and I. You think we don't have enough water?"

He laughs hoarsely, like the large birds that soar over the lake at dawn. He has the same cold, beady eyes. "Dead water! Ours is living. Ours is living forever."

He keeps laughing. Scilla hates him.

"Maybe I'm on my way to your mother," she says. "I'm tired of you, but I might want to talk to her."

"Lie." The boy gives her a grumpy look, as if her words have stung him. "No time for you, Mama has."

Scilla walks past him. Up the hill, to the butchers' house. "I need food."

"You go drink your poison water." The boy doesn't try to stop her. "When the old man dies, you'll be thirsty and you'll be starving."

The butcher woman stands in the yard and hangs wet, heavy linen over the washing line. The house is full of babies; they're crawling by the woman's feet. Once, Scilla heard Cain say that all the children born on the isles are damaged. You can't always see it on their bodies, but if you look them in the eye, you know.

"What do you want?" The butcher woman shakes a dripping shirt in the air as if she wants to shoo Scilla away with it. "What did you say to my boy?"

Scilla makes her face soft, though her muscles moan and struggle. "Swan couldn't come by himself today, but we need some food." She sees the woman's contempt, the glimpse of a worn-down canine. "Swan will head over as soon as he can and pay you for the meat, of course. He never forgets things like that."

The woman's eyes narrow. A baby clings to her leg like a tick and she pushes it away. "No," she says slowly. "We know Swan and we do trust him, just a bit. But you, what purpose do you have? You think I don't know what kids are like, and how they lie?"

"But I'm not lying."

The woman walks toward the house, where the door stands open. She digs into a bucket with her large red hand and throws whatever she's found in there toward Scilla.

It's a piece of meat. Raw and stringy, gray at the edges. The little children gape at it and a dog starts barking, but it must be tied up because it doesn't come running. Scilla knows what can happen with old meat, but her belly screams and she grabs it with both hands. Opens her mouth and chews, swallows, feels no taste at all because of how fast she's eating.

The woman's laugh is as hard and rough as the tree trunks. "I pity you, girl. Swan won't live long, and after that, you're on your own on that shore. Make yourself pretty, and maybe Cain will have you. You won't get any more from us until you learn to pay for it."

The worst, most painful hunger is gone. Chewing the meat is getting harder. It's tough like leather and it tastes stale, stale and foul. Scilla throws it away. She looks into the face of the butcher woman, and inside her, the truth about Swan boils and quivers. The nausea rises like a flood, and she drops down on the ground. Vomits undigested meat, vomits until there's nothing left but bile.

The woman laughs. The ugly boy stands among the trees and grins, his eyes darting between Scilla and his mother.

"You forgot to say thanks, you little thief!" the woman shouts as Scilla staggers away from them. Back to the lake.

She feels lighter inside when she reaches the shore and the waterline glitters in the distance. The lake is pretty—it's part of the sea, really, the sea which Cain views as his own, but Swan has always called it a lake. Maybe so it can be theirs, and no one else's.

Swan talks about the lake a lot. He watches it, as if he's waiting for something to rise to the surface. It's been many years since he told her why he can never move out of the cottage on the shore. The woman who lived with him a long time ago didn't understand that the water was dangerous. She used to swim every morning before the Accident, and she missed her lake. Once, when he was asleep, she went down to the water for a swim. He woke up at the sound of her screaming. When he reached the shore, her skin was already peeling off, and it was too late for anything.

Swan is on the bed snoring with the quilt on top of him when Scilla enters the cottage. She doesn't want to wake him—Swan is tired, pained by his ancient joints, and they don't have any food. Cain is the last person she wants to depend on, but who else is there? Maybe he'll come by tonight with the black bottles and stir Swan from his stupor.

The dizziness slithers through Scilla's head like a viper, and the taste of bile is on her tongue still. The air is fresh outside and there's a sea-wind blowing, so she heads down to the waterline. The shore isn't much—it's as stripped and ugly as the cottage, with bird droppings in the sand and rocks sharp as knives. It doesn't matter. Not today, because the weather is clear and there are no clouds ahead. She can see the City.

Maybe Swan remembers what it was once called, but he has never told her. It must have been grand, beautiful, what is now nothing but ruins and deserted streets. A world mirroring their own, a world as dead as the woods and the sea. Cain says that the City is where the Accident happened. Swan sighs when Cain talks that way, but he doesn't protest.

Scilla walks along the waterline. Not too close—never. She knows. Her eyes are drawn to the City, then to the colorless sand in front of her. *Crunch-crunch-crunch*, say the rocks and the grains and Swan's old boots.

She's reached the spot where the shore ends and the cliffs begin when she sees it. The flower. It has pale, paper-thin leaves, and it shoots out of the ground like a tiny hand. The petals are wrinkly but the color is as red as blood. As life.

Scilla gasps. She stares at the flower, caressing the stalk with her index finger. Then she grabs hold of it, hard, and tears it up. The flower is in her fist, pulsating like a heart fresh out of someone's chest. She rushes back to the cottage. Swan sleeps on while she sacrifices one of Cain's bottles to use as a vase, like she's seen in one of the old magazines. The red petals light up the cottage like a fire and she thinks she can smell the flower, too—a smell as faint and soft as the memory of a dream.

She sits at the table when Swan wakes up. She's eager, waiting, but she doesn't want to mention anything until he's noticed it by himself.

Swan gets out of bed with a heavy sigh. Yes, he does move slower these days. His face tenses up with every step he takes. For how long has it pained him so much to walk?

"Here you are." He pats her shoulder. Hasn't seen the surprise yet. "Did Cain...did Cain...?"

"No," Scilla replies quickly. "I'm sure he's here soon."

Swan heads for the hearth, but stops mid-step. He turns toward the table and his eyes widen. Scilla smiles.

"I found it on the beach!" The words burst out of her. "It grew right there, right beside the water! Swan, I...I don't think the water's bad anymore."

Swan makes a sound—a drawn-out groan. It reminds her of the butchers' house and what goes on up there at night.

He grabs the bottle, snatches it out of Scilla's reach, and throws it out of the house. Once he's done that he sinks to the floor, pale and broken. "Scilla…"

"I wanted to make you happy." Scilla cries. She can't stop crying. "I wanted…It was a living thing."

Swan watches her. He has the same look in his eyes as when he told her about the woman who went for a swim and died. The woman who was Scilla's mother. "Living things can be bad, too."

Cain arrives late that night. He and Swan get drunk, and Swan's eyes are far away. Once Cain has left them, Swan sleeps heavily, and Scilla knows that the butcher woman is right about him. About everything. She hums the tune, hums louder than ever, but nothing can wake Swan and in the end the tune is lost and she's just wailing.

The air is chilly when Scilla leaves the cottage. The one sound in the world is the waves hitting the shore. Their shore. The night is dark but she finds the bottle. The flower droops, but it hasn't wilted.

Her hands dig into the sand. She digs deep, before she plants the flower and refills the hole around it. Tears stream down her face—she laps them up, tasting the salt. Hungry. Thirsty.

"Please," she whispers, her hands stroking red petals. "Keep living. Don't leave me alone."

The Moor

We live on the Moor. Grandma used to say that water flowed here in the olden days, stubborn river water with strong fists. She knew everything about fists, Grandma did. The river was a storm beast, a blind rage, but now it is nothing at all and Grandma has ended up in the same dense dark earth it once tore apart. We buried her on the southside of the Church Rock, because that was how she told Dorte that it should be done. Every Sunday, Dorte, my sister Dorte, stands in front of the Rock and sings. She does it at dawn and when I explain to her that it disturbs my sleep, she replies that things can't be done differently. Tyra sleeps like a corpse and can show the whites of her eyes like a corpse, too. My sister Tyra has white eyes and Dorte sings God-songs before anyone else has risen.

Tyra takes care of the rabbits. The grindstone stands in our shed, made of sandstone from the old quarry where Granddad and Great-granddad and all the other men used to work. The tools belonged to Granddad, too, the longknives and hammer and the wood axe. Tyra is out in the shed a lot, but never Dorte. Tyra likes things that are sharp and things that are downy. Dorte sews clothing from most of the pelts, but sometimes Tyra hides parts and keeps them with her in the shed. She strokes the fur when she thinks no one is looking. The rabbits push through the earth that was once river—they are their own river in endless tunnels under my feet. I think that the rabbits should stay in their tunnels but I only ever tell Dorte, never Tyra. Maybe it's one of those thoughts I forget to tell anyone at all.

There is a road across the Moor but the ground is hilly between it and us, ridges with hunching trees and thickets lit up by poisonous yellow berries hiding the road from sight. A stranger knocked on our door once, when Grandma was in charge. I'm glad it happened then and not now when it's just Dorte, Tyra, and I. My singing sister and my sister with corpse-like eyes.

Granddad started working at the sandstone quarry when he was eight years old. That's what the men do, they break in the middle, and that's why we are girls and wouldn't have it any other way. The boy Granddad bled from his hands and turned ugly and crooked. Grandma married him out of pity and had many children who spread themselves out over the Moor. They are called Erid and Halvar and Meta and Laren and they are our kin. They have children who are our kin. I don't think any of them are as skilled at trapping rabbits as my sister Tyra.

When the Moor was a river there was salmon and trout and maybe pike—I've read the species names in Granddad's book about animals. *Salmo salar. Salmo trutta. Esox lucius.* Maybe they didn't exist at all. Dorte says that the world looked different then and that Grandma liked making up stories. Dorte's head is as grown-up as her body, and sometimes I get very tired of her.

I'm good at hammering nails and at hiding. Sometimes I run all the way up to the cairn, and before they've reached me, I'm hidden among the stones and invisible.

"Mei," Dorte says. Her voice is pointy and heavy, and her head jerks like an animal's. She's a large brown bird, my sister is, and I have to press my hands over my mouth to keep from giggling.

"Stupid brat," Tyra shouts and kicks into the dirt with Granddad's boots. This is why I like the cairn—no one dares to go near the rocks except me. Granddad never talked about the cairn and never looked at it. It has to do with death, but I'm too small to die.

"We'll go home without you," Dorte says. "Mei, do you hear? We'll leave you alone now."

"You won't get any food until tomorrow," Tyra adds. "Just sit out here. I hope the spirits take you."

I hear the slap when Dorte's palm hits Tyra in the face.

"Come out now," Dorte begs. Tyra stands behind her, covering her cheek—I see them through cracks and cavities. "You can't be in there. You know that."

The river flows forth when I close my eyes. I'll sing to it once Dorte and Tyra have gone.

***

I return to our house once the ground inside the cairn has gone cold and the earth has started squeaking. Dorte pretends as though I haven't been away but Tyra glares. Meat juice runs from her mouth, and it's shiny with grease. She's scrawny everywhere except for her swollen lips. After eating we pray, our mouths moving around the words at different speeds. It's forbidden to open your eyes during prayer, but they don't know that I do it so it doesn't matter. Once Tyra peeked, too—we looked at each other. Murmured the words like Dorte does and sat there with our eyes open.

"You'll help me with the dishes, Mei," Dorte says and looks straight at me. Prayer is over. I lower my hands into the dishpan and wonder if the water in our well is river water. Fairytale water. I stay there longer than I need to just to feel it between my fingers.

We sleep in the room that has always been ours. Sometimes Tyra sleeps out in the shed and sometimes Dorte doesn't sleep at all. I'm always where I'm supposed to be. My eyes are heavy but I hear that hum from the earth, and I listen to it. I sink, cold and blue and lonely.

***

It's morning. We eat greasy bread, and drink, and go to the hole behind the house. Dorte has a tiny brush to clean her nails with. Tyra sits with her legs spread and carves at a piece of wood, her face as rough and knotty as Granddad's. She aims longlegged kicks at me when I ask her to tell me a story. Summer mornings, fall mornings—the year takes giant leaps around the house, and sometimes I run to the cairn. Their voices follow, Dorte's tired and Tyra's angry one. Tyra wants to throw sharp sticks at the cairn but Dorte stops her. The river murmurs through the night and I wonder if Tyra would let me have a woolly little rabbit to tame. No, I don't wonder. I know.

***

The road lies splayed out beyond the hills, ugly and uneven. Dorte goes to the road sometimes but Tyra and I never go with her anymore. We went with her once but we never do it now. There is a woman who sells fabrics, Dorte waits for her. Returns with thin strips of colored linen that's no good for anything but mending tears. The woman is old, as thin as her fabrics but with a swollen lump of a stomach. She walks very slowly. Dorte comes back with her colors and the woman's chatter like fluttering birdwings in the air around her. When the words flutter in my ears I search the river instead. We live on the Moor. We don't need anything but the Moor.

It's from the road he comes. The stranger. He comes on Fabric Day and Dorte stands by the road beyond our hills with her basket. I'm in the kitchen and Tyra in the shed when she returns, without fabrics but with the stranger in tow. He's a man with long legs and boots. There hasn't been any man here since Granddad. And Dorte claims to revere the Church Rock! She throws her braids around, the basket hanging empty and forgotten over her arm. Tyra comes inside and puts her knife away on the window sill. Blood dribbles over the wood—she's been busy. No one is as skilled at trapping rabbits as she is.

"It's ruined now," Tyra says, watching Dorte and the stranger.

I want to run to the cairn and hide, but now Tyra is here and would catch me if I tried. She never scrubs her nails like Dorte does and they are black, thick and long. She's quick, and mean most of the time.

Dorte enters together with the man. Her voice is light and syrupy, false. The man has to hunker down inside the house—he's taller than Granddad. Taller than Granddad's sons, the ones that spread out over the Moor.

"Matteus," Dorte says and he grins with a too-wide mouth and too-white teeth. "His name is Matteus. Will you make the tea, Mei?"

The stranger's head moves in all directions as he surveys the lamp and the rugs and the knife on the sill. "You hunt?"

"It's just Tyra," Dorte tells him. "This is my sister Tyra, and that's Mei."

"Not what I'd expected out here on the Moor." What does he know about the Moor, this stranger? "I've passed this place many times, but your cottage isn't visible from the road. There are people further down, towards the woods. I usually speak a word with them when I walk past, but up here I've never seen a living soul until today."

I slam the cups against each other in the cupboard. Dorte doesn't seem to notice.

"Granddad built away from people," she says as if we talk about Granddad with anyone. "It's a good house, it's been here for a long time. So has the shed."

The stranger looks a fool when he smiles. His lower lip isn't beautiful like Tyra's, just fat and spongy. "To think that you live out here alone, three girls. Not bad."

I drop the tea tin on purpose, crushing the leaves between my fingertips. The counter turns gray and grainy. "We've only got three cups," I say, and Dorte's eyes sharpen.

"We have five, so you just take four of those." She's impatient, not as sweet-voiced as when she's talking to the stranger.

We only have three cups. The two at the back of the cupboard belong to Grandma and Granddad, and we never use them. When Granddad passed, Grandma pushed his cup to the back of the cupboard, and when Grandma passed, Dorte did the same with hers. The Granddad cup is blackened on the outside from all the fires he's heated it over. The Grandma cup has a dent on one side. They are Granddad's and Grandma's, and that's why they can't be used by anyone else.

"Not the Grandma cup," I say.

"Grandma knew what hospitality means." Dorte comes up to me and takes the cups out herself. Places them on the table. "That's more than you know."

I'm not trusted with a single thing after that. Dorte pours steaming tea into the cups and shows the stranger to the seat of honor. Tyra sits by the window, quiet. I'm by the door, though Dorte tries to push me around with her glares.

Dorte wants to know why the stranger walks across the Moor. He tastes his tea. His hands are too big for the Grandma cup—they cover it until it's gone.

"I'm from a village far away from town, so I go there once in a while to see my old mother. The bus fare is too costly for me, and even if you take the bus you have to walk the last mile or so. I've always been fond of the Moor. There's a sort of serenity here, I like that. No sounds, nothing. It allows you to think."

I have to speak. "There are plenty of sounds on the Moor. The earth squeaks, it whines, it lives. The soil buzzes because of the river but I bet you can't hear it, since you don't belong here."

Dorte flies from her seat. "Stop it with that river talk!" Her voice is loud, almost a scream. "It's a story, Mei, don't you understand? Don't you understand anything?"

Tyra laughs. She draws her knees to her chin and laughs, low and croaky like a bird.

"I do understand," I say and go outside. Once I've closed the door I run, past the shed and the Church Rock, toward the cairn. I fight my way inside and I'm hidden. Invisible.

The door to the house opens. Their voices trail toward me, mingling with the sound of stomping feet.

"…just a child," the stranger says. Some words reach me but not all. "Could get sick…the earth is cold."

"Damn kid!" Tyra calls, and Dorte looks like she wants to do the same. They come up to the cairn, all three of them, stopping in front of it. One tall, black shadow and two little ones.

"Sorry, but I don't see what the problem is." The stranger laughs. "The girl is right there. I can see her watching us."

Dorte turns her eyes away from the rocks. Murmurs, "She's not allowed…it's no place for us. She's not supposed to be there."

"Damn kid," Tyra says again, but this time her voice is almost sad.

The stranger's laughter hits us again. "What, you believe such old nonsense? It's just a heap of stones, nothing more. You can't be serious."

Dorte tightens her hands to fists. "It's the resting place of the fathers. It's the sacred place. The women can only touch the stones when a man of the family is to be buried—the men can't ever go up here. The spirits watch, they make sure things are done correctly. Grandma taught us that night when it was Granddad's turn to rest. We have tools in the shed—hoes and spades. We have what we need."

"Mei ruins everything," Tyra says. "Mei doesn't know how things are supposed to be."

The stranger steps forward. "You're lucky that I came by. I'm not afraid of any old superstition. Your spirits may do their best to fight me." He comes all the way up to the cairn. I don't have time to back away before he reaches into my hole and grabs my ankle. His other hand comes for me too and he pulls, stronger than me and the cairn together. I'm dragged into the open, aiming kicks at him but he laughs, pinching my arm.

"There she is. See, that wasn't so hard. The spirits must be asleep." He watches me with his wide face that is far above mine, halfway to the heavens. "You need to be nicer to your big sisters from now on. They know what's best for you."

Back in the kitchen, the tea has gone cold and bitter. I sit opposite Tyra because they've made me.

"You have to agree with me now that there are no spirits." The stranger eats—Dorte has brought out her honey cakes. He's had three already.

Dorte shakes her head. "The spirits can't reach you since you don't belong to the family. You're not from the Moor."

"And little Mei?"

"Mei hasn't become a woman yet. No blood. Once you have your blood you're a woman, and then the spirits know what you are. Tyra and I can't touch the stones—they won't let us. Mei can." Her eyes harden. "But she shouldn't."

I have never heard the bit about the blood before. I don't like it. "It's the river," I say. "It's because I can hear the river, and you can't."

The stranger laughs with his fat lips and pearly teeth. "Water out here? I'd like to see that. Dry as dust it is, drier than any place I've seen."

I watch him. Still I don't see him.

He stays in the house that night. It's the kind of night when Dorte doesn't sleep. He doesn't sleep either. The bed thumps and screeches, and they make vile noises that slice through my head. He goes still after a while and Dorte rises. Her nightgown hangs off one shoulder, unbuttoned. I hear her walk out of the house and to the Church Rock. She's singing. The stranger sleeps but Dorte is singing. Tyra's in the shed, caressing silky furs with unwashed hands. She does it in her sleep.

It roars and rushes. I hear it over Dorte's song, over all the songs in the world. The river, the fairytale water—Grandma's promise. There has been a river once, and there shall be a river again. What once was will exist again.

It lies on the window sill, forgotten. The wood under it is dark and sticky. I grab it in my hand and it only weighs a little, is as light and soft as an animal.

My feet move over the floor toward the bed where he sleeps. I turn the knife this way and that in my hand. The earth laughs. The earth lives and breathes and waits for me to set things right.

Once you have your blood you're a woman.

Maybe it's the flowing blood I'm hearing?

Rose and Caramel

Lucia came riding the dawn with that here-and-there hair and the carmine coat whispering forgotten poems around her fleshy thighs. Amelia leaned out of the doorway, breathing in the fading bus fumes and the rose-and-caramel scent that was Lucia. It had been too long; too many days without speaking, too many nights with loneliness and house groans keeping her awake. All that was gone now, the lonely nights carved away like worm holes in an apple. Lucia had come home.

"But you know I don't live here," she said on the porch steps with Amelia's stick-figure arms squeezing her, with Amelia's weird little brain drowning in a sea of rose petals and caramel bonbons. "Sweetie, I've got to go back to town now and then. I need my job."

"I know, I know," Amelia sang, rose-drunk, face hidden in Lucia's hair. "Please don't talk about your job, Luce, because I hate it."

"Yes, yes." Lucia patted Amelia's shoulders. "Shall we go inside? You haven't even let me put down my bags, you little monster."

Amelia giggled as she darted inside to put the kettle on. She skipped through the kitchen opening and closing cupboards, setting the table with Lucia's favorite cup and her own kitten-adorned one. The house filled with good sounds now, sounds like Lucia taking off her boots, Lucia hanging her coat, Lucia heading upstairs with the bags. When she came back down Amelia poured the lavender tea and waved at her to come sit down.

"How have you been?" Lucia had calm, normal-colored eyes that Amelia had been jealous of at first, because hers were strange and broken. But Lucia said they were pretty and as long as Amelia didn't look too long into the mirror, she believed it.

"Good. Bored." Amelia fidgeted with the tablecloth. The questions. She didn't much like the questions. Lucia should know better than to ask them, because they made her love Amelia less.

"Bored?" Lucia's eyes narrowed. "Honey…"

"It doesn't mean what you think it does." Except it did. The boredom was a sickness that ate at her, and it came crawling in through the window on lonely days. It was a tall pale man with burning eyes and a smile that went all the way around his head. It was hungry and mean and it played naughty games. "It was only once, anyway."

Lucia closed her eyes. Amelia quietly counted the wrinkles around them, one-two-three, one-two-three.

"It's bad," Lucia said at last, and opened her eyes again. "You know it is."

"But he doesn't. The man." Amelia hanged her head. Her hands were curled in her lap like withered, useless claws. "I've told him, but he won't listen."

"Show me." Lucia stood, her tea untasted. "Better just get it over with."

Amelia held Lucia's hand and led her through the tall grass, over to the shed. The sun peeking through the holes in the walls was so bright that no flashlight was needed to spot the bundle in the corner. She hadn't been to see him for a few days and he had started to smell quite bad.

"Amelia…" Lucia didn't vomit, like she'd done the first few times. "Who?"

"He knocked on the door. He's not supposed to do that." She tried to remember more, but whatever the boy had said or done had gone lost in the maze that was her brain. She did recall that his eyes were an impossible shade of blue. A sea that was still or stormy depending on the light.

"Right. We have to bury him." Lucia tied her hair into a bun and grabbed the shovel and the wheelbarrow. The sounds she made as she was lifting the boy off the ground were just like the sounds he himself had made when Amelia killed him. Lucia pushed the wheelbarrow to the backyard and Amelia came after with the shovel. Her thoughts were fluffy and light as clouds.

"I don't want to do this again." Lucia dug the hole away from the other ones, beneath the cherry tree. The boy slipped into the ground as if he felt at home there. Amelia enjoyed that thought. His face was pale, as pale as that of the man with the smile going around his head, but now that Lucia was here Amelia knew that the wicked man didn't really exist. He was a nightmare that felt real but wasn't.

When the hole had been filled up again it was a patch of bare soil in a sea of swaying grass. Amelia said that it looked as small as if they'd buried a baby, not a boy, but Lucia's wrinkles had multiplied and she didn't smile. Back inside she washed her hands and showered and wept loudly in the bathroom, and then she came out and finished her cold tea.

"You need to learn how to be lonely." Her hand fell on top of Amelia's, warm and just a little dry. "You can't keep doing this."

"I won't do a thing when you're here." Amelia tilted her head the way she had a lifetime ago, when her parents had been alive and could be persuaded to buy her sweets and curly-haired dollies.

"Not just then, Amy. You have to behave yourself when I'm off working, even when I'm gone for months."

Months. Something clicked inside Amelia's curly-haired head. Months was the wrong word, it was twisted and foul. Lucia had never used it before and she shouldn't start now.

"You're not on your own. Even when I'm not here, sweetheart, you're never on your own."

Amelia saw his bony fingers land on the window sill. A pale man, a man with burning eyes and a smile that went all the way around his head. Lucia kept talking but his smile, smile, smile drowned out her words. His raspy voice danced through Amelia's mind, stopping here and there to inhale the scent of rose and caramel.

Months? We can't have that.
Months? We can't
We can't have

The Ice

Nina is hiding behind the raspberry bushes when she spots the cat. From that moment on his name is Tail, and she loves him.

"Come here, then. Come, kitty!"

He trots up to her, a shadow snaking through the meadow-grass. His coat is the same midnight black as her sisters' veils.

"Where'd you come from?" She touches his fur with filthy hands. "Did you run away from home?"

Tail meows, rubbing his head against her naked calf. Nina wants to pick him up and bring him inside, but her sisters wouldn't allow it.

"They don't like cats. They don't like anything." She's particularly mad at them this afternoon since they've told her to pick the blackcurrant bushes clean. They're too frail to do it themselves—Emilia can help out for an hour or two before she starts whining about backache. Even then, her work is sloppy, and she huffs and wheezes whenever it's sunny like today. Sibylla and Henrietta are the eldest, and they're practically useless. Sibylla's spindly like a scarecrow, and walking takes her forever. Her hands are icy, with too-thick nails and too-bony fingers.

"But I have to be nice," Nina murmurs into the cat fur. "You can't tell anyone that I had a bad thought about my sister."

Tail watches her with green eyes—she would like to compare them to some rare gemstone, but she only knows sapphires and rubies. Does he belong to anyone? There are no neighbors, as far as she's aware. There's just the house, the road, the meadows, the woods. And the lake, watching them day and night.

"You'll be mine, won't you?" A horse-fly lands on her arm, and she slaps it. The moment it falls into the grass, Tail traps it under his paw before gobbling it up. His tiny chewing noises make Nina laugh.

"And they can't say a thing about it." She glances toward the house, where something dark is stirring—Emilia has stepped out on the porch. "It's just between you and me."

"Child?" Emilia calls. Her voice is like a piece of string, stretched out so far, it's on the verge of breaking. "Where did you get to?"

"I have to go." Nina pops a raspberry into her mouth, chewing it to mush like Tail did the horse-fly. "Don't let them see you."

Emilia waits for her on the porch. "No playing until you're done picking." Her gray braid reaches down to her waist. Sometimes Nina wants to tug at it, just to see what will happen.

"But it's hot."

"It's summer." Emilia's eyes trail past Nina, toward the lake, and they narrow. "Soon the berries will go bad, and they'll be no use to anyone but the jackdaws."

Nina knows about jackdaws. They flock in the treetops and soar over the roof. "There are horse-flies everywhere."

Emilia pats her shoulder. Her long, wide sleeve brushes against Nina's cheek. "They're mean little bities. We've always had plenty of them here."

"I'll pick more tomorrow. I promise."

"Very well." When Emilia smiles, her eyes sink into the wrinkles and disappear. "Enjoy your playtime, then. But don't tell Sibylla I allowed it."

Nina runs off to look for Tail, who's dozing off in the shade behind the clothes line. She sings him songs about girls and cats until the bell calls her inside for supper. The sisters are seated when she comes, their hands locked in prayer.

"Late," Henrietta says, the word slipping through her pursed lips.

"Very late." Sibylla's nostrils twitch, as if Nina carries an unpleasant smell with her from outside. But cats don't smell like anything. "Wash your hands."

They don't say grace until she's seated opposite Emilia. Sibylla closes her eyes and uses that God-voice that Nina can't stand, since it's warm and soft and nothing like how she usually talks.

"Amen," Sibylla finishes, and Mother's old soup tureen is passed around. Carrots, cauliflower, and pearls of fat swimming on top. Nina has told them many times that she hates carrots, but they never seem to remember. The earthy, sweet-but-not-sweet taste grows in her mouth, and she has to think hard about Tail to keep from spitting it out.

Washing dishes is Nina's task, and so is bringing in firewood. The sisters sit on the sofa, muttering to each other every now and then. At a glance, it's impossible to tell them apart. Nina's wrists smart from carrying the firewood, and splinters dig into her fingers when she piles it next to the tiled stove. *Your fault*, her thoughts hiss at Sibylla, Henrietta, and Emilia. *All your fault*.

They don't speak to her until her tasks are done and she's changed into the nightgown with the lace-trimmed collar.

"You're growing, child," Sibylla declares, toying with the silver key around her neck.

"Our little sister is not so little anymore." Emilia smiles. "We've agreed that it's time you got your own room, instead of sharing with me."

"Come." Henrietta stands, her gray eyes pinning Nina like a butterfly to the wall. "I'm sure you're most grateful for this."

They head upstairs, and Sibylla unlocks the door that shouldn't be opened. The door to Viola's room.

"Too old for bed-sharing," Sibylla says, still clutching the key. It's dull and heavy-looking, rusty like the spade in the shed.

"It's what dear Viola would have wanted." Henrietta has her hands clasped. The black cuffs of her dress hang loose around her wrists.

The room makes Nina wrinkle her nose. Creaky floorboards shiver under her soles as she follows Henrietta inside. Everything spins, as if the whole room is about to be swallowed by a gaping mouth. A maroon quilt slumbers on top of the bed. On the wall is the picture of Viola, the one that worries her, the one she always skips in the photo album.

"Your own room, eh?" Emilia says. "What a lucky girl you are."

"A girl who needs to be good and show respect for her eldest sister." Henrietta nods to the portrait. It hangs there watching—Viola watching them with wintry eyes.

"I will." Nina curtseys, wishing someone would take the picture down. She isn't a good girl and she never will be, because she doesn't want her dead sister's portrait in her room.

She's alone with it after the others have left. If only Tail were here, but he's probably out hunting. For a while, she stands by the open window, but there are no cat movements in the swaying grass. When she slept in Emilia's room, the view outside was the woods and the road, but here she can only see the lake. The blue lake, the cold, dangerous lake. Nina has never seen it up close, because she isn't allowed to leave the garden. The sisters have told her stories about snakes in the meadow-grass and wild beasts prowling the woods. And they have told her about the lake, the ice, the luring ice. The ice that took Viola.

She barely sleeps that night, which is no wonder because of the heat. It's windless outside but the house creaks, its old wooden floors and drafty windows bursting and beating. Emilia gets thirsty in the middle of the night. She used to make Nina fetch water for her, but now she'll have to go herself. That must be why stairs and floorboards are swaying—just a glass of water. Still Nina hides under the quilt, inhaling its musty smell, and forces her eyes shut. Viola's portrait is a pitch-black square on the wall.

***

One night is enough. The next evening, she sneaks out to find Tail, and when she does, she hides him in her apron and carries him to her room. He's warm and heavy like a sun-heated rock. She puts him under the quilt, and he's asleep by the time she slips into bed with damp strands of hair glued to her brow after the face-wash. Tail purrs loudly in his sleep. It's lucky that Emilia doesn't notice, when she stands in the doorway listening to Nina's prayer. She prays that God will protect Sibylla, Henrietta, and Emilia. She prays for Father and Mother and Viola, who are in Heaven, to which Emilia nods and interlaces her own hands.

"Yes," she says, and her voice is sad. "Not a day goes by when we don't remember Father and Mother and dear Viola." She bids Nina a good night and shuts the door. Nina reaches out for Tail and pulls him close.

"But I don't remember," she tells him, and wishes ripple and multiply under her skin. "I'm the only one who can't remember."

***

The accident shouldn't have happened, but it does. Nina sleeps for too long the next morning and is torn awake by the scream, when Henrietta shoves Tail off the bed.

"Are you out of your mind, girl, to bring a cat inside? And a black one, too!" Henrietta's thin arm lashes out again but Tail is quicker, and he darts out of the room. Nina thinks about the front door that is usually ajar on hot days, and if it isn't there should be a window open somewhere. Tail will find his way.

"What a mess! And there's cat hair all over the linen." Henrietta slaps her cheek, hard. Sibylla stands in the doorway—Sibylla, with those same sharp, gray eyes that Viola has in the portrait.

"Listen to your sister," she says. Her voice is more brittle than the others', like the dried roses hanging in the kitchen windows, with thorns that are just as treacherous. "You're bringing ruin down on all of us. Is that how you repay us for dear Viola's chamber?"

"But he's mine!" Nina hates them. They're her sisters, but she hates them.

"Viola didn't like cats, that's for sure," says Henrietta who has stopped slapping Nina but is straightening the linen with jerky movements.

"No." Sibylla drops the word like a needle. "She certainly did not."

In her head, Nina is returning every single slap. Until they'll never hit her again.

Emilia doesn't darken when they tell her a while later, but not even she is happy about Tail although she's said that they used to have cats before. Maybe she's forgotten.

"Play with him in the garden if you have to," she tells Nina when they're alone in the kitchen. "But you shouldn't have animals in bed with you."

Nina wants to say that the portrait didn't frighten her when Tail slept on her arm, and that the house stayed quiet all night. But she must never say out loud that the portrait is scary. You mustn't be afraid of your own sister, even if she has cruel eyes and wrinkles so deep that they distort her face. You must love your sister.

The dream comes to her that night. Nina is so small between the sheets and she wants to stay there, but something makes her feet touch the cold floor. Something forces her chin up and makes her look at the portrait—but there's no one looking back. The frame is empty. Viola is gone. That fact should have made Nina relieved, but it doesn't. It scares her. She's lost in a dream, but for a split second, she wonders where Tail is in the world outside.

It's dark on the stairs and she's dragged down, down, though she doesn't want to go further. The rail is slippery, slick with moisture like the snakes lurking in the grass. She comes downstairs and sees the front door, and the quiet kitchen with moonbeams stroking the table. She wants to go outside, search for black fur and velvet paws. But the dream forces her to the left, to the parlor, where the lamplight flickers and the clock has stopped ticking. *The clock has stopped ticking.* Her feet stick to the floor, moving step by step, until she's in the doorway. And she sees.

The moon spews pale light over the shape on the sofa. The black petticoat falls to the floor, just like the ones the sisters wear—their dark robes, the black fabrics covering steely hair. It looks like one of the sisters but it's not one of them, not Sibylla, not Henrietta, not Emilia. Nina never got to meet her but she has the portrait in her room and she knows Viola, dear Viola who was the eldest sister, dear Viola who was taken by the ice.

It's been ten years since they locked Viola's room. Ten years since the crack in the ice and the lake's treason. Still she's here now, a dark form against the sofa's dusty velvet, and something about her interlaced hands makes Nina want to look away. *Claws,* she thinks. *Roots.* Viola doesn't move, but her sunken chest falls and rises under the veil. It's lace, too pretty for daily life, but Emilia has said that they had to look nice when they had their portraits taken. They were all there, everyone except Nina. Emilia has never properly explained what a photographer is, but she has talked about how they brought their funeral veils with them, the leaf-thin ones with lace trimmings, and how solemn they had to be in the photographs. Sibylla, Henrietta, and Emilia appear in their veils in the photo album and they look different, smoother, more like Mother in the one picture they have of her. Viola sits with her back straight in the center of the sofa—and Nina can't breathe, because Viola looks different, too.

You can't see much under the veil. It doesn't hang like this in the portrait, not like this soft, black film obscuring her face. Heavy breathing makes the fabric rustle. Nina's eyes dart to the clock on the wall. It has stopped on the 10 and the 3, the inky hands pointing away from each other. Nina knows, like everyone knows, that Viola died at ten to three on that winter night. She knows, even though she wasn't born.

A sudden noise, a hoarse gasp of breath, makes the veil billow. Something wicked glints behind the lace. Nina wakes up, her toes like ice, her knowledge sharp and cold and terrible. What she heard was a laugh, what she saw was her dead sister's eye. The quilt reeks like rotting autumn leaves but she buries her nose in the stench, too scared to lift her head. She doesn't want to know if the frame on the wall is still empty, or if Viola's dead eyes are watching her.

***

The summer burns Nina's feet, and Tail catches fat voles in the grass. The sisters move like crooked stick figures under their dark layers of fabric. Sibylla craves strong coffee early in the morning, and lets Nina know that it's her duty to make it. She's doing most of the cooking, too, now that she's old enough to use the stove. In the kitchen cupboards, she finds mouse droppings behind the plates and saucers, and she thinks about Tail's teeth and his high leaps out on the meadow. Not even Emilia seems to remember that they used to have cats when Mother was alive.

Sibylla makes sure that there's always a fire going. She moves slowly through the rooms, twisting her hands. Nina sees Viola in her dreams every night, and she notices the similarities and differences between them. Viola is the eldest sister—she's drier and colder and paler than the others. *Is*, Nina thinks, as if Viola was still alive.

The dreams don't change. Every night she walks down the stairs and into the parlor, where Viola sits. Every time, the clock has stopped at ten to three. Not once does Nina think about asking her sisters to move back to Emilia's room. Emilia is kind, most of the time, but Nina doesn't want to bed-share with her again. And she knows, somehow, that nothing can make the nightmares disappear. Someone wants her to have them, again and again.

Every other Tuesday afternoon, Nina is forbidden from playing outside. The sisters make her stay upstairs, but it usually doesn't bother her since it's the only time she's allowed a pencil and some pieces of drawing paper. Her Tuesday drawings are crammed with big-eyed girls and flowers as large as trees. Once, Emilia praised a drawing and put it on the wall in her room, though Sibylla made her take it down again. Nina itches to fill the blank paper with teary eyes, but it's the last days of summer, and Tail is waiting for her under the oak-tree. She doesn't want to stay inside.

"Don't give me that sour look!" Henrietta says and shuts the door. Nina is left alone with the sheets of paper and Viola's eyes on the wall. Viola's face, unveiled.

The sisters are in the garden—Nina hears their voices from outside. They won't know whether she's drawing or not, so after a while she leaves her room and moves into Emilia's instead. From there she can see the road and the front yard. Nina has heard things before, on other Tuesdays, and she's old enough to know that Tuesday evenings are when the pantry is filled with fresh eggs and milk bottles. She stands on the tips of her toes and looks out of the window.

Someone stands by the gate together with Henrietta. A stranger. *Boy*, she knows from Emilia's description of such creatures. A human being but with short hair—this boy's hair is light, the same color as her own. An odd-looking thing with wheels, two at the front and one at the back, stands next to him. There's a wooden box between the front wheels, and that's where the eggs and the milk bottles come from. Plenty of other groceries, too—Henrietta has a piece of paper in her hands, and she seems to be reading out loud from it. The boy is taller than Henrietta, much taller. If Nina stood next to him, he wouldn't even see her. He'd walk right past as if she were a ghost. His fingers are stubby and tan, and his skin is as smooth as hers. He's a living, breathing thing with skin as smooth as hers.

Nina grabs hold of the sill to bring herself closer to the window, but she slips and knocks her forehead against the glass. The boy looks up at her. He frowns, saying something, and Henrietta twists her neck like a big, black bird and stings Nina with a glare that has her backing away from the window. But it's too late. She's barely returned to her own room before they ascend the stairs, hissing and rambling.

"It's a disaster," Emilia cries, "a disaster!"

Henrietta digs her nails into Nina's arm, and Sibylla blocks the doorway. Her head is bowed, and the veil covers most of her sunken face.

"To think that our little sister is such a wicked creature," she spits. "After everything we've done for you. Is this the thanks we get?"

Henrietta shakes Nina hard, keeping her eyes on Sibylla. "What are we going to do if he tells anyone?"

Emilia whimpers, fingers toying with her braid.

"There'll be no more playtime for you." Sibylla has a mean little smile lurking in the corner of her mouth, as she fixes Nina with one steely eye. "We've been lenient with you, sister, but that time is over."

Nina imagines that Tail is there, brushing his head against her leg. Scratching the smile from Sibylla's face. When she's thrown into the dream that night, everything has changed.

She enters the parlor at ten to three, and Viola has pulled her veil aside. Nina wants to stay in the doorway, but the room tears and pushes until her feet keep moving. She's not allowed to stop, until she stands in front of her dead sister's face.

And it is a dead face. Brown patches cover the forehead, reminding her of rotting apples. The skin looks like it would break if she touched it—it's like a spider's web, so thin it's barely there, and if even a single thread burst, the whole face would collapse. Worst are the eyes, though—fogged-over, glassy, as if they're trapped under the ice, but there's a glint of something living in them. Something living and breathing and mean, just like Nina herself.

Viola stares at her, twisting and turning her hands in her lap. Tufts of hair stick out under the veil, iron gray like the porch stairs or the lake in spring. A grin dances over her lips, flashing broken teeth. Then, her mouth opens to form words.

Nina has never heard a voice like Viola's. It's as if someone has carved her innards out with a spoon, until only a hollow space remained. From that space, the words are pressed out, in stinking puffs of air, as mauled and distorted as the dead woman's eyes.

Afterwards, back in her bed, Nina buries herself under the covers and reaches for Tail, though he isn't there. In her head Viola's voice repeats its foul words over and over again.

You are not my sister.

***

The room forces her to stand in front of Viola the next night, too. Viola's laugh dips filthy fingers into her mind, and the moonlight paints deformed shadows on the floor. Nina stares at Viola, and Viola talks.

"I don't care much for sisters, little one."

It's a strange thing to say. Sisters are all they've got, for better or worse. That's the way it's always been.

"You shouldn't either, child. Not if you know what's good for you."

Nina is used to the night-thoughts, the secrets only Tail can ever know. Why does Viola seem to know them, too?

"I was the eldest, I was." Viola grins with the few rotting teeth she has. The other sisters don't have a lot of teeth left, either, but still Nina shivers staring into that dark hollow, with the tongue that writhes like a spongy worm. Viola's eyes are burning and she's dead, dear Viola who went through the ice is dead.

"I was in charge," she says, "and they didn't much like that, you see. They didn't like it at all, when I told them we were moving away."

Moving away? Birds move in winter. People don't move; the sisters don't move from the house that Father once built.

"Oh, I see what you're thinking." Viola laughs. "A little thing your age, you don't know a lot about anything. You don't know that you get old, and you die, and you want a bit of comfort in your final years...You don't know that at all." Something creaks under the veil when she turns her head.

"But you're small enough for one thing," she says, and the smile melts into a scowl. "You're small enough to dance on the ice."

***

September blends into October, and Nina is made to rid the garden of dead leaves and moldy apples. Tail watches from a hiding spot between the birches but doesn't dare to come closer, since Henrietta stands on the porch and cries out whenever she spots him. Nina makes them coffee, and rye bread using Mother's recipe, and she washes Emilia's hair though she hates the smell from Emilia's body and the spotty skin on her shoulders. Every night she says her evening prayer, shivering when Viola's name fills the room.

"That damn cat, we should get someone to shoot it," Sibylla says at supper one night. Henrietta agrees, complaining about ruined flowerbeds. Nina watches them quietly, her imagination painting scratch marks all over their faces. Painting blood.

October turns into November, and frost frames the window in Nina's room.

"Take shelter," she tells Tail, though he's not there and isn't allowed inside ever again. "Grow your coat thick and warm, and watch out for the sisters."

When the frost comes, Viola keeps talking about the ice.

"They won't let you go down to the lake," she says, "but they have no reason. You're light and lean as a feather, girl. The ice won't hurt you." It's what Viola's always claiming. *It will carry you.*

"I'd be in charge," she says like she has many times, but there's more behind the words now. A shadow, clinging to each syllable. "I'd be in charge after Mother and Father were gone. But they didn't want any of that. Sibylla, Henrietta, and Emilia." The names sound filthy coming from her mouth, as if they tasted foul. "No, they wouldn't have it. You shouldn't trust people, just because they're kin. If they could do what they did to me, then you don't want to know what they might do to you…who's not part of the family."

The dream ends there. Nina tears her eyes open under the covers, hugging her legs to her chest to keep away the cold and the fear and what Viola just told her. It's like what she said that first night. *You are not my sister.* Nina has tried to forget it. The bad words, the lies that aren't real and must never be. She's the youngest sister. They're all sisters—Viola, Sibylla, Henrietta, Emilia, Nina. They belong to the family, and they live in the house that Father once built. That's all there is. It can't be any other way, no matter how much she hates Sibylla's cold stares, Henrietta's tugging hands, and Emilia who pretends to be nice but isn't. They're kin, though Nina is small and smooth and fair and doesn't look at all like any of the others. She doesn't even look like Mother, in that one photograph they have from when she was young. But Nina is the youngest sister. She always will be.

The next morning, the first snow of the year falls. It covers the woods, the meadows, the road. The lake is pale, foggy like Viola's eyes, and Nina knows what that means. The ice.

Viola tells her at ten to three that night, as if she knows.

"It will freeze tonight," she says. "Tomorrow there will be enough ice for you to walk on, girl. Tomorrow, with your little feet."

Nina shivers, as if she's on the ice already.

"You shouldn't listen to what they tell you," Viola continues. "Sibylla, Henrietta, and Emilia. They thought it was blasphemy when I said we ought to move away from here. Blasphemy and treason against Father and Mother."

"Father built the house," Nina says. It's the first time she's ever spoken to Viola.

"You don't know a lot, but they've taught you that. Oh, he did all right, and he beat Mother to a pulp, too." A shadow flashes by in Viola's broken eyes.

"I bet they never told you that we were the ones who gave him what he deserved, either. But Mother wasn't grateful...oh, no she wasn't."

Nina thinks about Mother's face in the photograph—her round, kind face. Maybe it's not Mother at all but someone else, another lie writhing under the house foundations.

"*The house that Father built.*" Viola huffs. "What of it, and what good was a drafty place like this to four old hags anyway? But when I told them that they got so very anxious, and it was after that that they—" She cranes her neck, glancing toward the silent clock. "It was after that that they chased me down there."

Her fingers twist like maggots in her lap, like starving creatures wanting to be let loose.

"They were younger," she says. "They were always younger. And Henrietta had the spade, and they didn't let me go. It was meant to be like an accident, of course, but it wasn't." She stares at Nina with burning eyes. "It wasn't an accident when I went through the ice." Her fingers tear at each other, and the sisters' voices echo in Nina's head. *Dear Viola, you mustn't forget to pray for Viola.*

"And then," Viola continues, "then they cried and moaned, but it was all an act. And when you came…"

Nina reaches for the words, hangs onto them. She's part of the story after all. She belongs in it.

"That woman showed up on the doorstep, and she had a child growing in her belly and she was alone. They were getting old, and they knew they'd have a hard time managing out here on their own. You see, little one, you have no ties to this family. You used to have a mother of your own once, but…" She giggles—it sounds as if a child has hidden away inside her rotting body, and it makes Nina freeze. "They couldn't kill her soon enough, once you were born. After that, they could tell you whatever they fancied, and you believed it."

Nina wonders if her mother is buried in the garden somewhere. She wonders if her mother liked cats. *Sibylla, Henrietta, and Emilia.* You must love your sisters…but only if they really are your sisters.

"Tomorrow," Viola says. "Tomorrow, with your little feet, you'll be dancing on the ice."

***

Nina wakes up to a snowy winter morning, and the lake has frozen. The soles of her feet tingle when she sees it. *You'll be dancing on the ice.*

She brushes the porch free of snow and searches the garden for Tail's tracks. It takes her forever to spot them. She bakes the rye bread using Mother's recipe—*their* mother—and listens in silence when Sibylla says grace. Nina waits for the night.

For the first time in months, she doesn't dream. She lies awake, watching as shadows tiptoe over the floor and up the walls. She's the only one who isn't sleeping—she, and someone who sits on the parlor sofa with her milky eyes wide open.

Then Nina puts her feet down on the floor. It's cold, but nothing compared to what is to come. The door opens without sound and the stairs don't creak until she reaches the very last step. As if it's meant that way—as if it's how Viola wants it. The wind tears at the front door when it falls open, and the snow beats against her neck and ankles. Everything is as it should be. Her feet sink deep into the snow, and the hem of her nightgown turns wet and heavy. Nina doesn't care. Snow and ice can't hurt her. Not her, because she has the small feet of a child.

She's reached the shore when she hears them. Their screams fill the silence, three ancient voices chanting her name. Nina has to turn her head and laugh at them. Emilia comes first with her long hair flowing free, then Sibylla and Henrietta who are leaning on each other. The front door is still beating in the wind. Ten years—ten years since Viola went through the ice. Ten years since they killed her, and tonight Nina will dance.

Emilia shrieks when Nina takes the first step. It's just as she thought—the ice holds, and it caresses her feet as she skips toward the center of the lake. Close up like this, the ice is uneven, with reeds sticking up here and there, but she still thinks it's beautiful. The nightgown billows around her and she raises her arms to the sky, laughing when the wind catches her hair.

"Nina!" Emilia cries. "Come back before it breaks!"

The sisters' voices rise and fall around her. Looking back, she sees them stumbling toward her over the ice. They hold onto each other, and Emilia reaches her hand out and keeps calling her name.

"Nina, little sister, why are you doing this?"

Nina stops. Smiles at them. "Because of my mother."

Her words are drowned, though, by the ice cracking. It tears, breaks, and where the sisters stood there's just a gaping hole. Black, slushy water, and three claw-like hands sticking out of it for a frozen moment. Their cries turn into one single terrible scream until they stop as abruptly as if they've been cut off with a knife. *Sibylla, Henrietta, and Emilia, the dear sisters who went through the ice.* The dark water goes still and quiet—it will freeze over before morning. Nina lifts her head and watches the house, the house that Father once built, standing all alone in a world of snow. She dances home over the ice, dances with her little feet.

Tail waits on the porch when she reaches the house. He rubs up against her legs, soft and black and just a little fat. The front door is still open, but she closes and bolts it before she heads upstairs together with her cat. Tail is sleeping in her room from now on, and there's no one who can say a thing about it. They hide under the covers and Tail falls asleep on her arm, purring so loudly that her bad thoughts drown and vanish.

On the wall, the frame is empty. No eldest sister staring down at her, because she doesn't have sisters anymore.

"Viola," Nina breathes into the darkness. "Where are you?"

Just as she knew it would, a voice fills her head. A voice, giggly, as if a child has hidden away inside a rotting corpse.

I'm right here, child. I'm not leaving anytime soon.

Fur

On Adela's thirtieth birthday, Cyrus said he would build her a house. Cyrus could make a promise like that because he was an architect, and he was rich, and he knew which forms to fill in and where to send them. It wasn't that Adela had asked for a house, exactly—the flat was small, but she didn't hate it. She did miss the woods from her childhood, though, the open fields and the snow that piled up in winter. She had talked to Cyrus, every once in a while, about leaving the city. Still, his plan came as a surprise. Adela tried to imagine Cyrus trudging through the woods, in rubber boots and a knitted sweater. It was impossible. Cyrus didn't own any knitwear, and he had no knowledge about chopping wood or foraging. Cyrus was bald like a seal and wore thick-framed glasses, and his dreams were as monochrome as his wardrobe. Adela wasn't particularly fond of the houses he designed—low, square buildings made out of steel and concrete, with either too few windows or too many. When Cyrus told her about the house he'd build just for her, her first reaction was *no*. But Cyrus told her he'd do everything different this time, because this house was hers.

"It will be everything you ever dreamed of," he said and took her hand in a rare display of affection. "In the middle of the woods, with no one around for miles. Just you and I."

So, Adela started sending him links to this or that she had seen online. Blog posts and magazine photographs where women in floral dresses stood on the porches of dainty cottages with chickens or cats or babies in their arms. Rural kitchens with wooden floors and trays of freshly-baked cookies, and romantic bedrooms with vintage wallpaper. She bought scented candles and fairy lights for the house, different scents and different colors for each room. Maybe they could have a dog? Something living, something to keep her company when Cyrus was away. Yes, the more she thought about a dog, the more she wanted one. A big, shaggy thing that would roam the woods with her.

Cyrus refused to show her the blueprints. "I want it to be a surprise," he said. "When it's done, I'll take you there and show it to you. It will blow your mind."

Adela ordered billowing, lace-collared dresses for her new life. She watered the plants and told them that they'd have a better life soon, away from car fumes and neon signs. She even contacted a kennel, but decided to wait until after the move.

"You seem happy," Cyrus said. "You finally seem happy."

She hugged him, which she hadn't done in forever. Everything was going to be fine. She would be like the women in the magazines, and she'd have no reason to cry again.

***

The house was finished a year later.

"Well, there are some minor details left," Cyrus told her as they drove out of the city. She was in the passenger seat, eyes darting from one streetlight to the next. "The basement needs some work before we can use it, but you wouldn't have a reason to be down there anyway."

"No." She chewed on her nail, remembering a rat she had seen in her parents' basement when she was small and how it had made her scream. "I don't like basements."

"I know that." Cyrus patted her leg while overtaking a truck. The increased speed made her chest ache. "I know you better than you know yourself."

The drive was lengthy. Adela fell asleep and when she woke up, they were deep in the woods. It was dark, the pine crowns blocking out the sun, but it made her happy. She thought about her little cottage, her dresses, her dog. The endless woods that would be all hers.

"Here we are," Cyrus said, driving past a bend. "Here's your new home."

Adela stared at it. At first, her brain couldn't comprehend what it was, or where she had seen it before—then she realized that it was the same square, anonymous block of concrete that Cyrus had designed a hundred times. Trees had been chopped down around the house, creating a sterile yard where nothing grew. The yard, more than anything, made her want to cry.

"What do you think?" Cyrus looked at her, smiling, and for the first time she hated him. "I'm quite proud of it. Every time I see it, it makes me think of you."

Adela breathed. In, out. The air inside the car smelled like plastic and leather, and it made her feel sick.

"Come on." Cyrus patted her hand. "Time for the house tour."

He guided her to the door, which had a fingerprint digital lock that was too shiny and too complicated. She saw her reflection in the steel handle; a ghost of a woman with a twitching mouth.

"Let's set it up right away, so you can come and go as you please." Cyrus pressed her fingertip to the display over and over, but the lock didn't react. "It's worked perfectly before." He sighed, letting go of her hand. When he put his own index finger on the display, the lock clicked. Adela wasn't surprised that the house didn't want her.

She followed Cyrus inside, pretending to be amazed by the state-of-the-art kitchen, the tall living room windows, the downstairs bathroom where every surface was obsidian black. There were no carpets, no curtains, not a single plant. The house was as sleek and efficient as Cyrus himself, as if he had carved flesh from his own body and shaped it into a building. It was the opposite of what she had hoped for. It was the opposite of everything that was her.

"Can I at least get a dog?" she asked, once they had reached the master bedroom where an enormous piece of abstract art covered the far wall. The black and white dots looked like grinning faces.

"You know I'm allergic," Cyrus said. "It really wouldn't work at all."

Adela nodded and grinned and told him the house was wonderful. Once Cyrus had gone to sleep, with his ear plugs in, Adela stood in the obsidian bathroom and stared at her own reflection. A ghost of a woman, her face breaking.

***

Cyrus went to the office each morning and came home at night. Adela was stuck in the house, because the door lock still refused to scan her fingerprint. She cooked tasteless meals in the microwave, because the gas stove scared her. She arranged her books on the shelf in the living room, but the colorful paperbacks looked as cheap and trashy as they were next to Cyrus' expensive art books. She sat googling dog images for hours, but it only made her chest tighten. When Cyrus was home, she pretended to be content. She lied about how many words she had written and how many new job offers she'd had. She told him that she was fine, and that he didn't have to worry about her.

"You see?" Cyrus kissed her forehead. "Moving out here did you good. I can tell that you're much better."

She nodded and smiled and pretended to go to sleep when he did, but once he started snoring, she went back downstairs. She hated the house, but she hated it less at night. The woods seemed to come to life then, as if all the furry things out there waited, just like her, for Cyrus to fall asleep. Adela stood by the tall living room windows, watching as the trees and birds and four-legged creatures moved. After a few nights, she pushed the windows open. Let the night air in, let the screeching and snarling in as well. Stood there in a billowing dress with her hair loose, and when the predators came close she didn't shut the window. She invited them in, the fire-eyed wolves, and they followed her through the quiet rooms. Explored the night world with her, and allowed her to bury her fingers deep in their fur. Their smells clung to her, and after they'd left, she found coarse, gray strands on the floor. She hid them in her hair and shut the windows, before slipping into bed next to Cyrus.

"You seem different," Cyrus told her when they were having breakfast together or watching the evening news. "Something about you is different."

Adela nodded and smiled. Once he'd left for work, she slept, and when he came home, she lied about all the things she'd done. After dark, she let the night in. Stroked its fur and stuck its hairs behind her ears.

Cyrus invited people over. His friends, because Adela didn't have any of her own. They took pictures of the house and told Adela that she must be so, so happy.

"If I had a place like this," they said, "I'd never want to leave."

Adela didn't tell them that she couldn't leave, because the house wouldn't let her. She thought about claws and fangs, and she smiled.

***

"I'm glad you could see reason about the whole dog thing," Cyrus said one night when they had lived in the house for three months. "We've got everything we need, don't we?" He told her that a magazine would come and take photos of the house. He didn't know when, but soon.

"You might want to make an appointment with the hairdresser," he said. "You're starting to look a bit…wild."

Adela stood in the obsidian bathroom that night, watching her reflection. Her hair had grown. She never bothered brushing it anymore, because it was too time-consuming. Here and there she saw the streaks of silver, the rugged whispers of fur. It made her laugh. She went to the living room to open the windows, and the pack flocked around her. They barked and growled, and she kept laughing. As she went up the stairs, her hair brushed against her arms, her thighs, her naked feet. Cyrus slept. With his ear plugs in, he heard nothing. Adela watched him. She didn't move, just watched as her hair slithered toward him. It covered him like a quilt, a warming pelt. Then it wormed itself in between his lips, and he started screaming.

"Adela," groaned the thing that had been Cyrus but was quickly becoming something else, something she'd have to bury in the morning. "Ade—"

She smiled. Around her, the wolves started howling. Adela howled with them.

Slither

I was sent to Aunt Vera because Mama started drinking again. My teachers saw me come to class in my jammies, with filthy nails and a rancid smell trailing after me, and I was put on that train. Where they put Mama, I don't know and I don't care. When I was small, I thought she resembled an angel, with her beauty queen mane and velvety soprano. Then I learned that the demons had once been angels, too.

Mama used to drag me off to pageants whenever she had the gas money. Once, I peed myself on stage and got the hairbrush treatment when we got home. My skin went from red to black to the purple of ripe plums. Thighs, ribs—those places no one would ever see but her. My own My Little Pony brush and her skeletal hand wrapped around it, *smack, whop*. My own goddamn fault, and why couldn't I be pretty like those other girls? Why was I so fucking useless?

Diane from Social Services told me that Mama was very sick and that I'd have it better at Aunt Vera's. I'd never met Aunt Vera and I'm sure Diane had never met her either, but grownups say these things because they want them to be true.

"Mama said I could have a puppy," I said, because Mama had told me that she'd get me a puppy if I ever won a pageant. She had a couple of nice days a month, and that had been on one of those. Of course, I'd never even got a tiara, and I didn't want one, but I had always dreamt about a dog.

"Did she?" Diane kneeled down to be level with me. People were moving around us on the platform, suitcases swinging in their hands. "That's nice. In the meantime, though, I'm sure you'll see a lot of animals at your aunt's. It's right in the middle of the forest, apparently. Maybe she even has a dog or two?"

Then it was time to step on the train and she gave me a stiff hug, her sleek tweed jacket barely brushing against me. She didn't smell like anything, just clean, unperfumed skin. "I'll call in a few days. See that everything's okay over there."

Of course, she didn't call. But it wasn't as if I had expected her to.

Aunt Vera wasn't there when I got off the train. She didn't arrive until half an hour later, pulling in outside the locked station building in a rusty skeleton of a car. The station was at the outskirts of town, surrounded by warehouses and deserted factories, and the only people around were an old man who smelled like Mama, but worse, and some teenage boys whose loud voices terrified me.

"Hi there, Alan," Aunt Vera greeted the old man as she grabbed my hand and lifted the sports trunk with my belongings—a nice man on the train had helped me get it onto the platform, since it was too heavy for me to carry. Aunt Vera was difficult to pinpoint—she was somewhat pretty, I suppose, with her red curls and majestic height, but she wore mud-streaked sandals and a fleece jacket that looked as if it had never been in a washing machine. Mama always wore too much makeup, but Aunt Vera didn't wear any at all.

"What do I call you then, tiny?" she asked after dropping my trunk in the backseat and fastening my seatbelt. I frowned, not sure what she meant, and she arched her birdwing eyebrows.

"What do you want to be called?" She turned the car key, and the radio started blaring some country song I'd never heard. Mama hated country music.

I shrugged. No one had asked me a question like that before. Diane had had plenty of questions, but they had all been about Mama.

"I think we should call you, hmm…" Aunt Vera smiled, ruffling my hair before she put the car in motion. "Aura. From now on, that's your name."

Aura. It was as good or bad as any other name, so I didn't protest. I sat there, watching the road that meandered through the woods like a ribbon, and when Aunt Vera started singing along to the radio I made my lips move as if I were her, or we were both the same person.

The first road was asphalt, cracked in places like my mirror after Mama broke it. The second, third, and fourth were dirt roads, each one narrower than the last. All the signs we passed looked handmade, worn red paint on a piece of wood. I had only just learned the alphabet, and Aunt Vera drove too fast for me to decipher more than a couple of letters here and there.

"Ivan made those," she told me when she caught me studying a sign. "There used to be proper road signs before, but the Transport Administration figured there was no use maintaining them. No one lives out here, after all." She rolled her eyes. It was an expression Mama used all the time, and it made the ball of anxiety in my belly curl up so tight it hurt. But Aunt Vera was nothing like Mama, or Diane wouldn't have sent me to her.

"Who's Ivan?"

She laughed. Her laughter reminded me of nice things, like rollercoasters and cotton candy, and I forgot about the eye-rolling. "Ivan is, well…We're not married or anything, but we've been living together for a while. It's good to have a man around; you'll see what I mean when you get older."

"Uh-huh," I said, pretending to understand. Aunt Vera laughed again. A while later, I caught a glimpse of roofs and flaking paint among the pines, and she reached her slim hand toward the windshield and pointed.

"There's Ivan's mother's house, and that's us over there. Cozy, isn't it? The two of them have been living out here since forever. She's a very old lady, so Ivan helps her out with things. You'll see for yourself how nice he is."

The house belonging to Ivan's mother looked lifeless and uncared for, with dark windows and outhouses where half the roof was missing. Aunt Vera's house was much tidier. It was a light shade of green, like the dress I wore for my first pageant, and the wooden gate was painted green, too. I liked it from the start, and if things had turned out different, I might still like it now.

"Welcome home." Aunt Vera parked in front of the porch and killed the engine. The woods wrapped us in silence, except for a rhythmic pounding from the backyard. Aunt Vera took my hand and brought me toward the sound, with a smile on her face that was nothing like cotton candy.

A man stood there, shirtless, chopping wood. His hair was graying, even though his face looked young. He gave me a short look and muttered something, before burying the axe in another log.

"Here's Aura," Aunt Vera said. "Our little runaway. You want some coffee?"

He grunted in response, before lowering the axe and inspecting me closer. "She's ugly," he said. "For a beauty queen."

"Ivan!" Aunt Vera glared at him but still looked smiley, like Mama whenever men sweet-talked her. "You're horrible. Did you see your mother yet?"

"Later." The axe looked like a toy in Ivan's meaty hand. If I had tried to lift it, it wouldn't even budge.

"Okay." Aunt Vera gave me a secretive look and shook her head. "Ivan has never been much for small talk. Or any talk, for that matter."

She led the way to the back door, and we entered a big kitchen with a large sack of potatoes in the corner and heaps of dirty dishes in the sink. But I was used to dirty dishes and didn't care.

"Better get something for you, too." Aunt Vera rummaged through the cupboards for cups and coffee powder. "Milk all right? Well, it's all I have, so it'll have to do. Want to see your room? The kettle takes forever, so we might as well go upstairs."

My room, as she called it, was a narrow space squeezed in between the roof and the master bedroom. The ceiling sloped too much for Aunt Vera to stand upright in there, but I fit. If I raised my arms over my head, I could press my palms against the ceiling. The room was drafty, and there was nothing in it but a white bed that looked fit for a toddler. The window at the opposite end of the room didn't let in any light, just a tiny square view of the woods.

"This is all yours." Aunt Vera patted my shoulder. "You can unpack your things later, but now I need some coffee. Come on."

We sat down at the kitchen table with our cups of milk and coffee.

"I bet you find it a bit lonely out here. So did I, at first, but now I'm used to it. I don't want it any other way." Aunt Vera smiled. "I wish I got along with Ruth, of course, but she's still not used to me. Ruth, that's Ivan's mother. She's set in her own ways, I guess you could say. Last time I went over, we got into a bit of an argument, so I'm just letting her be for now. It's best for everyone."

I sipped the milk, which tasted as if it had cream at the bottom. The name *Ruth* whirled through my head like autumn leaves.

After a while, Ivan joined us. He downed his coffee in big gulps, though it was steaming hot. Aunt Vera put her hand on his arm every now and then, and he let her.

"I saw Alan in town," she said. "He's let himself go."

"Haven't we all?" Ivan muttered, glaring at me.

Aunt Vera pushed her cup round, round in a little circle on the table. "Let me know if you need any help out there. Otherwise I'm going to make sure Aura settles in all right."

"You do that," Ivan said, standing. He was tall, like the giant in a story Mama had once read to me, and I thought to myself that he could never fit inside my room. "I can manage on my own."

"Ivan doesn't like kids," Aunt Vera said after he'd left. "But don't you worry. He'll come around eventually."

I spent the remainder of the day playing in the yard, while Ivan piled firewood in the shed and Aunt Vera dozed in the hammock. The yard was wide—perfect for soccer, if I'd had anyone to play with. When I grew tired of studying the ants in the gravel by the gate, I heaved myself up on my toes until I could rest my elbows on the wooden fence. From there I saw the neighboring house. I really didn't like the look of it. The garden was overgrown, and there was no car signaling that the place might be inhabited. But maybe Ivan's mother was too old for driving.

There was a sound coming from the house. Nothing strange about that, but something about the sound made me scrunch my face together. It was wet, somehow, like puddles hit by rain or mud when you step into it. But it wasn't raining, and the ground was bone-dry.

"What are you up to, tiny?" Aunt Vera came over and ran her hand over my head. Her voice was soft and drowsy.

"There's a strange sound. From Ruth's house."

"Oh…whatever it is, I'm sure it's nothing to worry about. If anything's amiss, Ivan will fix it when he goes over there tonight. You and I should get inside now, okay? See what we can whip up for dinner."

I followed her inside. We cooked and ate, and I got to watch five minutes of cartoons until Ivan came in and switched channels. Aunt Vera rolled her eyes in that Mama-like fashion and told me it was my bedtime anyway.

"Ruth's dinner is on the counter," she told Ivan. "Let's hope she's got no complaints this time."

"Yeah, yeah." He kept his eyes on the TV. "I'll take it to her in a while."

Aunt Vera accompanied me upstairs. She made sure I brushed my teeth, but didn't tell me a story.

"Be a good kid now," she told me after saying goodnight. "No bad dreams."

I don't know why she told me that. All I know is I woke up in the middle of the night from a wet, slithering sound that had my heart racing. The end of the bed was freezing so I curled up, hugging my legs. The sound came and went, as if whoever was making it was circling the house. I thought about slipping into Aunt Vera's room, but then I remembered Ivan.

"Go away," I hissed under my covers, like I had done whenever Mama had come into my room drunk. Though back then I had never said it out loud, or she would only have hit harder. Something rattled right below my window—and I heard the slithering again. The anxiety ball in my belly grew and ached.

It's just a dream. Go back to sleep.

But it wasn't, and I knew it all too well. After a while the sound died away, though, and I fell asleep again. In the morning, the sound was the first thing on my mind. I asked Aunt Vera about it during breakfast, and she sighed.

"You're just not used to living in the woods, that's all. We get all sorts of weird sounds here. Now I need you to stop asking about it, okay?"

"Why?"

"Aura." She fixed her eyes on me, and I was reminded again of Mama. "Forget about it."

I wondered why I couldn't ask, but I didn't push it. Mama had taught me to do as grownups told me. I played outside, and I helped Aunt Vera dry the dishes, and I wished I wouldn't hear the sound again. But I did, and this time it seemed closer—swooshing, slithering right outside my window, but I was on the top floor and there could be nothing there.

In the morning, before I went downstairs, I stopped at the sound of arguing. Aunt Vera did most of the shouting, while Ivan muttered something every now and then. They were in the kitchen—I heard him pacing the creaky floorboards.

"The timing is pretty fucking awful," he said. "And you know it."

"What was I to do? It's my goddamn niece. If I didn't take her in, they'd put her in foster care or something."

"So what? It's not our problem."

"Easy for you to say." Aunt Vera was quiet for a long while. "She says she's hearing sounds. I don't know where she gets it from."

Ivan cursed. "Do I look like I care?" He must have slammed his fist into the wall, because the whole house rattled.

"It's only for a while," Aunt Vera said. "Until Annie's out of rehab."

"Let's hope she's out quick, then," Ivan said before stomping outside and closing the backdoor with a bang. When I came down fifteen minutes later, Aunt Vera smiled and chatted and made me pancakes. As if she knew I'd heard, and she wanted me to forget it.

Later that day, Ivan had a call and told Aunt Vera he had to go to town.

"You know what it's like," he said, squeezing his bulk into a leather jacket. "Keep an eye on the kid."

"Of course," Aunt Vera said. "Come back soon."

But Ivan stayed gone. Aunt Vera kept glancing out of the window, fidgeting with the hem of her fleece jacket. After dinner, she gave him a call, then came into the TV room where I sat in front of the cartoons. Her face looked lined and old.

"He's got some car trouble, so he's not getting back until tomorrow. Aura, would you mind getting Ruth her dinner? I feel bad for asking you, but she'd never let me in, and things got so ugly last time…You'll help me out, won't you?"

I knew that it was wrong of her to ask me, just like I knew that Mama was wrong to beat me up when she got angry. But Aunt Vera's eyes looked sad and the lines in her face just kept spreading, so I went with her to the kitchen. She put a lukewarm Tupperware container in my hand and gave me a flashlight.

"Just tell her that you're our kid. I mean, it's easiest that way. Ruth is very old and she gets confused a lot. You understand, right? Just give her this and make sure she eats it all up. She can be stubborn at times, but she won't be able to refuse if you ask her."

I put my jacket on before leaving, though I was only heading next door. The outside air was cool, and it was getting dusky. I thought about the night sounds, the slithering, and I wanted to tell Aunt Vera no, but she had already closed the door. I had no choice. I crossed the yard and squeezed through a hole in the fence, then padded through the tall grass with the flashlight pointing forward and the food container pressed to my chest.

There was no fence, only the sagging outhouses marking where the yard began. The house looked scary up close, with missing roof tiles, and broken glass on the ground outside. Bracing myself, I went up to the porch and knocked on the door. No one opened. I waited for a while before knocking again, but there was no answer. Maybe Ruth was hard of hearing, or was she in a wheelchair? I recalled the presentation Mama had written about me for a pageant last year. *She's got a heart of gold and she loves to help others.* I had no idea if it were true, but I sort of wanted it to be. A heart of gold sounded better than a ball of anxiety. Reluctantly, I pressed down the handle, and the door opened. A nasty smell slipped out, making me retch. It reminded me of the garbage can in our backyard in the city, and the dead cat they once found in it.

"Hello?" I didn't want to enter, but what if the old lady was hurt? Maybe if I helped her things would be okay—Mama would stay gone, and I would get a dog, and Aunt Vera wouldn't look sad. I started breathing through my mouth before heading inside. The place was filthy, littered with trash bags and old newspapers. How could anyone live like this? The kitchen was too crammed with junk for me to get into— also, there was something rustling in the sink. I went instead into a gloomy living room where empty bottles covered every inch of the table. It wasn't until I reached the next door that I heard it—a wet, slithering sound I knew well. It was faint, like the rustling in the kitchen sink, but this was different. Somehow it was very different.

It was a bathroom. The door was open just a sliver, and the smell was so bad I had to put the Tupperware container down and press my hand over my nose and mouth.

"Ruth?" I said, but the sound of my own small voice made everything worse. It was there, the slithering. It was coming from behind that door. I don't know why I pushed it open. I wish I had known better.

I can't describe what I saw in there. I won't. Only the tub, the water, the stained tiles...the stench that buried itself in my nostrils, mouth, lungs. The wound splitting her head open, and her *eyes*. I knew what I saw. I knew that she was beyond helping. The flashlight dropped to the floor, and I didn't pick it up. When I rushed out of the house, the slithering filled my ears, as if she was reaching for me. As if she stirred in that slimy water, mouth twisted in a demented grin.

I don't remember what I told Aunt Vera. I don't think I said anything. When Ivan returned the next morning, she told him I had brought Ruth her dinner, praising me to the skies.

"Aura is a good kid, see? What would we do without her?" She squeezed my shoulders so hard it hurt, but I didn't say anything. I was used to things hurting.

"Hm." Ivan gave me a long look. He chewed a big piece off the sandwich Aunt Vera had made for him, without breaking eye contact. Finally, he said, "So...you saw my mama."

"She was upstairs," I lied. "She said I should put the food on the table, so I did."

"Aura." Aunt Vera frowned. "I told you to make sure she ate it. She's so very particular with food. Especially my food. You should—"

Ivan put his hand up, and she stopped talking. "Well, then. Everything's as it should be." But his eyes stayed on my face, and there was something in them that reminded me of Mama when she was drunk. Something that made me shrink while he grew.

That night, when the dead woman dragged her hands over the wall, Ivan and Aunt Vera started fighting again.

"*I* handle Mama," Ivan said. His voice was so loud I could hear it through the flimsy wall separating my room from theirs. "Why the hell would you send a kid there?"

"I just thought…" Aunt Vera sounded insecure, like a child being scolded by her parents.

"No…You never think. From now on, you leave everything to me, all right? Mama's scared of strangers. She needs her peace and quiet."

"I know, baby, but Aura did really well."

Ivan laughed—the sort of cold laugh that could mean all sorts of bad things. "Did she? She put the container on the floor and forgot the flashlight. Mama was really upset about it when I came over tonight. You know how she gets when something's out of the ordinary."

Slither, slither…

"Oh, well, Aura won't do it again. It was just a mistake." Aunt Vera's voice was warm when she talked about me, but for some reason, it didn't make me happy.

"It's making me crazy." Something about Ivan's voice scared me. It was weak and small like mine, and it shouldn't be. "That goddamn noise."

"Noise? What noise?"

The thing in the tub hissed against my window. I imagined it climbing the wall, staring at me, listening.

"You don't understand anything, do you?" Ivan was shouting now. "Mama tried her best to be friends, but you were never happy. And now look what you've done."

"Come back to bed," Aunt Vera said, all smooth and soft like milk. "My Ivan…it's no use, all that shouting. We need our sleep now. You'll feel better in the morning."

He said something, but it was too low for me to hear. I guess he went back to bed, because they didn't talk more after that. We all slept, and I learned to ignore the house next door and the sounds that came at night. What else could I do? Ivan went over there every night with food in gaudy containers, and at daytime he left for the woods, coming home with thick logs he chopped to splinters with the axe. I watched him work, burying that blade in the logs, and I thought of Ruth's head.

Mama came for me some weeks later. Her dress sparkled, she smelled like cotton candy, and I thought that maybe everything would be different from now on.

"Come on, sweetie, let's get out of here. Jesus, look at this place." She wrinkled her nose at everything, and refused to come upstairs and see my room.

"All sobered up already?" Aunt Vera asked when we were in the kitchen and I was getting my shoes on. Ivan was out in the back, hiding. "You know I can't let you take her unless you've changed."

"We're leaving," Mama said. As soon as we were alone in the car, she threw a glance in the rearview mirror and huffed. "I don't know what they were thinking when they sent you to those freaks. They're literally crazy, both of them. I bet Social Services never thought to check."

"Why's that?" I asked, my skin going shivery.

"That Ivan, I don't know what she's doing with him. I mean, she's always been a weirdo, but Ivan is something else. Back when me and Vera lived in this hellhole, when we were kids, Ivan went to our school. Even then he was a freak. Lived out here with his crazy mom, with no one around for miles, and he was obsessed with her. Vera is hopeless, sure, but even she could do better."

I turned my head to watch the little green house. Aunt Vera stood on the porch, waving. Her face was turned away.

"Mama, I need—" I stopped myself. *Mama, I need to warn Aunt Vera.* As if grownups ever listen to what kids tell them. We passed Ruth's house, and I fixed my eyes on the road ahead. But the sound trailed after me: *slither, slither.*

"Can I get a dog, Mama?"

"Of course," she quipped, and I knew she was lying. Once we had driven past all of Ivan's homemade signs, she pulled in by the side of the road and frowned at me.

"Look at you, your hair's a mess." From her purse she took the My Little Pony brush and started untangling my hair. "There's a pageant this weekend that you just have to enter. I've bought you the cutest dress, but it's in the trunk so I'll show you later. You'll win this thing for sure, okay?"

It only hurt a little when she brushed my hair.

"Okay, Mama. I'll win."

Chatterbox

Some kids talk too much. It's obvious from the start that she's one of them. Pigtails, gingham dress, a lisp. Far too young to be in a place like this, but Joe doesn't ask where her parents are. I debate with myself whether I should say something.

"I'm hungry," she states and plops down on a chair, skinny legs dangling. "No, don't offer me anything, that wasn't why I said it. But you should always say what's on your mind, shouldn't you?"

Joe glares, but she doesn't notice.

"I saw a magpie taking a bath in a puddle yesterday. It seemed to be enjoying itself so much and I could have watched it forever. I never wanted to go home." Her hands are folded in her lap. "I wish I could have a pet bird," she continues, "but I don't think that will happen. They need to be taken care of just as much as a cat or dog. You have to love them and bury them when they die."

Joe snorts. "That's a strange way of looking at it."

"But you do," the girl says, frowning at him. "If you don't bury things properly they come back. They stand around in the garden and they're not very nice to look at."

Joe wipes the counter, ignoring her. She watches him with her round eyes.

"You don't say much, do you? But Papa doesn't say much either and we love him all the same." She draws a breath. "Papa used to work in a mine. One time, a pile of rocks fell over him and everyone thought he was a goner. They left him alone in the dark and he was trapped for days, until they came back down and realized he was still alive. Poor Papa." Her face contorts into a tragic mask, the corners of her mouth drooping.

"He wasn't harmed physically," she goes on, her voice light, the grimace gone. "But the doctor said Papa couldn't ever work underground again. Because being trapped in a mine for three days makes your brain funny, and no wonder! You wouldn't like it if that happened to you, would you?" She looks straight at me but averts her eyes before I put on a smile. "Mama didn't notice until they'd been married for three years and had both me and Chloe. That's when they moved to our house and Papa got locked in the basement. It was a bad door that got stuck at times, and Mama was upstairs with us and didn't hear him. Poor Papa," she says again, shaking her head. "He was good to us but then he was wicked, too. It's not his fault but the mine's, though I suppose it doesn't really matter."

Joe clears his throat. "Kids like you should stay quiet."

"Oh, I know," she says. "I really should stay quiet. Papa always told me as much! He didn't like to be disturbed and I, well, I only wanted to talk to him. See, I needed to know what the darkness was like, and the solitude. But Papa never wanted to talk to me about anything. He said—" She sniffles. "He said I was a nuisance and a freak."

Joe rolls his eyes, which enrages me. "You poor thing," I say. "It was awful of your father to call you such things."

The girl nods, as if she expected me to say something like that. My hands are clammy when I reach for my glass.

"According to Mama, I should stay out of his way. Papa had a hard time, she told me. There was always this or that bothering Papa. He tore down the door to the basement with an axe even though he knew it scared Chloe and me to stare down that dark opening. And it was cold down there, it made the whole house cold, but Mama told us we couldn't say anything. It would only make Papa angry. Rats lived in the basement too, and they came up into the kitchen and made Mama cry. Papa took out his rifle and shot them. He loved shooting them."

I wish she would stop talking. Her gingham dress is dirty, I didn't notice before. The hem is torn over her knobby knees.

"When Chloe fell down the stairs, Mama didn't blame Papa for it, though we all knew it was his fault. Well, the mine's fault. Mama wrapped Chloe in the only duvet we had because you have to sacrifice something to the dead, or it's just no good. Papa dug the hole in the basement and made the cross, and I sang to keep the rats away."

My glass is empty but I'm still holding it. "Your sister died?"

The little girl tilts her head. "Well, of course! Oh, I suppose you couldn't know because you never did see those stairs. She landed on her head and her neck snapped. You should have heard the sound Papa made, lady. Like a bull or a moose or a tall, bawling baby. *It should have been me*, he said. And it really should, because Chloe was kind and Papa was wicked. Mama sat in the basement all night, to keep Chloe company as she said. No one kept me company. Papa drank beer and cried and smashed things upstairs. I tell you that I didn't like it one bit. After he went quiet I walked upstairs and…no." She giggles. "You can figure the rest out for yourselves." She swings her legs and there are stains, dark stains all over her white sandals. "But I'm an orphan now and it's quite boring, and there's no food left in the kitchen at all." She looks at me and smiles, a pretty smile, angelic and saccharine and false. "Lady, won't you let me stay with you?" She jumps down from the chair and stands, her smile widening. "You won't even know I'm there."

Howl

Eva passed the gates of Greyling Hall with smarting feet and sweat gluing the blouse to her armpits. She would have called a cab if she'd known how far from town the house was located, but it was too late now. The garden was unkempt, haphazard, with a heavy canopy shadowing the path and shutting out the dying daylight. She was a city girl, she preferred neat garden patches and well-lit parks. So far, Greyling bewildered her.

The house came into view five minutes later. Eva's shoulders ached so bad, she considered leaving the suitcase outside and coming back for it in the morning, but that would be a bad decision. Eva never made bad decisions.

The manor house was absurdly large, swelling out in all directions like a blood-filled tick. It must have been grand once, but now the windows were dark and the vegetation ran its fat limbs over the façade. There was no lawn, no yard, just plants sprouting everywhere. Eva didn't like it. It was her new home, and she most certainly didn't like it.

After dragging her suitcase to the front stairs, she knocked and waited. The garden seemed to breathe into her neck, hot and revolting. She longed for a bath and a change of clothes.

The howling came from nowhere. It scuttled up her legs like beetles, like nasty things from below the ground, and she twisted her neck to locate the sound. Were there dogs? How many, and why hadn't she been informed? Eva had never liked dogs. She wasn't fond of any animals, really, but dogs were the worst. Dirty and smelly, but their owners doted on them all the same. The air filled with howls again, closer this time, and she rapped her knuckles against the door so hard, it stung.

"Just get inside, will you?" someone shouted from the other side of the door. "It's open."

Eva stumbled into a foyer with plaster cherubs in the ceiling and a wide staircase that dominated the room. It took a while before her eyes adjusted to the dusk and she discovered the woman standing in a doorway to the left. It was the largest woman she had ever seen—tall and fat, with meaty hands and a face that was red but free of lines. Her gray hair was thin and woolly like that of a baby.

"Are you her? Mrs. Landon?"

The woman huffed. "Who else would I be? And you're Eva, I bet."

"Yes." Eva recalled the first line from the ad. *Loyal housekeeper needed in charming country home.* Who in their right mind would describe this place as *charming?*

"Follow me, then." Mrs. Landon waddled away and Eva hurried after. They came to a small parlor, which was hot and stuffy from the crackling fireplace. Mrs. Landon dropped herself into one of the armchairs in front of the fireplace and motioned for Eva to take the other. The floor was sticky, littered with books and used napkins, and Eva breathed through her mouth to avoid the stale, unwashed odor from Mrs. Landon's body.

"So," Mrs. Landon said, "this is it. It's a mess, you don't have to tell me that. We've been alone out here these last few years, me and the boys, and I'm not as agile as I was back in the day."

"Boys?" Eva asked. The ad had only mentioned Mrs. Landon herself.

"My grandsons. But never mind that now—I'm sure you can't wait to get acquainted with the place."

"Well, I…It's a bit larger than I expected. Do you have any other staff?"

Mrs. Landon grunted. "You think I'm made of money? No, it's just us. Don't worry, you don't need to concern yourself with the old parts of the house. We only ever use the parlor, the kitchen, and our bedrooms upstairs. No need to overdo it."

"I see." The fire made her face tingle. "Mrs. Landon, are there dogs here?"

Mrs. Landon's eyes narrowed. "No, there damn well aren't. Now, would you mind getting me a cup of tea? You'll find the kitchen just past the foyer."

Eva had reached the doorway when Mrs. Landon said her name.

"Listen, don't climb those stairs whatever you do. Rotten to the core. We use the servants' stairs, and it works just fine." She paused. The flames made her eyes seem golden. "And call me Helena from now on. I've had enough of people groveling in the dirt."

The state of the kitchen was even worse than expected. The counter was brimming with old cartons of milk and yogurt, empty cereal boxes, and used tea bags. A quick glance inside the fridge made her wrinkle her nose at the rancid smell that slipped out. She would need to sanitize this place—but first, tea for Mrs. Landon. There was a plastic kettle behind the wall of milk cartons, and she found mugs and tea bags in the cupboard to the left. Even the tea smelled funky, but maybe it was just the trash on the counter taking over. She couldn't wait to bring a hoover in here, a mop, bleach. Cleaning had become almost a hobby lately. It was so simple, after all, to turn a room spotless. It was different with people.

When she entered the parlor with the steaming mug, Mrs. Landon grinned. She had stained, uneven teeth, and Eva thought again of bleach.

"There you are! I thought maybe you'd gotten yourself lost. Wouldn't be the first time in this damn place." She grabbed the mug and took a swig. "Sit down again, will you? Tell me what brought you here."

"Well, I…" Eva sat down at the edge of the seat, longing for bathwater and silence. "I saw the ad. It made me interested."

Mrs. Landon frowned. "Of course you saw the ad. I don't need you to tell me about the ad, Eva, because I wrote it myself. What was it about the job that made you apply, though? Why do you think you'd make a good housekeeper?"

Eva didn't like the house, and she certainly didn't like the stuffy parlor with its foggy landscape paintings and drawn curtains. The room seemed like an extension of Mrs. Landon herself, a shadowed corner of her being. "I never worked as a housekeeper before, as I said in my letter, but I was my mother's caretaker for many years. I figure I learned a thing or two then."

"Were you and your mother close?"

"What sort of a question is that?" The noise started scratching at the back of Eva's head. The same noise as always. "Naturally we were close."

Mrs. Landon seemed content with that. "And loyal? Are you loyal, Eva?"

Squeak-squeak-squeak. "Loyal?"

"Perhaps I should explain myself." Mrs. Landon put the mug down on the cluttered side table. "I've invited you to my home. My family. We've had plenty of bad stuff happen to us over the years, me and the boys, and we don't need any more. I need to know that you're someone I can trust. Are you?"

Eva brushed her hands over her skirt. The fabric was coarse, ugly, cheap. "Yes, Mrs. Landon. I am."

Mrs. Landon put her hand up. "Pardon the language, Eva, but would you cut the crap? I've told you to use my first name, and I don't like asking for things twice. We're not fancy people, me and my grandsons—you'll realize that soon enough, if you haven't already."

"I'm sorry. Helena, then."

Mrs. Landon clapped her hands together. "See, you can do it!"

As if it matters, Eva thought, then decided to forget about it. There was no reason to be angry. Anger would only put her in trouble.

"Your grandsons…How old are they?"

Mrs. Landon thought about the question, toying with her mug of tea. "Now, let's see. June turned fifteen this spring, or was that last year? Anyway, Jules is thirteen months younger."

Eva had never been able to stand teenage boys. "Those are some pretty names. Unusual."

Mrs. Landon scoffed. "Oh, they certainly weren't my doing! My girl, Christina, she was a whimsical little thing. Married a man who had great looks and not much else, least of all an intellect. They had all sorts of romantic ideas about child-rearing, though they were a bit disgruntled when they had boys instead of girls. Christina always wanted daughters. As if that'd be any guarantee."

Guarantee for what? Eva wanted to ask but didn't. She was tired after the trip, and she still hadn't had that bath. "Would you mind if I turned in early? It's just, I've had a long day, and—"

"Oh, sure." Mrs. Landon patted her leg. Eva kept herself from recoiling. "Just mind those stairs, like I said. Take any bedroom you want up there, though mine's at the top of the servants' stairs, and the boys are next door to me. We'll talk more about your duties tomorrow."

"Thank you. Goodnight." Eva left the heated parlor, went back to the foyer and grabbed her suitcase before locating the servants' stairs and ascending. The hallway upstairs was gloomy, and the clicking of her heels bounced between the naked walls. She chose a door at random, one opposite Mrs. Landon's, and entered a bedroom that smelled like the attic in her mother's house and had dust piling up beneath the bed—but there was a bathroom next door, a tub, a tiny window to let the steam out of. Eva sank into the water and closed her eyes. The *squeak-squeak-squeak* had gone. All she heard was the night wind, the trees, and distant howling.

***

She woke up early, as was her habit, and started cleaning. Opened the kitchen windows wide, found binbags for the trash on the counter and filled them up. After leaving the dirty dishes to soak in hot water, she started mopping the floor, humming. This was good. This was a whole lot better than the therapy they'd suggested at the hospital. It would take days to rub all the stains out, purge the smell of rot and garbage. Eva had days. She had all the time in the world.

She was on all fours examining a hole beneath the pantry door—mice? rats?—when the hallway floorboards sighed. She looked up, turning her head, but didn't see anyone.

"Hello?" It was probably nothing. This vermin infestation needed to be taken care of, though; she made a mental note to ask Mrs. Landon about traps, poison. If there weren't any in the house, she might have to head out to the nearest supermarket. Not today—tomorrow. She had to stick to the plan, do things in the right order. The house was a mess, but Eva was going to sort it out. Piece by revolting piece.

A moment later, the floorboards creaked again. Louder this time, or was it her imagination? Eva busied herself by the counter, glancing toward the doorway every other second. There was nothing. Just that sound, every now and then, as if someone were hiding right behind the door.

She went over to the pantry to collect some moldy marmalade jars for the binbags. When she turned around, they stood by the counter—the boys—and the jars crashed to the floor.

They were beautiful. She had expected coarse features and bulky frames, inherited from the grandmother, but June and Jules were lithe and angelic. They had sweet faces, plump-lipped and rosy-cheeked, and golden hair falling to their shoulders. If one had not been slightly taller than the other, she wouldn't have been able to tell them apart.

"Oh, I'm sorry." She picked the jars up. One had broken, emitting a stomach-turning odor of apricots gone foul. "You startled me. You are June and Jules, aren't you? Your grandmother told me about you yesterday."

No reaction. They watched her calmly, standing side by side with their arms touching.

Eva's hand was sticky from the broken jar. The smell clung to her face, nasty, vile. She needed to be rid of it. "It's nice to meet you. I'm Eva. Would you boys care to help me take these binbags out? If you're not too busy?"

They kept watching her, but didn't say anything. Then one of them opened the fridge and grabbed a carton of milk. The other boy took one of the open boxes of cereal from the counter. After giving her one last look, they slipped away, and she was alone again. Eva turned on the faucet and poured dishwashing liquid in her open palm, then scrubbed until her hands were red and raw. Her eyes welled up; she didn't know why. There was a sound, an awful sound at the back of her mind. The boys had made it appear, and she hated them for it.

When Mrs. Landon came down an hour later, Eva heard her heavy footsteps long before she entered the kitchen. She was in a silk nightgown that had burst in places, and her feet were bare.

"I appreciate your dedication, Eva, but you don't need to do this. We've managed just fine so far, so you're wasting your time." She opened a cupboard and brought out a package of chocolate chip cookies, ripping it open and popping a cookie into her mouth as she spoke. "Boys up yet?"

"Yes." Eva tried not to notice the crumbles raining over Mrs. Landon's nightgown and the newly-mopped floor. "They weren't very talkative."

Mrs. Landon laughed. "Teenagers! You know what they're like." She filled the kettle with water and put it on, then grabbed the cookie package again. "Would you mind bringing me the tea when it's done? I'll be in my chair."

"What about lunch?" Eva asked. She was trying very hard not to think about crumbles, or squeaking, or the boys' vacant stares. "Do you...I mean, should I prepare lunch? Do you eat together?"

Mrs. Landon looked past her, toward the open window, before her eyes settled on Eva's face. "Sure, if you want. Been a while since we did that. The boys tend to grab something whenever they get hungry. But if you want to cook something, go right ahead. I won't stop you."

After she'd left, Eva mopped the floor again. Pantry; counter; dishes. Lunch. Her head filled with tasks, until there was no room left for any sounds at all.

***

Hours later, she had the food ready. Pasta, olives, and tomato sauce from a can—back home she'd been taught to serve greens with every meal, but there were no vegetables in the fridge or the claustrophobic pantry. Mrs. Landon and her grandsons would hardly care, but it didn't feel right. It wasn't proper. She went to the parlor when the food was ready, still in the apron she'd found neatly folded in a drawer next to the stove. Mrs. Landon was in a shapeless dress that went to her knees. She sat watching the fire, her mouth slack.

"Mrs. Landon—Helena. I just wanted to let you know that lunch is ready. Where would you like to eat? Do you have a dining room?"

Mrs. Landon coughed once, a sharp noise that shot through Eva's head. "Dining room? We've got all sorts of rooms in this place, Eva, but we don't use them. They're locked, unheated. Kitchen will do fine. Call the boys inside, will you? There's a bell on a side table in the foyer—use that, and they'll hear you. They're good children; they always come when they hear the bell."

Eva felt stupid, stepping out on the porch and sounding the bell. Its chime reminded her of school—the gravel out in the yard, the swings, and her mother's shape on the other side of the fence. *School is fun, Eva. You just have to try.*

Back in the kitchen, she set the table. Three plates, three glasses, three sets of cutleries. When Mrs. Landon came in and saw it, she scoffed and told Eva to bring out another plate.

"Not eating with us, is that how you want it? Think that's what I want to teach my boys—that some people are better than others?"

In fact, Eva had looked forward to eating alone. "Thank you," she murmured, and they sat. A while later, the boys padded inside, stopping by the fridge and eyeing the food on the table, the plates, Eva. Mostly Eva.

"Come, darlings," Mrs. Landon said. "Sit. We're eating together as a family again, see? You remember when we used to do that?"

They didn't answer, but they slid through the room and into the two remaining chairs. The tallest boy—June?—had a twig stuck in his hair, and the ends of Jules' golden curls were damp. They pulled the bowls and pans toward them and heaped pasta on their plates. When June helped himself to the tomato sauce, he was so careless that he stained the tablecloth. Eva watched those splotches of red and counted, very slowly, in her head.

"Good work," Mrs. Landon said around a mouthful of pasta. She made a thumbs-up, and Eva saw how long her nails were. The boys, too, had long nails with dirt caked around the edges. Her stomach turned at the sight of them digging into their food, shoveling it into their pretty mouths. When they were done, there was tomato sauce dribbling down their chins, staining their white t-shirts. They stood, wiping their mouths with their hands and giving Eva a look before leaving.

"My pride and joy," Mrs. Landon said. There was sauce on her face, too, and Eva could smell it now—it was spoiled, bad, inedible. She cut her pasta in pieces, pretending to eat while fighting the nausea. As soon as Mrs. Landon left, she threw up in the sink. When she cleared the table, the taste of vomit glued to the roof of her mouth, she thought she heard laughter.

***

That evening, Mrs. Landon wanted to talk. Eva would have preferred to stay in the kitchen, cleaning—there was so much to clean, so many corners and cupboards to scrub free of dust and grime. She didn't want to sit in the parlor with Mrs. Landon's eyes sticking to her, but she was an employee and couldn't do as she pleased. The fire whispered like a creature from a nightmare, but Mrs. Landon reached her hands toward it and smiled.

"We have a good life here," she said, looking into the flames. "All things considered. Think I'm crazy for saying that?"

"What? No."

Mrs. Landon chuckled. "Well, I guess you don't know what happened. If you did, you'd pity me."

"Maybe." Eva wondered where the boys were. If she rang the bell, would they show?

"It was eight years ago. My Richard was still with us back then. But the whole thing ate at him, so he passed away not long afterwards." Mrs. Landon sighed. "Christina and her family lived with us. That good-for-nothing husband of hers could never keep a job, and it wasn't as if we didn't have rooms to spare. She'd had a baby that spring, a little girl called May. But May was always sick from this or that, always crying, and Christina hired a nanny to help her. She shouldn't have done that."

"Why?"

"The nanny wasn't right in the head. Real nutjob. She was madly in love with Christina's husband—we all saw it; it was clear as day. Pathetic, how she sucked up to him and did whatever he asked. Well, one night she killed all three of them. Poisoned the girl's formula, then the peppermint tea Christina and her husband drank before bed every night. I guess she wanted what Christina had, and when she couldn't have it…"

"Oh," Eva said. A tiny baby called May, killed by poison. She wanted to throw up again.

"There's nothing anyone can do about it now. It's done. She had Richard's eyes, May did…Would've grown up to be a beauty, if she'd lived."

"I'm sorry."

"No, no." Mrs. Landon shifted in her seat, as if Eva's sympathy made her itch. "I've got the boys, don't I? And you can be sure they'll never leave old Granny."

"Where do they go to school?" It was summer, but fall would come soon. Secretly, she hoped that June and Jules would go away, only coming home for Christmas.

Mrs. Landon frowned. "Oh, they had this private tutor, but he left. Without any notice whatsoever, and I'd paid him six months in advance. Shows you can't trust people, no matter how reliable they might seem."

She's talking about me, Eva thought, and there it was, at the back of her mind—the squeaking.

"They're such lovely children," Mrs. Landon continued, sweet-voiced now. "They play so nicely together, and school might ruin them. How was it for you, Eva? Did it ruin you?"

School is fun, Eva. "My memory isn't very good. I'm sorry."

Mrs. Landon looked into the fire again. Her round face shifted, as if a cloud passed over it. "Mine's crystal clear. Unfortunately."

***

Eva talked to Mrs. Landon about the possible vermin infestation the next day. She hadn't seen any droppings, but there was that hole. You needed to take care of these things immediately. Spawn and eat, that was all they did, steadily growing in number until they were everywhere. She couldn't let that happen now that the kitchen was passably tidy. It smelled like it should, of bleach and citrusy detergents. It was going to stay that way.

"Rats?" Mrs. Landon's eyes sparkled, as if Eva had told her a joke. "Well, who knows. Big old house like this, there are a few lurking about, though mainly in the basement. But don't worry yourself—the boys take care of that. It's a bit of a game for them, you know, setting the traps, outsmarting the little bastards. They've had that responsibility since they were kids. You just ask them to have a look around in the kitchen, if you want, and I'm sure they'll catch whatever it is that's bothering you."

Eva remembered asking June and Jules about the binbags, earning nothing but vacant stares. "Okay. Maybe."

For dinner that night she found some ready-made lasagna in the freezer, and Mrs. Landon asked to have some red wine with it.

"The wine cellar is in the basement, just below the stairs. Take any bottle; I'm not picky."

Eva thought about their earlier conversation. "Of course. I'll go see to it."

The basement door was in the foyer, behind the rotten staircase. *Just grab a bottle*, she told herself. *Grab one, go back up, be done with it.* She'd never cared for wine, unlike her mother. She couldn't understand the appeal.

The door made no sound. The light she switched on was greenish, a fluorescent shimmer that didn't do much more than show her the outline of the steps in front of her. When she heard a rasping noise she stopped, thinking about teeth and fur and naked tails.

You could never do a thing right.

She trudged on, ignoring the voice in her head. The same voice as always. Just one bottle, just the one, and Mrs. Landon would be pleased and nothing would go wrong and when the bottle was empty she'd wash it clean, wash away the sour and sticky, and leave it for recycling.

The rasping noise came at her again, louder this time. Eva squinted. There, along the wall: bottles, rows of them, waiting. On the floor, something moved. Something on all fours, something far too big to be a rat. Two somethings, two shiny pairs of eyes.

Eva looked into those eyes and retraced her steps. She heard their heavy breathing, the sound of nails dragged over the concrete floor. *Rats*, she thought. *Rat traps.*

At dinner, Mrs. Landon didn't comment on the lack of wine, as if she knew why it wasn't there. Eva sat opposite June and Jules, staring down at her lasagna, repulsed by the greasy smell. The boys played with their food, pushing it here and there on the plate, smearing every inch of china with sauce and fat.

"Boys," said Mrs. Landon. "Aren't you hungry?"

"We've already eaten," said beautiful Jules loudly. It was the first time Eva heard him speak, and she turned to him. He locked eyes with her and smiled, his teeth glistening red.

***

They needed groceries. Eva asked Mrs. Landon how it was usually done, and Mrs. Landon pointed to a stained post-it note on the fridge with a number scribbled on it.

"That's to the store manager—he'll fix everything and make the delivery. I've got a deal with him since way back. The girl who was here before used to make lists and send them to him; it was every other week or so. Just text him what you need, and he'll let you know when to pick up the stuff."

"What happened to the girl?" Eva pictured manicured nails, neat handwriting. "She quit?"

Mrs. Landon scoffed. "You could say that! I haven't had much luck with the people I've hired in the past. I sure hope you're not planning to abandon me."

"No." Not that she wanted to stay, but Greyling was the only place that would have her. It was a house where you could be swallowed and forgotten. "Is there anything in particular you'd like me to buy?"

"I'll leave it up to you." Mrs. Landon looked older for a moment, as if those few words had drained her. "Just be sure to get the boys their milk and cereal. They like that sugary brand, the one that tastes like chocolate."

Eva recalled the basement, the crouching shapes in the dark. Jules, his teeth stained with blood. "Yes. I know the one."

"Perfect." Mrs. Landon sighed as she walked away. "I think I'll go for a nap now. Take a look every now and then, will you, just to make sure the fire doesn't die."

Eva got to work on her list. Her handwriting was messy, and her nails were chewed to the flesh.

The delivery was made the next day. The store manager, whose name she didn't know, wrote that she could pick the groceries up outside the gate at ten am. Eva wanted to ask why he couldn't drive up to the house, but she didn't. The walk through the garden did her good—it was nice to be out of the house, and the plants and shrubs sprouting everywhere didn't look too bad in the sharp sunlight. When she reached the gate there was no one waiting, just two grocery bags left by one of the gateposts. The deserted road wormed away from her, leading to town or away from it. If she went in the unknown direction, where would she end up? If she walked on and on until the squeaking lost track of her and she became yet another lost employee of Mrs. Landon's.

But Eva wasn't like those other people. She was loyal, just as the ad had demanded. She grabbed the bags, ignoring how the handles dug into her palms. The walk along the garden path was slow, the bags weighing her down. She'd have to take a wheelbarrow next time, a cart, something. It had been stupid of her not to think of it now.

Rustling from the side of the path made her turn her head, and a gasp slipped between her lips. It was the boys. They were hunched over, wild-eyed, naked. Wet hair, grimy hands and feet—*there must be a pond*, she thought, *somewhere in the garden there's a hidden pond*. Her mind reeled, grasping at every possible logical explanation. *It's a hot day, so they've had a swim. As boys do.*

June and Jules opened their mouths. Eva saw in their eyes that they weren't going to speak, that there was something else coming, and she ran. The bags cut into her hands, slammed into her thighs. The howling rose, grew. Followed her until she was inside the foyer, panting, sinking to the dusty floor. Kept sounding in her head while she dragged herself to the kitchen and unpacked the groceries. Giant boxes of cereal, cartoon animals on the front. *They like that sugary brand.* Eva's mother had told her that sugar was bad, but she was dead and gone. It was like that with old people— they died easily. It had nothing to do with Eva. Her head squeaked, her palms were blistering. From beneath the pantry door the rat hole taunted her.

An hour later, while she dusted the bookshelves in the parlor, the boys entered. Dressed in their usual jeans and t-shirts, hair hanging around their faces. They came up to Mrs. Landon and sat down on the armrests of her chair, leaning into her.

"There you are, my angels." Mrs. Landon patted their arms, shoulders. "Give Granny a kiss."

June and Jules stuck their tongues out and licked her cheeks. Then they turned to Eva, showing their teeth. As the dust whirled around her she stared into their faces, and from that dark place in her memory came the sound of her mother's wheelchair. *Squeak-squeak-squeak.*

***

She woke up that night, knowing that something was in her room. Someone. It was too dark to see anything, but she heard breathing. Low, raspy breathing, laced by giggles.

When she'd been very young and tormented by nightmares, she had called for her mother. Her screams had ripped the house apart, but her mother had never come. *You're too old for that*, she'd said. *You should know better.*

This wasn't a nightmare. This was reality, and her mother was dead, and Eva's brain was crammed with things she didn't want to remember.

Something moved in the darkness, brushing against the bed. *They're watching me*, she thought. *They want something, and it's bad.*

Minutes later they were gone. They hadn't touched her, but Eva felt covered in dirty fingerprints. Their smell was on her, rancid, old blood, and she wondered if it was hers now, too. If she was part of Greyling now and could never leave, because she smelled like insanity.

***

Eva cooked them meals, the good kind, nutritious homemade food with real cream and butter. It soothed her to see a cake rise in the oven or a quiche come out with a perfect, golden crust. And it gave her a reason to wipe the counter and wash the dishes, to stay away from the parlor. She made the kitchen hers, moved plates from one cupboard to another, threw away anything that reeked. Mrs. Landon told her she was too thorough but didn't stop her, so she kept at it. With hands that were chapped and dry from detergents and scalding water.

On her first Sunday at Greyling, she made a roast from a sirloin she'd got with the store delivery. Mrs. Landon praised her when she entered the kitchen, inhaling the aroma with a smile.

"We always had a Sunday roast when I was a little girl. Of course, back then, we sat in the dining room, and us kids didn't get to leave the table until we'd finished everything on the plate."

When June and Jules sauntered in, a while later, she beamed at them and repeated the same story Eva had just heard. "Richard was so mad at Mama because of that. He always was a fussy eater."

She cut a fat slice of beef from the tray as she spoke and divided it into pieces on her plate. Then she put a piece between her lips and leaned close to June. "Here you are."

June caught the meat hanging from her mouth with his teeth, then turned to his brother who repeated the process before devouring the roast beef. Eva cut her own food, small, smaller, and when the blade of the knife showed her own blurred reflection she felt that smell that stuck to her, them. Her mother moved through the hallways of her mind, wheels turning, and outside, the garden was crawling toward the house with long, twisted fingers. And the beasts howled.

She found the grave at the back of the house later that day, when she was putting away another binbag. Did anyone come to collect the garbage or would it stay, rotting, attracting vermin? Eva didn't know. She dropped the bag next to the others, and then she spotted the grave and went over to dig it up. It was among the rhododendrons, half-hidden, an oblong patch of soil staining the lawn. Eva sank to her knees and dug, burrowing into the dry earth with her hands. Dirt landed on her skirt, the hems of her cardigan. She stared at her own hands, filthy, she would have to scrub her nails. Scrub, rinse, remove every trace.

She was down to her elbows when she backed away, scared of what she might find. Hurriedly she refilled the hole she'd made, thinking about the tutor and the housekeeper with the neat handwriting. In her head that voice, chanting. *You can't do anything right, Eva.*

The boys squatted by Mrs. Landon's armchair that night, gobbling up meatballs from a plate on the floor. They had never come to dinner, so Mrs. Landon had told Eva to fetch something for them. She sat there, face glossy with sweat, caressing their golden heads.

"Lovely boys."

Eva heard the fire roar and whisper about her. June and Jules looked up at her and smiled like angels, with meat sauce glistening on their lips and faces twitching from silent laughter.

***

The house closed in on her like a pair of hands, large, grimy. Eva went between the kitchen, the parlor, and her faceless bedroom, a ghost-walk across the same floors. Beneath the pantry door the rat hole grew, spread. She stopped cooking, because the smell of food sickened her. The fridge started stinking again, like it had when she came, and the boys piled their empty boxes of cereal on the counter. How long had she been at Greyling? She sat in bed, using her fingers to count, but they were too few and she couldn't concentrate because of the walls. Because of the sounds in the walls, and the howling.

When she entered the parlor one bleak afternoon, Mrs. Landon sat with a velvety photo album clutched to her bosom. She stroked it as if it were a pet, a tiny thing to love.

"Eva? You should see this. It's my family...my wonderful family."

Eva leaned over her chair, inhaling sweat and filth. Mrs. Landon's hair was sparse on top of her head, the scalp shining through.

"Here, look." Mrs. Landon opened the album, prodding the photographs with her finger. The first one showed a handsome man, middle-aged, looking away from the camera. "That's my Richard. Ellen, he called me. He was the only one who ever did that." She turned the page. There she was, decades younger and many pounds lighter, in her chair by the fireplace, hugging two lapdogs to her chest. Mrs. Landon stroked the image of the dogs, covering them in fingerprints, but she didn't say anything. There were other pictures—blurry photographs of two angelic, solemn boys, always together, never smiling.

"And here they are, everyone together. My daughter and her children before the murders." Mrs. Landon flipped another page open. The portrait showed a beautiful young family—blonde, slender Christina and her princely husband, both of them watching the sleeping baby in Christina's arms.

Behind them, in the shadows, were June and Jules. Doll-like, hand in hand, staring darkly into the camera.

"Such a tragedy." Mrs. Landon spoke slowly, as if she was dozing off. "The nanny...the nanny killed them. Richard never got over it. Those pills he took, you know...You know about the pills. His skin was gray when I found him. Concrete gray. At least he didn't get those bulging eyes, like Christina did."

"And Baby May," Eva said, staring at the picture, at the boys and their sullen faces. Rat traps. Poison.

"There was blood in the crib. The lace frock she was wearing, it used to be Mama's, but we had to throw it away. Richard tried to save it, though—he was always opposed to Mama when she was alive, but after she died he clung to her gowns and jewelry. Her bedroom is still somewhere in this house, untouched. If May had lived she might have inherited it."

Eva thought of the boys, small, angel-faced. She thought of little hands and rat traps and howling. "Where are the boys, Helena?"

"Here and there." Mrs. Landon let the album fall shut and turned her head to the fire. It rose, flamed. "My grandsons. My pride and joy."

Eva wondered if she would make it to the gate. To that road outside, the one that might lead back or forward. If she pretended to have an errand, would they let her go?

As if the previous housekeeper, the one with the handwriting, hadn't tried.

"I'm tired." Mrs. Landon leaned her head back, sighing. The album dropped to the floor, and she didn't pick it up.

Eva went upstairs. She curled up in bed, fully dressed, listening to the howling from outside. It had seemed like a good idea to get away after her mother died. The neighbors, the sick-smell, all the empty rooms. The tasks that clung to her though she didn't have to perform them anymore. It wasn't her fault, was it? It was just, the chair was so heavy. Things would have been easier if her mother had agreed to sleep on the ground floor. If they could have hired a nurse, but her mother didn't want any strangers in the house. *You're my daughter; it's your duty to take care of me.* The chair crossing the floorboards, *squeak-squeak-squeak...*

"It wasn't me," she told the darkness, the garden, the rats in the walls. "It wasn't."

She closed her eyes and her mother stared at her, ashen, skin peeling off. *Look at me, Eva. Look what you did.*

***

Mrs. Landon was dead the next morning. Eva came down and found her in the chair, the fire smothered, smothered at last. Mrs. Landon's eyes were open and the photo album was on her lap, showing the picture of the boys and their dead parents and sister. Baby May, killed by poison.

"Mrs. Landon. Helena." Eva shook her, shook until the album fell and the picture stopped staring at her. Mrs. Landon's head lolled to one side and her mouth fell open, showing mud-colored teeth. Her mother's teeth had been bad, too, brownish, rotten—

Because you didn't take care of me, Eva. Because you're a selfish girl and you always have been.

"Mrs. Landon, I think you had it all wrong. About the nanny." She twisted her head as the shadows moved, but there was no one there. Only Greyling's ghosts and her own.

Mrs. Landon watched her with dead eyes, face sagging like a shirt on a hanger. *Look what you did,* she said with Mother's voice. *Look what you did.*

Then came the howling. It was inside the house, growing, trailing through the locked rooms. They were on their way. They were coming for her.

Seventh Floor

When Paloma had her child, she told everyone that it looked like a hummingbird. Small, colorful like summer or a sequined dress. She was high on whatever the doctors had given her—she had never seen a hummingbird in real life and might as well have likened the baby to a bluebell. Back then, there was still time for beauty. If you saw a pretty bird now, heard its celestial singing, you caught it and roasted it over the fire. Women who gave birth rarely wanted hummingbird babies, or wanted anything at all. Paloma had taken in a few—sharp-edged women, women with gaps and cavities in their chests where there used to be husbands, wives, children. They had listened to her stories but shared none of their own.

Antoine had been a good husband, a passable father for the little bird. When he died, she looked around her and saw that the world had lost a color—it used to be brighter, warmer, the missing link between blood and fire. She buried him herself because no one else could; she buried her husband while her child watched, coal-eyed, autumn-haired. Years later, the man came. He took the child, and Paloma became sharp-edged, too. She left her belongings; she wandered. Time carved deep lines in her skin and no one knew her name, so she whispered it to herself:

Paloma, Paloma, Paloma.

The wind and the clouds and the flurrying sand caught it and ate it and spat the bitter core back at her:

Murderer, murderer, murderer.

***

Zeke first saw the asylum hours before he reached the gate. It was a lousy hideout, the worst one yet, but he wasn't sure he still had people to hide from.

He didn't know it was an asylum until he pressed his palm to the cool brick wall and read the sign. The structure towered over him—massive concrete with squares of barred windows twinkling here and there, like nuggets of gold in a muddy river. He counted to seven floors, counted quietly in his head. There couldn't be anyone still alive in there. He wondered if they had died in their cells or if they had been let loose, if hordes of patients had swarmed the desert. The thought made him chuckle as he pushed the unlocked gate open and went inside. The yard was narrow, devoid of anything but sand, patches of asphalt visible underneath. The entrance to the asylum was wide, ugly like the rest of the building—steel doors surrounded by barely readable signs prohibiting cigarettes, alcohol, pets.

"I don't have any of it," he muttered. "Sadly." Breaking in was easy—it must have been done before, by others like him. The foyer was dim, smelly with mold and tiny cadavers. By the stairs he stopped, leaning in to get a glimpse of what was above him. Darkness; silence. He thought about the seven floors, the patients who were dead and gone. In the basement, he found an array of rooms—a deserted lodging for a caretaker, a warden, anyone. There was a heap of bone-dry firewood in a corner, a stove, and when he turned the faucets, brownish water spurted out. Zeke washed his clothes and himself, ate the jerky in his pocket, and fell asleep on the bed with the iron frame. When he woke up, the old woman stood there, wrapped in shawls of blue and green, and told him that her name was Paloma.

***

She didn't like the idea of sharing the asylum with a man, but it was either that or walk on. Paloma was old; she needed shade and liquids and something soft to lie on. She had entered the asylum expecting it to be empty, but he had been there, asleep. She had always found sleeping people beautiful. Zeke was rough-faced and tall, but the beard made him look like Antoine if she squinted hard enough. In the morning, they shared some of the bread she had brought with her, and she told him why she wandered.

"I used to have a child," she said, and her head filled with birdsong as it always did. "A girl who followed me around like a cat, or a friendly ghost."

"Cats don't follow anyone," Zeke said, but she ignored him.

"I was a seamstress. Rich women came to me with their hopes and dreams and a few lengths of silk, and I gave them what they wanted. The scraps of fabric ended up in a trunk under the bed—shiny and smooth, any color you could think of. As my child grew, I made her dresses from the scraps. Dresses, skirts, wide coats where she could hide. She danced around me while I worked, sparkling, glowing. That was how I lived back then."

"Sounds like a fine old time." Zeke's face was still too new for her to recognize the curl of his mouth as either a sneer or a sympathetic smile. Or something else entirely.

"It didn't last." Paloma smoothed the shift she wore, the faded linen. "She grew too beautiful, and I was a fool for enhancing that beauty with tulle and velvet. The town boys started flocking in our backyard at night—after Antoine died, that is." She couldn't remember if she had told Zeke about Antoine, but maybe it didn't matter.

"Then the man came." The shadows crept closer, gathering at her feet. "He had a car...the child had never seen one. She ogled, demanding to know how it worked. He showed her the wheel, the gear shift, the dusty engine. Placed her in the driving seat and turned the key. She drove round and round in our backyard and he laughed, and after a week he left and took her with him."

Liar, the shadows hissed at her. *That wasn't how it happened.*

"*Child*, you say?" Zeke watched her with eyes like storms and thunder. "How old was she?"

Paloma sank into her shawls, sank to that place where all her lies were born. "Old enough to have children of her own. Young enough to be broken." She watched his face. Lines, sharp edges. "Did you lose someone?"

Zeke locked his eyes with hers. She realized that he wasn't like Antoine at all. Zeke wouldn't have let anyone outlive him; Zeke wouldn't have been buried like a dog out in the yard. Zeke would have done the digging.

"I used to have a wife," he said. "And now I don't."

***

It wasn't as if he had planned to talk about his wife. He'd made it a rule not to talk about anything from the past. Lili was dead, he supposed, and in a way, she had always been—too starry-eyed to be real, too wrapped up in herself to see through him. Their first year together had been good, whatever that meant these days. Lili filled their tiny hole-in-the-wall with song, sometimes even laughter. She sweet-talked the butcher at the end of the street to give her whatever was left at the end of the day, the worst bits, the graying meat no one wanted. At night, she told him he was the only one who had ever loved her. *I thought I was loved before, but I was wrong.*

The first episode came a month into their second year together. Zeke had work in the quarries, he only came home on weekends. When he entered the flat that Saturday morning, she was in bed, motionless, and the place reeked with old sweat and meat gone bad. She didn't respond when he spoke to her, shook her, dragged her out of bed. Her hair hung around her face, matted, oily, and her body had glaring red marks where the elbow creased, where the thigh began.

She didn't love me, she told him when he slapped her face. *She didn't love me, and neither do you.*

The next day, she was better. It became a pattern, irregular at first but then steadying into a dark rhythm. For months, she was air and light, until she fell and turned into the other girl, the girl he hated. It was as if his wife had died, and in her place was this creature, this hollow-eyed specter whose presence revolted him. He took work further away from the city, spent weeks excavating rock. She was rarely in the flat when he returned. He found her in the streets, dolled up in cheap lace, snaking her arms around men twice her age. Zeke was stupid, got himself involved when he shouldn't. He fled the city right after she disappeared, and he hadn't been back since. There was nothing left. He'd had a wife, and now he didn't.

"I loved her very much," he lied. "I wish I could get her back."

***

The girl on the seventh floor opened her eyes. The voices of the asylum rippled through her as they always did, but there hadn't been any ripples in a long while. Just rats crawling inside to die. Around her the hair billowed, rose and sank with her movements like the oceans of the old world. She sucked on a strand, let it tickle her tongue. The hair sustained her—she didn't know how, but it did. That was why she was the only one left and all the others were dead. Not that she knew much about them—she'd heard their screams, but that was it. The doctor had told her not to concern herself with the outside world, but hadn't he been part of that world, too? He was most likely dead now, though, so it didn't matter. There was very little that mattered.

Burying her fingers into her hair, she thought about the Man with the Crow's Face. He had come by in the night, watching her while she slept. His eyes were the same as hers, dark like the space under her bed when she grew up. Dark like home, if there was such a thing.

"You'll be here tonight, won't you? You'll be here until I'm well enough to go outside?"

He didn't answer, but his spindly shadow moved at the back of her mind. Her friend, her only friend in the whole wide world.

"There are voices," she told him. "I'm not sure if I like them."

Then he was there, the Man with the Crow's Face, speaking with his mouth an inch from hers. *I don't like them either, darling. We're going to have to do something about it.*

***

They came to an agreement of sorts. Zeke went out at dawn to hunt and forage, while Paloma started the fire and boiled water. He skinned the animals before handing them to her for cooking, and she was grateful—she didn't want to know what kind of creatures they ate or what color their furs had been.

Zeke didn't talk much. He guarded himself, and she respected it. They weren't friends; they cohabitated out of necessity or perhaps loneliness. In a few days, maybe a week, they would leave the asylum and go their separate ways. Paloma wasn't sure if she would be able to cross the desert again. There was a dull ache in her lungs at night, as if she were breathing sand. As if the desert were growing inside of her, grain by grain, and there was nothing she could do to get rid of it.

It was Zeke who suggested that they should investigate the building. "There might be stuff we need," he said, chewing the last strip of meat off a miniscule bone. "Medical supplies, canned goods, whatever. I'm taking a look, anyway. You're free to join me."

Paloma thought about the people who had been locked up on the floors above. Years ago, screams must have bounced between the concrete walls, growing, multiplying. Would they find corpses? She'd seen her share of dead people, but still. Back when she was a young girl, she had been afraid of death. It had been a faraway terror, the stuff of ghost tales and horror movies.

"The world changed," she told Zeke, turning a bone round and round between her fingers. It looked like a needle, but she had no shiny fabric and no one to sew for. "I thought my life would be different."

Zeke raked his nails over his shorn head. The gesture turned him into Antoine, and the needle twitched in Paloma's grip.

"I shouldn't have married," Zeke said. "She was unhappy before I met her, but I didn't make her any better."

Paloma's ears filled with hummingbird laughter, and she shielded her eyes. *I thought I was doing the right thing. I only wanted what was best for her.*

The shadows pressed against her, writhing, hissing. *You knew what you did. You're a murderer.*

"We'd better get a move on before it turns dark." Zeke stood, wiping his mouth. He was too tall for the room, for their ugly desert world. "Let's go."

***

The cells lined the sterile corridors like teeth in a stinking mouth. Zeke reckoned that the stench had been much worse a few years back, though—the corpses they glimpsed through the barred doors had been dead so long that there was little but bones left. Paloma huddled in her shawls, pressing her fingertips together for every corpse they passed. Zeke remembered the gesture from his childhood—the memory smelled like raisin-studded cookies, but he had no idea why. He'd grown up with his dad and brothers, and no one had ever baked him anything.

"What a sad place," Paloma said. "People shouldn't die like this. Was there no one who could bury them?"

"If I'd worked here, I would have left, too." He gave each cell a look-over, keeping his eyes out for useful stuff, but there was very little. Some locks were broken, doors hanging askew—there had been scavengers here before. The asylum was yet another place that would lead him no further.

"Someone should be told about this." Paloma coughed, following him up yet another flight of stairs. "It can't have been legal what they were doing here."

"We don't have much of a law these days, far as I know. I'm sure they were better off out here than back in the city." He saw Lili's face in front of him. Her cherry-mouth, stretched out into a stiff smile as she chanted her own name. *Lililililililililili.*

Paloma gasped and sank into a sitting position, rocking her head. "I'm sorry, I'm having some trouble breathing. I should return downstairs. You keep going."

Zeke grabbed her and helped her down to their lodgings at the base of the building. Paloma panted and sweated and pointed, pointed at something behind his back.

"There's my girl," she said. "My angel, my little bird."

***

The girl on the seventh floor dreamt about sand. It danced, burrowed in her hair, pooled at her feet. It was alive like her, and the Man with the Crow's Face said that it would always be.

The voices in the walls had been louder today. There had been footsteps, too, gnawing on the stairs with rodent teeth. She didn't want them there. She had been very clear about it, but they refused to leave her be.

"They have to go," she said. "The man and the old woman…they make me sad."

The Man with the Crow's Face ran his cold fingers through her hair, from the scalp and down. *I'll look after you, Little Bird. I won't let anyone hurt you again.*

For a moment, he sounded like someone else, a man with a big smile, a man they had buried in the backyard. Dirt had rained over his face until he was out of sight, and she was told that he wouldn't be back again.

"Who are you?" she asked the Man with the Crow's Face, and his laughter filled her head. In a flash, she realized that she had asked him before, and he had answered. Different answers each time, as if they were playing a game.

I'm a friend. Your only friend in the world, remember?

"Yes." She leaned into the touch of his skeletal hands. Her mind filled with fluttering wings, silks, and sand.

***

Paloma knew that she would die in the desert. Maybe that was what she had come to do. Her chest burned with every breath, and Zeke winced at her coughing. He served her broth, and otherwise he stayed out of her way.

"You should get away from here," she told him, and he didn't argue. His storm-cloud eyes flickered when she looked at him, as if he had secret thoughts about leaving.

"My husband was like you," she said one evening, when the fire threw tall shadows across the room. She was on the bed and he on the floor, carving the edges off a bone. "Tall and strong. I didn't know what to do when he died. It took me the whole day just to dig a hole big enough to fit him."

Zeke lifted his hunting knife and sent splinters of bone raining over the floor. "I wish I'd buried my wife. She would have been better off dead."

Paloma ignored him. "The child kept asking about him. No matter how many pretty dresses I made her, she wouldn't stop asking. And it was hard, being without a man. There weren't a lot of rich ladies left, and the few that remained had other concerns than renewing their wardrobe. I managed to find a piece of food here and there, but it wasn't enough. She was always hungry. She woke up crying from how her stomach ached."

"My wife got us meat," Zeke said. "She laughed, she danced through the flat."

Paloma felt the shadows press against her chest. Antoine's body had been heavy on top of hers in another lifetime, but this weight was ice-cold. "When the man came, I knew right away what he wanted. Girls disappeared sometimes, and we knew that they ended up in the city. We knew what they did there. The man came with sugary words, he talked to me about marriage. I knew he was lying, and I still took the money. I sold my child, though I knew that the city would kill her."

Zeke put down the knife and held the bone up into the light. It was a girl, a girl with eyes like coal and hair like autumn. "I'm going to see the seventh floor," he said. "And you're coming with me."

***

The old woman clung to his back like a child, feather-light and scrawny. Zeke strode upwards, inhaling dust and filth. This was the last night—there wouldn't be any more. He'd seen death settle into the lines of Paloma's face, and he knew this was his last chance to see what was at the top floor of the asylum. He wouldn't go without her—when she died, he'd bury her outside the brick wall and leave. Continue into the night, with Lili's face carved into his skull.

Paloma shook from her coughing fits, clawing at his shoulders. Three floors, four, five, six. Sweat poured into his eyes.

"Her name was Elise," Paloma said. "When she was born, I told everyone that she looked like a hummingbird."

The seventh floor. It smelled different—sweet and putrid like rotting leaves, like autumn. Like Lili when she'd been in bed for weeks, muttering her own name as if it were a spell.

"There is something here." Paloma got down from his back and stood behind him. "Oh, it smells like sugar. My little girl would have liked that. She loved anything sweet."

"Come on." He started walking, not because he wanted but because he had to. There was something in the air, flurrying, whirling. Sand.

"She called herself Lili," Paloma said, her voice dream-like. "She would repeat it over and over until it melted into a single word. *Lililililililili.*"

Her voice faded, but the chanting continued. From the walls, the desert, the six floors below. From a cell at the end of the corridor—a cell at the end of the world.

***

The girl on the seventh floor heard them coming. She twisted her neck, and the hair rippled around her.

"Are you there?" she asked the Man with the Crow's Face, but he didn't answer. She tugged at the hair, ran it through her hands. They were coming, even though they shouldn't. They had been people with names once, names she knew and cherished.

"But they didn't love me. No one loved me, so I ended up here."

Footsteps struck the concrete floor. The girl thought about wings, beaks, and the softest feathers.

She smiled when they stood in front of her. The old woman, draped in colors and sickness, and the man with the thunder-eyes.

"I don't want them here," she told the Man with the Crow's Face. "They should go."

He appeared behind their backs, smiling at her with glowing eyes. The girl stood. She reached her hands out toward him, smiling back, and the hair whirled around her like silks and sand.

It'll be just you and me, Little Bird. Just us, in here, forever.

Lineage

The house is larger than I expected. Not that I've given it much thought—I never had any romantic ideas about country life. The only time I ever spent out of the city were those years at The Home, and while I was there, I rarely left my room. I had no reason to.

The cab driver is too chatty for my taste. I'd prefer silence, but for the past hour he's told me pointless stories about his wife, his new apartment, and his favorite gym and how many hours a day he spends lifting weights. He goes on about his baby, too, even shows me blurry cell phone snapshots.

"I don't know who I was until she was born. It's like, I don't know, I wasn't even real."

He's a joker, too, which is one of the traits I like the least in people. *Man, you look like shit*, was how he greeted me at the station. *Just kidding, just kidding.* Except he wasn't, and we both know it.

"Sure you want me to drop you off here?" he asks after making a dangerous U-turn on the narrow dirt road. "Who'd you say you were going to visit, was it your brother? Are you sure he's not a serial killer? Nah, I'm just kidding." He laughs heartily and drops my bags to the ground.

I hope your baby dies. Just kidding.

After he's left, I'm alone with the house. It towers to my right, hiding behind the trees like a tittering child, spying from behind a curtain. It's the first building I've seen for miles. It's three stories high, brick-built, with tall windows reflecting the garden's apple trees, blackcurrant shrubs, and swaying grass. *The garden looks alive*, I think, *and the house doesn't*. I don't like the thought and don't know where it came from. There had better be someone alive in that house, or I'm fucked. My phone has no signal—I checked as soon as the cab was out of sight. The only one who can save me is the man who's supposed to live out here. The man who claims to be my brother.

I push open the rusty gate and walk across the garden, wary of snakes. There are shrubs and flowerbeds everywhere, bursting with bloom and berries. Insects whir in the hot air, lazily droning from one flower to the next. I suppose a lot of people would find it beautiful. Calming. But I feel more at home surrounded by concrete, and I wish my brother would come out on the porch and greet me.

He doesn't, so I rap my knuckles against the door. I knock a few times before it is unlocked from inside and swings open.

"Little brother!" Matthew beams at me. My first impression is that I wish that we were alike. He's taller than I am, annoyingly handsome, and smartly dressed in a suit that looks tailor-made. "You found your way. Excellent."

"Yes." How much older can he be? Ten years? Fifteen? "Thank you for inviting me. You didn't have to."

"Nonsense!" He slaps my back before ushering me inside and grabbing my bags. "We're brothers. It's what anyone would have done."

The entrance hall is glum, sparsely furnished and with nothing on the walls but the navy-blue wallpaper. It doesn't tell me anything about who Matthew is.

"Was it a tedious ride out here?" he asks as we ascend the stairs together. "Oh, of course it was. And costly, I imagine. I'm sorry about that. I would have come to town to pick you up, but we had a bit of an emergency here, and I couldn't leave."

"Emergency?" The stairs whine under my soles.

"No, nothing. It resolved just fine, as it always does. Being a parent is wondrous, but it does have its drawbacks."

I try to recall that letter he sent me. Now that I think of it, he did mention a wife and children. "How many kids?"

"Three. Two girls and a boy." His voice softens. "You'll meet them in a while. They're all very excited to get to know their uncle."

"I look forward to meeting them, too." I've never really been around children. There weren't any at The Home.

We reach the third floor, and Matthew leads me down a hallway.

"Here is your room. I'm certain you'll like it." He takes a bunch of keys from his pocket and unlocks the door. "Go on, open it."

I do. It's dark in there, but there's something behind the door that makes me gasp out loud. Something with gleaming eyes and fangs, ready to strike.

Matthew laughs and reaches for the beast. He grabs it and shows it to me—it's a taxidermy caiman, ancient-looking and dusty. "Oh, you should have seen your face! Pure terror. The children are so naughty, they must have put it here when they heard you arrive. Do you not recognize this little fella?" He pushes the caiman toward me, and I look away from its dead eyes. "Why, it's good old Willie! Surely you remember him—Grandma had him in her bedroom. Said he reminded her of Granddad. Every Christmas, the whole clan gathered in her house, and us children used Willie for all sorts of pranks. You used to love it. I remember you sitting on my shoulders, laughing…Your laughter was like birdsong." He puts the crocodile under his arm and shakes his head, as if he wants to wipe the memories away.

"I don't remember," I tell him.

"No, no, how could you?" He smiles. "Well, I'll leave you to it. Unpack your things, have some rest, feel at home. I'll see you in a while."

Once he's left, I sit down on the plain single bed by the window. The sunlight that filters through is pale and makes my hands look ashen.

I can't remember ever laughing as a child. I wish I did.

***

An hour later, Matthew knocks on my door. He doesn't enter before I've told him to, which is something I value. At The Home, no one ever knocked.

"Settling in all right?" With a smile like that, I imagine that he could fit in anywhere. Women must adore him.

"Yes." I stand. "Am I getting the house tour now?"

"Not yet. It's tea time. Though I fear that the children are having too much fun playing and are refusing to join us. We'll go to the nursery once we've had our tea."

I follow him back downstairs. The house is strangely silent, considering a whole family lives here. The hallways are carpeted, and all the doors we pass by are shut. I wonder where the nursery is.

Downstairs, Matthew guides me from the entrance hall to a well-lit dining room, with an oblong table at the center. The windowsills are crammed with plants, and in between them are tiny wooden figurines. Matthew holds one up between his thumb and his index finger.

"Charming, isn't it?" The figurine is a female form, naked, and obviously hand-carved. It has no face, just a blank space in between lumps of hair.

"Yes," I lie.

"Oh, here's Rita!" Matthew puts the figurine down and turns to the woman who's appeared in the doorway. "Darling, come meet Tom. My little brother."

The woman—Rita—looks at me without really looking. She's small, gaunt like a dying tree, with leathery skin wrapped snugly over her hands. She's in an ankle-length petticoat, and there's a knitted shawl draped over her shoulders. Even in her youth, she can't have been very pretty. The one beautiful thing about her is her hair, which cascades down her thin frame, thick and mahogany brown. In it there are braids, ribbons, pearls of various colors. The difference between it and the rest of her appearance is stark, as if the mane were a parasite, sucking her dry. I force myself to stop staring, hoping Matthew hasn't noticed.

"Welcome," she says. Her voice is deeper than I would have thought, and it has a monotony to it that I instantly dislike. *Wel-come.*

"Thank you. You're very kind to take me in."

She nods, then puts a tray on the table. It's only then that I realize that her pinky fingers are little more than stumps. I'm relieved when she leaves us alone. Matthew pours tea in fragile cups and offers me freshly baked scones with jam and butter.

"I suppose you're wondering why we live out here." He bites into a scone, smeared with jam so red it makes me think of blood. "The main reason is that my wife has certain…weaknesses. Allergies, if you will, but ones that the medical profession refuses to accept as of yet. It's better for Rita out here, where modern technology won't interfere with our daily lives. There's no electricity, no wireless communication, none of these horrid masts that they're putting up everywhere. You may have noticed already that your phone has no reception."

"Yeah, I saw that. Do you really live without electricity?" Surely, he is winding me up.

"Oh, it's quite easy once you get used to it. You know, I want this to be a safe haven for the children. I want them to grow up unpolluted by modern life. There are so many things about society today that corrupts people's souls. Enslaves them. Here, we teach our young how to live a simpler life. We make everything ourselves. We collaborate, as families should. I teach them History, Geography, all that theoretical stuff, and Rita shows them how to cook and craft what we need. It's the sort of life I dreamed of when I was young. Now I get to give it to them." He pauses. "And to you."

I don't know how to reply. "How did you find out about me?" I ask instead.

He shrugs, as if he doesn't find the question interesting. "I'm your brother. It's my duty."

"Well, thank you. You know, after Mom and Dad died, I didn't really have anyone. I sort of…ended up in a bad place." My mouth goes dry. *A bad place indeed.*

Matthew presses a linen napkin to his lips. "There's no need to talk about the past. You're here now. If you're ready, we should head to the nursery. See what sort of shenanigans the little ones are up to."

***

Except they aren't little. I stand in the doorway next to my brother, trying to make sense of what I'm seeing. The nursery is a bright room, all pastels, a shelf brimming with toys lining the wall. One girl and a boy sit cross-legged on the floor, engrossed in a chess game, while the other girl is by the window leafing through a book. None of them are children. They're a few years younger than me at most, in their late teens. The boy is strikingly pretty, with thick eyelashes and shiny dark hair, while the girl next to him on the floor is scrawny and pale, with hair so blond it seems white. Neither of them looks up from their game, but the girl by the window puts her book down and meets my gaze. Her large, brown eyes are kind, too kind, and remind me of a cow's.

"Children!" Matthew claps his hands together, and they turn their faces to him. "This is my brother Tom, your uncle who I've been telling you about." He puts his hand on my shoulder, smiling. "This is Nathan and Agnes. Over there is little Juliette." He nods to the girl by the window, who curtseys. She's in a billowing petticoat, just like Rita was. Agnes' dress is ankle-long, too, and she's got a big white ribbon in her hair. Matthew doesn't seem opposed to just modern technology, but modern style of dress as well.

"Hello," says Nathan, watching me from under his thick lashes. "Will you be here long?"

Agnes pokes his wrist with her finger. "Father already told us, remember?"

Father. There is no way that Matthew could have fathered these three teens, or he would have been exceptionally young at the time. They don't look like him, neither, nor like each other.

Cow-eyed Juliette doesn't talk, but she keeps looking at me. No—I realize after a while that it's Matthew she's watching. Her brown hair hangs around her face, reaching her breasts. I wish I could spot the title of the book in her hand.

"It's nice to meet you," says pale-eyed Agnes and smiles. Her teeth are too big; her thin lips vanish behind them.

It's as if the smile distorts her face, takes over, and I think to myself that she's ugly. She closes her mouth, as if she knows what I'm thinking, and her fingers ghost over the chess board. Nathan exchanges a look with her, but both of them have gone strangely expressionless and I can't read them.

"I'm sure we'll all become the best of friends." Matthew turns to me, grinning. "Aren't they cute?" he adds in a whisper.

I don't know what to say, but he doesn't seem to want an answer. We go back downstairs, to the dining room where the tea tray has vanished from the table. There is no sign of Rita.

Matthew stands by the window, watching the lush, blossoming world outside. He grabs one of the figurines again, closing his fist around it as if he wants to warm it up. Or hide it from view. "I want you to know that I'm delighted to have you here. I always regretted that I left you with them when you were little."

Them—our parents?

"We're finally together, just as it should be. The whole family."

I don't care that he doesn't look like me. I don't care that I can't use my phone, or that I'm in the middle of nowhere. *Family.* I lap the word up; I chew and swallow. I want it to become part of me.

***

We all gather for supper a few hours later. When I enter the dining room together with Matthew, the children are seated already, Agnes eyeing us keenly while Nathan ignores our presence. Matthew takes a seat at the end of the table, and I sit down on his right side, across from Nathan. Juliette is next to me, hands folded neatly in her lap. Her index finger twitches, as if it's tapping along to some soundless rhythm. I wonder what sort of music she likes—if she's heard any, that is.

Across from me, Agnes leans in and whispers in Nathan's ear. His eyes light up, and he gives me a quick look before turning away.

"Anything you'd like to share with the rest of us, Agnes?" Matthew asks.

"No, Father."

"Very well." He turns to the doorway and smiles when Rita enters, carrying the silver tray I recall from teatime. If the steaming pot on it would slip, it would cause burn marks all over her chest.

"Stew," she says as she places the pot on the table, before disappearing again with her tray.

"Ah, yes. Rabbit stew." Matthew nods at me, as if I've made a guess and chosen the correct answer. "We live off the land here, accepting what Mother Nature is willing to give us...in our case, an abundance of rabbits. Adorable little creatures, I know, but if we don't take care of them, they'll feast on all our crops."

"Which would be awfully sad," Nathan says, face blank.

"Yes, Nathan, it would." Matthew seems annoyed for a moment, but his face relaxes when Rita comes back in with potatoes and a platter piled with whole-boiled carrots. Once she's taken her seat at the far end of the table, Matthew pushes the stew toward me and urges me to eat my fill.

"You must be starving after your trip. Some homemade cooking will do you good, put some meat on you."

"Thank you." I try to ignore the fact that they're all watching me. I've had enough of being watched. "I haven't had homemade stew for years. Mom made it every other day, but…" I don't know what it is that I want to tell them. I fall silent.

"Your girlfriend should have cooked it for you," Agnes says. "If you have one."

"Agnes." Matthew sighs. When I hand him the ladle, he serves himself a generous portion before slapping some stew on Nathan's plate. "You have to excuse the children. They don't meet a lot of people, and they're excited."

"I understand. Don't worry. But there has got to be some neighbors around, right?" I inhale the creamy stew smell, longing to taste it. I haven't eaten a proper meal in days.

"No. Why?" Matthew frowns. "I wish to give my children the very best upbringing; I already told you. It is my belief that society of today is harmful to children, even when its intentions are admirable. Other people—neighbors, as you say—might be well-meaning and kind, but they are part of society whether they want to or not. They would interfere, simply because they have been taught to do so. They would disapprove of our lifestyle, because it is unlike their own. Do you see now, brother? Do you understand why my wife and I decided to build a home away from judgmental strangers?"

"I didn't mean to question you, Matthew." I don't like the way Nathan and Agnes are watching me. It's as if they're both holding back laughter.

"Of course not. I'm sorry, I fear I'm too passionate about this. I shouldn't take it out on a family member."

Out of the corner of my eye I notice Rita putting a potato and some carrots on her plate. No stew. Matthew starts eating, and the rest of us dig in, too. He loudly praises the food. Rita nods, but doesn't show any other reaction to his words.

Once the meal is over, Rita stands to clear the table. Juliette joins her, quietly stacking greasy plates.

"Nathan, tell me." Matthew puts his long, slender fingers together while eyeing the boy. "How is the chess going? Are you still beating your sister?"

Nathan pouts. "Agnes is useless. She hasn't won a single game in days."

Agnes' colorless eyes flare up with rage, but she doesn't speak. Juliette leans in to grab her emptied glass, her long hair touching Agnes' shoulder.

Matthew laughs. "Oh, well, I'm sure the tables will turn eventually. If it's any consolation, Agnes, remember that Nathan is two years older and has had more time to practice."

Agnes doesn't reply, but her anger seems to subside. She looks at me as if she expects me to say something. I don't think I've ever seen anyone with eyes like hers—like water, when it's not reflecting anything.

***

I go to bed early. It's a habit I can't shake, a remnant from those eventless days in the square white room at The Home. Matthew escorts me to my chamber, the dusky hallway lit up by his candlestick. I can't imagine being in this place in winter, with no ceiling lamps or central heating. If it weren't for the working plumbing, I'd feel as if I'd gone back to the 19th century.

"Thank you," Matthew tells me. "You don't know what this means to me. It always pained me that our bond was severed, but now things have finally been set right." The candlelight makes his blond hair appear golden.

"I'm the one who should be thanking you. Really, Matthew. I mean, I don't think a lot of people would take someone in like this, let alone someone they don't know."

"I know you," he says, smiling.

"Well, you knew me back when I was…I have no idea, honestly. How old was I when you left home? Five? Six?"

He shakes his head. I'm not sure if it's because I'm wrong, or because he doesn't want to be asked that question. "I should go back down. Rita and I usually have a cup of tea before bed."

"Oh. Right."

He reaches into his pocket and picks up a key that he hands to me. "I thought you might be the type of person who prefers to keep their door locked at night. Take the candlestick, too. I can find my way around this house even in total darkness."

Once he's gone, I slip into the room and place the candlestick by the bed. The key is cool—I close my fist around it, like Matthew did that figurine. Then I head back to the door and twist the key in the lock, just because I can.

A tapping noise wakes me up in the middle of the night. It takes me a while to recognize it as someone knocking on the door. Matthew? I shuffle over, turning the key, expecting to see my brother. But the small shape waiting in the hallway is Agnes, in a long-sleeved, white nightgown that brushes against the carpet.

"I didn't mean to wake you," she says, as if she knocked by mistake. "I just wanted to explain. Father and my brother are asleep now."

"Explain what?"

She puts her hand on my arm. I'm not wearing a shirt; I wish I did.

"Father says the world outside is bad. But you're from there, aren't you?" Her twig fingers are cold against my skin.

"I don't know, Agnes. You should go back to bed."

She huffs. "You don't know where you're from? You can't be very clever."

I push her hand away. "Your father wouldn't approve of you speaking like that."

She folds her arms over her flat chest. "Father disapproves of plenty of things. I'm sure you're nothing like him." She tilts her head, flashing that ugly smile at me. I can barely make out her face in the dusk, but I see those two rows of gleaming teeth all too clearly.

"Let's talk tomorrow," I tell her. "We both need our sleep."

Agnes' smile dies. Her lips move, but I can't hear what she's saying. After I've closed the door and locked it, I imagine her staying out there, waiting. I sink to the floor, the room shifting around me. We weren't allowed keys at The Home. It was one of many things we couldn't have. One night, I woke up in that white room to find a naked woman next to the bed. She was crying, her thighs smeared with blood. I'm not sure who she was or what happened afterwards. Incidents like that were common, after all, and people came and went, transferring to other wards or leaving altogether. I think about that woman and about Agnes, and I squeeze the key so hard that it claws my skin.

***

We spend the following afternoon in the parlor, which is one door down from the dining room. Matthew and I are reading in the two armchairs by the window, and Rita is knitting in an ancient-looking rocking chair in the corner. Juliette sits beside her, mending one of Matthew's shirts. Nathan and Agnes are on the floor close to Matthew's chair, hunched over their chess board. Despite the discussion yesterday, neither of them seems to care about who wins or loses. They make their moves swiftly, throwing the pieces aside as soon as they are out of the game. Whenever Agnes catches me looking at her, she glares before turning her attention back to the board. We haven't said a word to each other all day. I've thought about talking to Matthew—he'd want to know about it, no doubt. Agnes is young, and she hasn't met a lot of men. That's all there is to it, really, but I can't shake my unease. The one thing stopping me from telling Matthew what happened is that I'm ashamed. I didn't lay a finger on her, but I feel as if I did. The skin on my arm itches where she touched it.

Juliette's needle moves, burying itself in the white bundle of fabric before reappearing. Her neck is bowed, but every now and then she lifts her head, eyes shifting to Nathan and Agnes. I don't understand why she won't play games like them. Perhaps she's too slow, unable to keep up.

That night, just before bed, I stop by my window to watch the garden. The full moon paints the trees and shrubberies a ghostly blue, as if I've entered a shadow world. The woods stretch out beyond the garden, never-ending, and I remember the cab driver. *Sure you want me to drop you off here?*

Something shifts down there, leaving the woods and entering the garden. A pale thing dressed in white, skipping through the tall grass. Agnes. Her swinging arms make her look like a child, coming home after playing outside all day. Then she turns her face up, noticing me, and stops moving. I draw the curtains. I don't know what to make of the fact that she seemed happy before she saw me.

***

I help out in the garden the next day—I don't know anything about gardening, but Matthew assures me that it's simple enough.

"Tiring, yes, but not difficult. You'll learn in no time." He strides through the grass in knee-high rubber boots, overseeing the work. The children look different in their garden clothes—Agnes and Juliette wear baggy linen shifts, straw hats covering their hair, while Nathan is in a pair of coarse dark pants, ripped at the knees. I tear at weeds, the soil sticking to my hands. When Matthew states that gardening time is finished, I'm sore all over. My nails are black and broken.

I feel sorry for Juliette at supper. When she reaches for her glass of water, she knocks the gravy boat over. Instantly she's stuttering excuses, dabbing at the stain with her napkin, cheeks an angry shade of red. Neither Matthew nor Rita say anything. Nathan and Agnes, on the other hand, watch their sister with gleaming eyes.

"Such a shame," Agnes says. "Our best table cloth, too."

Nathan smiles. "You have to learn how to behave yourself, Juliette."

Agnes starts giggling, but stops when Matthew gives her a look. Juliette sits back down, interlacing her hands in her lap. I can't stop watching that one twitching finger.

After supper, Matthew invites me to the library. It's locked, but he doesn't tell me why. We sink into comfortable armchairs, surrounded by bookshelves, and he pours us both a brandy.

"Are you settling in yet?" He sips his drink, calmly watching me. "It takes some time getting used to, I'm sure. Our way of life is different."

"I think it's good for me." It's not a lie. At The Home, I felt as though they were trying to separate my soul from my body. Here, I'm blending together again.

"I'm happy to hear it. Rita told me yesterday that you seem comfortable."

I shudder; I'm not sure why. I haven't heard Rita utter more than a couple of words, and somehow, I don't want her to talk about me.

"Yes. Very."

"A game?" he asks, picking up a deck of cards and dealing the cards without waiting for my answer. "It's good for the children, too, having another adult around," he continues while studying the hand he's been dealt. I have no idea which game we're playing, and I probably wouldn't know it even if he told me.

"I'm not that much older," I say, staring at my cards. All two's and three's, which might be good but most likely isn't. "I'm only twenty-four."

"You don't have to tell me your age, Tom. December fifth—see, I remember your birthday, too." He flashes a grin at me.

"When is yours?"

"In March. Ages away." He picks up a card, then throws it aside.

"I wish I could remember. Our childhood, I mean. You seem to know all these details that I don't."

"Naturally. I'm the eldest."

"Matthew, don't take this the wrong way, but…When I grew up, there were no pictures of you in the house. Mom and Dad never talked about you. That's why I, I don't know, I've got all these questions and I—"

He holds his hand up, the cards obscuring the lower half of his face. "Can we do that some other time? I'm sure you understand that it pains me. I never talk about those years, not even with Rita. Of course I want to share everything with you, but I couldn't do it yet."

"Yeah. Sure." I pick the King of Spades up, not sure if I should save him or not. When the door creaks I start, but it's only Nathan. He comes up to Matthew's chair, sitting himself down on the armrest.

"What are you doing?" He watches Matthew's hand of cards with interest.

"I'd think that was quite obvious," Matthew says without looking at him. "Nathan, why are you here?"

"I can play cards, too." He shoots me a look. "Better than he can. And you've promised to let me try the brandy." He places his hand on Matthew's shoulder. Matthew removes it.

"If you want to play cards, you can ask your sister. As for the brandy, I believe I've told you that you can try it once you're old enough." He turns his head to face Nathan. "Do we understand each other? In a few years you'll be of age, but for now you belong in the nursery with the girls. Now leave, and don't interrupt us again."

Nathan slinks away, glaring at me before shutting the door. Matthew chuckles.

"I'm sorry about that. Nathan is such an eager boy, and he thinks he's older than he really is. I'm sure you remember what it was like at that age."

All I can remember are white walls and an unlocked door.

Matthew puts his hand of cards on the table, and I do the same. He smiles, pointing at his three Aces. "Better luck next time. Practice makes perfect—the children could testify to that."

Not Juliette, I think, recalling her twitching hand. *Juliette doesn't play.*

***

The only bathroom in the house is claustrophobically small and has no mirror over the sink, just liver-colored tiles that seem to suck up the light. It's on the ground floor, and when I wake up that night with the urgent need to pee, it's not the bathroom I dread so much as the winding stairs. I try and fall back to sleep, but it proves impossible. The silent house seems to mock me as my bare feet sink into the hallway carpet. I feel stupid, letting the candlestick guide my way as if I'm the heroine of a gothic novel. The stairs groan under my slight weight, and it's a relief to reach the entrance hall and the bathroom, which is all the way at the back of the house. I do my business quickly, somehow grateful for the lack of a mirror. The last thing I want to see in the middle of the night is my own sunken face.

When I'm back at the stairs I hear creaking. Someone is descending. I stop, not sure if I should say something. The candlelight only allows me to see a few inches or so in front of me—anything further than that is in total darkness. I wait, the creaking coming closer. Whoever it is doesn't seem to be carrying any light.

I don't spot her until she's right in front of me. Rita. My heartbeat races, but I manage to push back the yelp trying to force its way out of me. There's something strange about her—there always is, but this is different. She doesn't look at me. She doesn't even seem to realize I'm there. Her gaunt face is vacant, her eyes staring blankly. I step aside and she passes, shambling toward the kitchen. I don't stop to see what she'll do. I rush up the stairs, and once I'm in my room I stay by the door for several minutes, pressing the handle down over and over to make sure it's locked.

***

In the morning, I let the light into the room and tell myself that nothing happened. Rita is downstairs serving breakfast, bringing coffee for me and Matthew and cocoa for the children. Matthew talks a lot and Rita not at all, and it's nothing out of the ordinary. I was seeing things, my brain reshaping mundane shadows into ghouls. It's not the first time.

In the afternoon, after a tiring day in the garden, we sit in the parlor. I read while Matthew scribbles in a notebook, and Rita knits in her rocking chair. Juliette is by the window, hunched over a watercolor painting, while Nathan and Agnes are playing as always. It's not chess today but a different board game I don't recognize, with stark red pawns and two dice. The dice rolling over the board is the only sound in the room, apart from the ticking clock.

"Juliette, dear," Matthew says without looking up from his notes. "Would you bring us the tea?"

She dumps her painting on the side table so carelessly that droplets of water run across the sheet, blurring the colors. Agnes and Nathan watch as she dashes out of the room, whispering together. When Juliette returns with the tray, she takes it to the oval table in the center of the room and puts it down before pouring tea into the six gold-rimmed cups. She hands each of us a cup—Matthew first, then me, then Rita, and the children last. When she sets the tea down next to the board game, Agnes huffs and lets the dice roll.

"You know I want it up to the brim."

Juliette scurries to the table and brings back the teapot. She lifts Agnes' cup and pours, but the pot's lid falls. It lands in the cup, and hot tea flows over the rim. Over Juliette's hand, and on the hem of Agnes' white skirt. Juliette squeaks— that's the only way to describe it—and drops the cup and pot to the floor.

Agnes stands. She doesn't say anything. When her fist crashes into Juliette's face, her expression is completely calm. Juliette covers her bloody nose, wailing, but Agnes sits back down and moves her pawn forward.

"Agnes, you really do need to learn how to control your temper." Matthew clicks his tongue and jots down something in his indecipherable handwriting. "Darling, I think Juliette requires your assistance."

Rita puts away her knitting. For a moment, she just sits there, staring at nothing, and I'm reminded of what I saw on the stairs. Then she walks through the room, without paying any attention to Juliette who has collapsed in a heap on the floor, hiding her face in her hands.

"Come along," Rita says. "Nothing is the matter. It needs cleaning up, that's all."

Juliette's head hangs when she follows Rita out of the room. Matthew writes down a short word and gives me a look, brimming with kindness. *I'm sorry*, he seems to be saying, *that you had to see that.*

***

I go for a walk together with my brother the next day. There's a bit of a breeze, and I'm wearing the denim jacket I haven't been needing since I got here. Matthew gives it a look and feels the fabric, then shakes his head.

"You know, I believe the girls have started sewing a little something for you. We want you to truly feel that you're part of the family, after all."

We walk down the dirt road, deeper into the woods. An ancient-looking car is parked around the bend, just out of sight from the house.

"Yours?" I stare at him, and he laughs.

"Of course it's mine. If it were possible to live without it I would, but as it is, I do need it occasionally. I feel it spoils the view if I were to park in front of the house, though, so I keep it here. You're welcome to use it whenever you like, of course."

"I can't drive, but thanks." I go quiet, wondering how to bring up the topic I really wanted to discuss with him. "Um, I was thinking…about Agnes."

"I see."

"It's just, I…I worry."

Matthew grabs my shoulder, pointing at a squirrel with his other hand. It stares at us for a moment before fleeing. "Wonderful creatures," he says. "Oh, but we were talking about Agnes. It's kind of you to care about her."

"I worry that her behavior might hurt Juliette. That's all." Juliette has walked around all day with a swollen, angrily blushing nose. No one has said a word about what happened in the parlor.

"I understand. I really do. Rest assured, though, that I had a lengthy talk with the girl yesterday. She won't do it again." He sighs. "I'm afraid that there is some rivalry between the children, the girls in particular. They'll outgrow such silly notions eventually."

"Yes. Of course they will."

Matthew strays off the road, onto a path. I follow along, eyes on his broad back.

"You've really acclimatized yourself here," he says. "Haven't you?"

"I think so," I say, trying not to think about Rita on the stairs. "I like the serenity."

My brother laughs. "And here I worried that we'd bore you with our country ways! I'm happy to hear it. The serenity—that was what we sought out here, Rita and I. She needs her peace and quiet. It really is most important."

We're alone in the woods, away from all the others. I wait for him to say more, to explain what is wrong with his wife. I want to know why she looks the way she does, why she barely talks, *why she walked past me as if I were a ghost.*

Matthew switches the subject to the garden—a broken fence, vermin, crops. I walk behind him, wrapping myself in his voice, letting my thoughts wander. When we come back to the house, I don't know any more than I did when we left.

***

He tells me to meet him in the library again that night. It's only nine thirty, but without electric lights the evenings are short and quickly over with. I imagine the children, tucked in their beds. I think about Rita as if she's some robot housekeeper, stored away in a closet until dawn.

When I reach the library, I hear talking. The door is open a sliver, just enough for Matthew's voice to squeeze through.

"My patience is growing very thin."

I pity whoever is in there with him. It might be Agnes, who made Juliette cry at supper. She didn't do more than glare at her, but still.

"You promised," says Nathan. He's pouting, judging from his whiny tone. "All you do is tell us to wait. I don't want to hear it anymore."

I recognize the metallic clang that follows as a glass placed on a silver tray.

"If you truly want something, Nathan, you have to wait."

"But—"

"Ah, ah, ah… We don't use that word to our elders. Remember?"

"You're always saying that."

"I say it because it's true, don't I? Now I want you to go up to your sister and tell her what I've just told you."

I step back into the shadows, but Nathan doesn't leave the room.

"She's not my sister."

When Matthew replies, his voice is too low for me to make out the words.

"No!" Nathan cries, ripping the silence in half. "I'm sorry, I'm sorry, I'll never say that again."

"I certainly hope not," Matthew replies. "Just imagine how it would have hurt Agnes to hear your lies."

"I'm sorry, Father."

"There, there. I'm not angry, Nathan. I could never be angry with you." He pauses. "Now, come here. Let us part as friends."

A moment later, the door swings open and Nathan comes out. I try to hide but he sees me, bowing his head carelessly in my direction before sauntering off. After a while I enter the library, where Matthew is refilling his glass.

"There you are. Come. A toast." He hands me my brandy and we clink our glasses together. "Did you meet Nathan on your way down? I just had a chat with him."

"I did." *Let us part as friends.* "He's a sweet boy."

"Yes." Matthew sips his drink, tracing the rim of the glass with his finger. "He certainly is."

***

It's almost midnight when we finish our endless poker game. Matthew heads out into the dark for a walk, and after bidding him goodnight I scramble to the kitchen to have a glass of water. I'm not used to drinking, and I wouldn't do it unless he wanted me to keep him company. In the kitchen doorway, I stop. Rita slouches on a stool in the middle of the room, hands in her lap. Behind her Juliette stands, lovingly brushing her hair. On the table lies all the little things that are usually tied in there—the ribbons, the lace, the pearls and colored paper. Rita doesn't acknowledge me, but Juliette gives me a look before turning her attention back to the brushing. The swollen nose changes her facial proportions, makes her dark eyes seem smaller. I tiptoe over to the sink, filling a glass with water and emptying it slowly. When I get back to the doorway Juliette has started putting the trinkets back in Rita's hair. She ties, braids, brushes, and neither of them utters a word. Once I'm locked in my room, I try to imagine it the other way around. Juliette, dolled up with lace and ribbons.

***

The next day is slow and hot. The sun seems to have crept closer, as if it wants to spy on us through the windows. Before supper I look for Matthew, in order to suggest a walk, but he's not around so I head out on my own. The shirt sticks to my arms—it was on my bed when I woke up, neatly folded, similar to the ones that Matthew wears. I have no idea who put it there. I try not to think about locks and keys.

The birdsong takes me from one path to another, skipping ahead like a playing child. I wonder how long I would have to walk before these woods ended. What would I find on the other side?

I'm on my way back when I hear a noise. Too throaty to be a bird, too raw and filthy. I don't want to hear it, don't want the images, the thighs, blood-smeared. Something grows in my chest, grows fast, so I turn around and take a different path. When I reach the house my lungs ache, and the new shirt is soaked with sweat. Nathan and Agnes meet me on the stairs, creasing their little foreheads at my appearance. In my room, I tear my clothes off and stare toward the bed. Become a girl, crying.

***

The new day comes with throbbing temples and a sour taste at the back of my throat. A glimpse through the window shows that it's early, too early, but my headache needs clearing. The house is quiet around me, as if I'm walking in circles in a padded cell. On my way to the bathroom I spot movement in the dining room. A low voice, gentle hands.

"You know you have to, darling." Matthew brings his open palm to Rita's face. "It really is most important."

His hand is full of pills. White ones, yellow, orange, of every size.

"I need you to be a good girl, Rita."

She stares into the wall, showing no reaction when he pries her mouth open and forces the pills inside. He presses a glass of water to her lips and she drinks, though half the contents spill down her blouse. The gray fabric darkens as if it has been bruised.

"There." Matthew kisses her brow. "That wasn't so difficult, now was it?"

Hours later, I'm in the garden harvesting potatoes together with Nathan and Agnes. They talk about this and that, shoving their hands into the soil and digging up shapeless lumps that go in the bucket. Agnes' straw hat shadows her face, but I feel the sting of her eyes anyway.

"Father says he might take me with him to town next time," Nathan says without looking at either of us. "He'll teach me how to drive, too."

"That's not true," Agnes says. "If anything, he'll take us both."

"And how do you think that would work? Who would look after Juliette and Rita?"

They both turn to me, as if they've only just realized that I'm there.

"I'm sure you could both go," I say, unnerved by Agnes' lake-water eyes and Nathan's prettiness. "Where is town, anyway? Is it the one with the train station?"

They exchange a look, before Nathan says, "I guess. There was a train station close to where we lived, anyway."

"You lived there?" I can't imagine them among other people. They belong in the house, the blossoming garden. "When?"

"Until we were ten," he says.

"But you're not the same age, are you?"

He shrugs; they both do.

"Where did you live, though? When you were in town?" I glance toward the house, hoping Matthew won't hear. Though I'm not sure why that would be a bad thing.

"In the apartment." The word sounds strange, coming from Agnes in her hat and old-fashioned dress. "But it was messy there. Rita was always screaming."

"Why?"

She looks at me as if I were a tiresome child, asking questions I should know the answer to. "Because she was clumsy. She kept breaking things that weren't supposed to be broken."

***

In the library that night, Matthew talks about Rita.

"It's not easy," he says, eyeing his cards. "I try to provide the very best care for her, I really do. If I had the means, I'd hire a nurse, but…it's not possible. We have to make do."

I remember his open palm, the heap of pills. "Was she always like this?"

"No. They say that childbirth can cause certain issues, and I fear that might have been the case with Rita. She wasn't very strong to begin with, and perhaps it would have been best if she had not become a mother." He pauses. "Between you and me, the truth is that she was in an institution when we first met. I knew it was unethical to become romantically involved with a patient, of course, but you should have seen her. She was beautiful."

I wonder what sort of institution he's talking about. The white-walled, no-lock kind?

"So…the children are hers?"

He chuckles. "Oh, no. Only little Juliette. From the moment she was born, she was a weak child. Crying constantly. We thought it would be beneficial for her to have older siblings—that's why we welcomed Nathan and Agnes into the family. They were supposed to be her role models…but I'm not sure how it has worked out."

"You must have been very young when you had Juliette." *Very young for a doctor, too.*

Matthew laughs. He shows me his cards—he has won, again. "Oh, she could be anyone's. Rita was a beauty, like I said. She had a lot of suitors."

***

A nightmare cuts through me that night. I'm back at The Home, wandering the corridors, fluorescent lights whispering over my head. I'm trying to find a nurse, but all the doors are gone. When I bang my fists against the wall, I hear crying— so I keep banging until my hands bleed.

I wake up in a cold sweat, breathing hard. In the dark, I push open the window and let in the tree-rustling. Leaning into it, I see movement in the garden. Matthew. Nathan, Agnes. Matthew is carrying something; I can't see what it is. If they're talking, I don't know what about.

After pulling on some clothes, I strike a match and light my bedside candle. It flickers, throwing the shadows around as I leave my room and rush through the hallway. The endless corridors from the dream sit at the back of my mind, laughing at me. I come downstairs, still not sure why I'm there. It's about Matthew, I suppose. Most things are.

Their voices trail toward me from the dining room. It's light in there, the usual candelabra glow. I'm drawn to that light like a moth, flapping my invisible wings. Will he be pleased to see me?

He smiles at me when I stop in the doorway. The table cloth has been removed. Nathan is on Rita's chair, knees drawn up to his chest, glancing at me. My brother stands at the opposite end of the table, with his arm around Agnes' bony shoulders. And Agnes...

It's an animal. A rabbit. There are all sorts of logical reasons for cutting rabbits open, I guess—Rita cooks rabbit every other day, and skinning and butchering are tasks the children need to learn. It's part of our lifestyle.

Still, it does seem odd to do the butchering on the dining table. With all the downy, brown fur left, and blood oozing over the table, staining the rag rug and Agnes' white socks.

"You look like you've seen a ghost. Bad dream?" Matthew throws a look at the woolly bundle and Agnes' slimy hands, before turning to me. "Just come on in! Agnes here is making real progress." He caresses her hair and she smiles, leaning so close to the animal that she dips her sleeves in the blood. She doesn't seem to notice. On the other side of the table, Nathan is toying with something. One of the figurines from the windowsill—the blank-faced one with long hair. He turns it this way and that, as if he wants to admire it from every angle. Reaching his other arm out over the table, he buries his fingertips in blood. Without saying anything, he smears the figurine with it, pressing his thumb against the spot where a face should have been.

"Good girl," Matthew tells Agnes, who won't stop carving. Looking up at me, he adds in a loud voice, "She deserves a round of applause, don't you agree?" He and Nathan start clapping, and I join in, slapping my sweaty palms together. Agnes curtseys, without letting go of the knife. Her smile is wide and ugly.

"Don't you want to sit down?" Matthew asks me, gesturing toward the row of empty chairs. "You look a little pale. I hope you're not coming down with a fever?"

Nathan drops the figurine on the table with a thud, then starts drawing patterns around it. Circles, each one smaller than the last.

"No," I say. "I should go back to sleep."

He nods. "Of course. Please let me know if you need anything. Good night, little brother."

On the stairs, I feel like I'm running through a maze. There are no doors, only the sound of crying.

***

It's just Matthew and I at the breakfast table in the morning. If there are any stains left, they are hidden under the table cloth. I sip my chamomile tea, trying not to think. Things are better when I'm not thinking.

"You look a little under the weather," he says, buttering his slice of bread. "You shouldn't do any gardening today. Just rest yourself."

"Thank you." My mother always used that expression. *You look a little under the weather.* It ties us together with a ribbon on top, Matthew and me. I want to ask him about the past, but I don't know how. I want him to hand me another story about birdsong. It would wash away the blood, the knife, Nathan's drawings on the table. When I glance over to the windowsill, the figurine is gone. It's somewhere in the house, faceless, but it's not here.

"Matthew, I was wondering..." I wet my lips. "I've got some things that I need to do in town. Could you drive me? I'll pay for the gas, of course."

He frowns. "I only go there once a month, I'm afraid, and it's a few weeks left until next time. Also, I've promised Nathan to come with me."

"Oh." Something boils right underneath my skin. I don't want to know what it is.

"Just give me a list of what you need, though, and we'll get it for you."

"Right. Well, I suppose that will have to do."

In the silence that follows I smell blood. Raw, pungent.

"Oh, do cheer up." Matthew slaps my back. "We've got an exciting day ahead of us. The children are inviting us to a stage performance tonight."

"Stage performance?"

"It's no grand affair, as I'm sure you realize. But they've been practicing all week, and they'll be very disappointed if you're not present."

***

I do as little as possible that day. I sleep for a while; I hold an open book in front of me though I can't focus on the words. Rita is in the parlor with me, her rocking chair whining. Whatever it is that she's knitting keeps growing—a heap of black wool in her lap, like a sleeping cat. Her face is impassive, but her deformed hands never stop moving. I don't want to be alone with her, but I feel as if it's my duty. Matthew would value it.

Juliette comes into the room as I'm dozing off in my corner, book in hand. Her hair is matte and tousled, and she is barefoot. She murmurs something to Rita, but I can't hear what she's saying and Rita shows no reaction. Juliette grabs her watercolors and sketchpad and sinks down on the floor with her knees drawn up. I can't see what she's drawing, but the brushstrokes are forceful and the only colors she's using are red and black.

It's rabbit for supper again that night. I struggle to swallow the slices, the smell of meat revolting. Matthew watches me now and again. The concern in his eyes is like sunlight, warming me.

"Excited for tonight?" he asks the children, and Agnes beams. She's got a new ribbon in her hair. It's the palest shade of pink I've ever seen, as pale as the rest of her.

"I just can't wait, Father."

Nathan whispers something in her ear, and she erupts with laughter. All of her too many teeth show, and she throws her head back. I expect Matthew to correct her but he doesn't, he just keeps cutting his meat. After a while, Agnes stops laughing, throwing a cold little look at me before resuming her meal. Nathan snorts, glancing at Matthew. Next to me, Juliette clasps her hands together. They're trembling. When she's helping Rita to clear the table a while later, she drops Matthew's plate. It crashes to the floor, the china breaking in a thousand pieces. She stands there watching the mess, arms hanging. No excuses, no crying.

Matthew tuts. "Juliette…What are we to do with you?"

Her eyes dart to him and she rushes out of the room, then returns with a broom to clean up. Her movements are jerky, and her sobs are like nails hammered into my brain.

"I hope you're excited about the performance, too." Matthew smiles at me, gently pulling me back to reality. "I'll come get you at midnight. You might want to have a few hours of sleep before then."

"Right. Thank you."

"It'll be spectacular," Agnes says, tilting her head like a little girl.

"Something you've never seen before." Nathan runs his fingertips over the table cloth, drawing circles. Each one smaller than the last.

***

Matthew comes for me at midnight, just as promised. When I stumble into the hallway, blinking against his flickering candle, he grins and squeezes my shoulder.

"I'm sorry about the time...the children insisted. I know I overindulge them occasionally, but I just can't help myself. You'll understand when you start your own family."

We reach the second floor. It's as eerily quiet as always, and sconces light up the hallway. Matthew doesn't let go of my shoulder until we're at the door to the nursery.

"They're thrilled about showing their favorite uncle what they've come up with." He smiles. "Of course, it's a shame that you walked in on our little rehearsal last night."

Chills weave themselves over my skin. *The rabbit.* I grin back at him because if I didn't, the fear would show. I follow him into the nursery, where there are lit candles on every shelf and table. Mismatched chairs are placed together at the center of the room and Matthew guides me to one of them, sits me down. He takes a seat to my left. To the right is Rita, staring ahead. The pearls in her hair shine and shimmer. On her other side is a dark shape on the floor—it's the caiman, Old Willie. On his back are some dolls and stuffed bears with beady eyes.

Agnes and Nathan stand in front of us. Agnes in a pink dress that goes with the ribbon, Nathan in all black. They're holding hands, watching Matthew every now and then.

Then they separate, the tall table behind them coming into view. A white sheet is thrown over it, and something is breathing underneath. Someone.

For a long while, Agnes and Nathan are quiet. Their excitement is only betrayed by their eager glances toward the table. Matthew leans back, putting one long leg over the other.

Finally, Agnes starts talking. "We'd like to honor our beloved uncle with a little performance. We might not be very good yet, but hopefully you will have a lovely time all the same."

"I'm sure we will," Matthew says.

Agnes looks straight at me, and the ugly smile lurks in the corners of her mouth. "Little Juliette has offered to assist us today." She snatches the sheet off the table and Juliette lies there, shivering, dressed in white.

Nathan turns to Agnes and gives her a short nod. She reaches for something by her feet, something I haven't noticed until now.

It's a knife. It might be the same one as yesterday. Now it's here in the nursery, cold and glossy like a dying fish on the carpet. Agnes grabs it and starts caressing the blade with her fingertip, but Nathan tells her to hand it over. She eyes him with fury, but does as she's told. Nathan holds it up into the light and feels the tip of the blade. Then he looks down at Juliette.

"You see," he says, "we truly love you but you've become so terribly clumsy lately."

"We can't have that," Agnes says. "It's just not very nice."

Nathan runs the tip of the knife slowly across Juliette's naked arm. "No, and that's why we need to teach you a bit of a lesson. We're awfully sorry, we really are, but there's just no other way."

Juliette's sobs claw at my temples, fighting their way in. "Please," she cries. "Please!"

Agnes doesn't seem to hear her. She presses Juliette's arm against the table, puts all her weight into it. Nathan raises the knife. Without hesitation, he slices off her pinky finger.

The scream sets my head on fire. It drowns the room, the house, the woods around us. Agnes frowns, shaking her head.

"Do try to be quiet."

Rita makes a choked sound. Her hand grips hard around the edge of the seat, knuckles whitening. Juliette struggles to free herself, but Agnes keeps pinning her down and Nathan has no trouble chopping off the ring finger. The scream is more of a distant wailing now, as if it isn't only fingers she's losing but her voice, too. Blood discolors her dress, ruins the table and the carpet beneath. Her fingers have dropped to the floor, tiny white stumps. Useless.

"I want to do it too," Agnes whines, trying to take the knife from Nathan. "You promised!"

Nathan shakes his head. "If you really want something, you have to wait." He smiles sweetly as he cuts Juliette's middle finger off. "You should know that, Agnes."

Matthew stands, clapping loudly. I join in, though I'm not sure if the hands I'm staring at are my own or someone else's. Rita is stiff and white like the doll, the robot she is.

Matthew walks toward the children with his arms outstretched. When his sole connects with Juliette's middle finger there's a wet, cracking noise. He leans over Nathan, murmuring something while taking the knife and placing it on the table. Then he gathers Nathan and Agnes in front of him and puts his hands on their shoulders. Kisses their hair.

"I love you so much."

"We love you," they echo.

Matthew leans forward and grabs Juliette's limp, deformed hand. "But how is little Juliette supposed to carry our tea trays now? You shouldn't be so eager, Nathan. I'm afraid Agnes will have to do some of Juliette's chores in the future, and who will you be playing with then?"

"You can play with me!" Nathan's eyes glow. "Agnes is stupid anyway, she's always losing and when she does, she mopes and whines."

Matthew laughs. "Adults can't amuse themselves with games all day like you children can. But of course I can play with you every now and then, if it's what you want."

"And the brandy?"

Matthew strokes his hair. "Let's discuss that when we're alone, Nathan."

Agnes glares at her brother. It looks as if she's concentrating hard on keeping her mouth shut.

"Well." Matthew turns toward me and Rita. "This has been quite an eventful night. I'm sure we've all learned something."

Nathan and Agnes bow their necks and leave the room together, quietly closing the door. Matthew comes over to me, and I stand.

"Thank you," he says. "Now, let me escort you back to your room."

Does he think I'll try to escape? I don't know what goes on in Matthew's mind—I barely know my own. Rita sits as before, a shell, as alive as Old Willie and the toys. Juliette has fainted, and her three little fingers will never break any plates again.

"I don't know what to say," I tell Matthew. He guides me to the door, through the hallway, up the stairs. He doesn't speak until we've reached my room.

"It might seem cruel," he says. "To discipline a child is painful for any parent, but it must be done. It is my regrettable duty to see to the wellbeing of everyone in the family."

I nod. "Good night."

"Good night, brother."

After he's left, that word sloshes around in my head. *Brother*. I recall the one time I asked my parents about him. He had vanished without saying goodbye, and I wanted to know why. My father's belt told me not to ask again; so did my mother's tears. In school, everyone thought I was an only child. I didn't correct them, since I never really talked. Matthew wasn't in the house anymore, so he moved into my head. I knew from the start that he was better and smarter and more good-looking than I was. I didn't care. When my mother was sick, I asked about him for the first time in fifteen years. My father was gone and his belt, too, and my mother was always in tears anyway.

She told me lies. In a way, I guess Matthew is doing the same. But every time he talks, I feel like I'm behind a door that's safely locked. And I can't hear the crying.

***

When I wake up, my throat aches, as if I've been screaming in my sleep. I dress without drawing open the curtain, stumbling around in the dusk. There's a new shirt for me, one that wasn't there last night. While buttoning up I remember how easily Juliette's fingers were sliced through. Like carrots, asparagus, or a loaf fresh from the oven.

Matthew is at the breakfast table when I come down, together with Nathan and Agnes. Little Juliette's chair is empty.

"Sleep well?" Matthew pours coffee into my cup and I drink, feeling it burn my tongue.

"I think so. You?" Agnes watches me keenly, as if my words have any hidden meaning. Her dress today is coral, the darkest color I've ever seen on her. Beside her, Nathan grabs the bread knife, and I try not to stare at those slender fingers stroking the handle. He cuts a roll in half and smiles when he catches me looking.

"I slept wonderfully," Matthew says. "The nights are blissfully cool now, aren't they?"

"They really are," Agnes pipes up like a precocious child. Matthew raises an eyebrow at her but doesn't say anything.

When Rita enters the room, it takes a while before I notice what's different about her. Her hair. All the pearls and ribbons and pretty things are gone. It looks as if they've been cut off—the hair is thick and wild just as before, but there are patches where the scalp shines through. She puts a jar of marmalade on the table, then leaves again. Her movements are slow, as if she's turned into a frail old woman overnight. I want to say something, but I can't think of the right words. No one else seems bothered by her appearance.

Matthew turns to the window, where one figurine is still missing. "Ah, looks like we'll have a fine day. Don't you think so?"

I wonder where Juliette is. And if the knife Rita attacked her hair with was the one that cut Juliette's fingers off.

***

None of us leave the house all day, despite the beautiful weather Matthew keeps commenting on. We sit in the parlor reading, while Nathan and Agnes play chess by our feet. Rita only comes in once to serve tea, without looking at any of us. When Agnes wins a match for the first time that day, she looks up at me, holding Nathan's defeated king up like a trophy.

"Aren't you proud of me?" she asks. I exchange a look with Matthew, who nods.

"Of course I am, Agnes."

She beams, but Nathan just collects the pawns and sets up another game. Matthew watches me, smiling. I have no idea what that smile means.

In the evening, after a glum supper of watery broth, Matthew stands and claps his hands together. We turn our eyes to him—everyone except Rita, who sits at her end of the table without touching her food.

"I thought we should go upstairs now and visit our poor little convalescent."

I don't want to. I don't want to see her.

"Juliette will be most grateful for some company, don't you think?" Matthew heads for the door, so I have to follow. Nathan and Agnes trot after him, too, but Rita stays at the table.

"You look a bit tired, dear." Matthew walks toward her and puts his arms around her, pulls her head to his chest. He sighs, lovingly caressing her tangled locks. "You just stay here and rest, while we keep Juliette company." After kissing her forehead, he returns to us, leading the way upstairs.

"It'll be so much fun to visit Juliette," Agnes says on the stairs, and Matthew smiles at her.

"How kind of you to think about your sister."

Juliette's door is on the second floor, at the end of the hallway. It's locked. Matthew turns the key, then looks at us and lowers his voice to a whisper, as if we're about to give someone a birthday surprise.

"Be quiet now. She's probably asleep." He puts his finger over his lips, and Agnes giggles.

The stench is the first thing I notice. A blend of sweat, pus, and blood. The curtains are drawn open, but the window is small and doesn't let in much light. In the bed in the center of the room she lies, sleeping. She's small, a tiny shape, and her face is a grayish white. One hand is clutching her chest, but I can't see the other one—the one with only two fingers left. Beside the bed is a stool, and clean cloths and a bowl of water on the bedside table. Rita must have been here all day. The missing figurine stands there, too—naked, faceless, soaked in blood.

Matthew sits down on the bed. Juliette stirs, whines. After giving me a look, Matthew strokes her matted hair.

"Juliette," he whispers. Nathan and Agnes close in on me, standing on both sides.

She opens her eyes and screams. "No! No!"

Matthew sighs as she tries to move away from him. "Dear me. Did you have a nightmare?"

Juliette cries, coughs. It hurts my lungs to hear her labored breathing.

"Juliette, you need to understand that you can trust me. It was only a dream. You're safe now. There, there…Won't you tell me what it was that upset you?" He tugs at the covers. Gently pushes them aside. Juliette's whimpers are ugly and wrong, and I don't like them.

Nathan puts his hand on my arm, and Agnes does the same. Matthew keeps soothing Juliette, and Juliette keeps crying. When he lands on top of her, she bangs her fists against his back. The bandaged hand is just as ugly as the sounds she's making, and blood oozes from it. It paints patterns all over Matthew's shirt—a sea of red flowers, spreading.

"Let's leave her to rest some more," he says once it's done and he's back with us. Juliette is asleep again—at least it looks that way. "I'm sure she'll feel much better in the morning."

I wonder where I would end up if I went into the woods and let the night take me. One way or another, there would be a white-walled room waiting.

***

Just as I'm about to fall asleep that night, someone knocks on my door. It's Agnes. She doesn't say anything, just slinks into the room and in between my covers.

"What are you doing?" I come over to the bed, and she puts her icy hand on my arm.

"You have to," she says. "You know that." As though I'm a feverish child and she's my mother, urging me to take my medicine.

It blurs after that—the room, the bed, her bony chest. The only thing I can see in the darkness are her teeth, shining at me like a row of gleaming eyes.

I wake up alone, like I have ever since I came to my brother's house. Agnes is a vague memory I choose not to think about. She ignores me at the breakfast table, but when I meet her on my way to the bathroom her face is overtaken by that twisted smile. I wish I could smash it out of her, until I never have to see it again.

At supper that night, Rita falls to the floor in front of our eyes. The bowl she is carrying breaks, and tomato soup soaks her hands and petticoat. At first, I think she's fainted, but her eyes are open—she just lies there, stained, surrounded by shards, staring into our faces. When her eyes meet mine, I shudder.

"Get up!" Agnes barks. "Don't just lie there, what's wrong with you?"

Rita shows no reaction, but Matthew stands. He grabs Agnes by the arm and tears her from her seat. She tries to speak, but his fist crashes into her face. Agnes flies through the air and lands with a sickening thud. Matthew shakes his head.

"Never. Never again, do you hear?" He hurries over to Rita and takes her into his arms, then carries her to her seat.

"Now sit," he says. "You've worked too hard…you need to take better care of yourself."

Rita stares straight ahead as he puts a shawl over her shoulders and kisses her hair. After a while, Matthew returns to his seat, without looking at Agnes who is still on the floor, unmoving. He seems troubled and doesn't touch his food.

Nathan looks at me, smiling. When I think about it, he's had that smile on his face ever since Agnes received her punishment.

Later in the evening, when Agnes has come to again, Matthew invites me to the library. There's a wary look in his eyes that I haven't seen before, and he downs the brandy faster than usual.

"I'm dreadfully sorry about tonight," he says. "It wasn't the peaceful family meal I wished for. You haven't had many of those in life, have you?" He watches me with a new glint in his eyes.

"Have you?" I want to tell him about The Home, and what I did to end up there. I think, in a way, that he is the only person in the world who wouldn't judge me.

Matthew chuckles. "You know, I believe in visualizing what you want and making it happen. Our parents never did understand me, but now I've got a new family. And I got you back, finally. That makes up for all the sorrows of the past."

"What's going to happen to Agnes?"

He frowns, putting his glass down. "Nothing. Why would anything happen? Agnes is at a difficult stage in life, and we have to support her. All of us."

"Right. Yes."

"It's such a shame that Juliette has taken ill." His forehead creases with worry. "The poor child. She really has taken a shine to you, did you know?"

"I'm glad to hear it," I lie.

"When she's better, I'd be grateful if you talked to her. Got to know her a little. Parents aren't supposed to favorize, I know, but she really is the apple of my eye. Just like you were, once."

My mother's lies itch under my skin like crawling beetles. *He hurt you. He did bad things to you.*

"Of course." The brandy makes me feel like vomiting.

"Good." Matthew smiles, patting my hand. "We all have to do our part, little brother."

***

Foul dreams torment me that night. Stretched-out fingers reaching for my face, my eyes, and heavy breathing from someone I can't see. When I wake up, soaked in sweat, I have no idea what time it is. It doesn't matter. I can't stay here. The doctor at The Home told me I'd become better, but he lied just like my mother did. My brain is breaking; I can feel it. It has happened before, after all.

I find my shirt and trousers and put them on, before I enter the hallway. Too dark, too quiet—why have I never realized that the house is a tomb? I remember that cab driver, and I start laughing. I can't stop.

The stairs hiss at me that I don't belong here. They could mean the house or the world, the entire universe. I've never belonged. What do I care what stairs think? Once I've reached the entrance hall, I throw the door open and step outside. The garden watches me with one yellow eye, like a cat. The grass is cool and wet under my naked soles. On the other side of the gate I turn left, grinning as the dirt road stings my feet.

"No one knows where I am," I tell the trees and sleeping ditches. "I've turned to dust."

I walk into the darkness. I walk until I find the car, and then I lean against the hood and start to cry. I'll never get out of here. I'm stuck.

"Tom." It's Nathan's voice. He's on the road, approaching me. "I saw you leave. You shouldn't do that."

I stare at him with tears streaming down my face. His white shirt billows in the breeze, and when he stretches his arm out toward me I do the same.

"You didn't really want to go, did you?" He comes up to me and grabs my hand. His skin is burning. It calms me, because it means he can't be dead. "Come back. I'm going to teach you how to play chess tomorrow."

"Agnes," I say.

"Yes. My sister Agnes." He snorts. "I could teach you other things, too. If you come with me."

The pebbles spike through my brain as I follow him back to the house. I wonder how sharp they would need to be to draw blood. Nathan holds the gate for me, then the door. Once we're inside he locks and bolts it, before returning to my side.

Agnes stands there, translucent in her nightgown. "You should have let me go," she tells Nathan.

"He wouldn't have followed you."

Their voices... I hear them through water. Something is slithering around in my head, trying to find its way out.

"Here you are!" Matthew comes up to us, smiling widely. "Lovely night for a walk, isn't it?"

"I found him by the car," Nathan says.

"Of course." Matthew pats my back. He glances toward the stairs, and I do the same. Rita stands there with Juliette leaning against her, both of them dressed in white. There is no kindness left in Juliette's cow eyes, only fear.

Matthew laughs. "What's this? I see no one is able to sleep tonight. Well, then. How about we play a game?" He lifts his other hand, and there it is. The knife. He hands it to me, and I take it. It's warm from his grip.

I smile at him, while my mother's dying words play over and over in my head.

You're just like your brother.

Acknowledgments

In a way, I've been working on this book for a decade. I wrote the first version of *Lineage* in Swedish in 2011, and *Snow White* and *The Ice* followed in 2012. Until 2021, I didn't think any of these stories would ever get published. I'm very happy that they finally are, along with seventeen others. It's a dream come true, and I'd like to thank some of the people who helped me achieve that dream:

Michael Aloisi at Dark Ink for publishing my book, and Rebecca Rowland for supporting me ever since I was one of the authors of Dark Ink's anthology *Shadowy Natures*. I owe so much to you.

All the publishers whose publications these stories have appeared in before. I've enjoyed working with all of you and hope to do so again.

Camilla, the most enthusiastic reader I know.

Millan, who knows the importance of art and poetry and nature. The illustrations you did for *Lineage* were breathtaking, and I hope more people will get to see them some day.

My family for your constant support and love. My parents for letting me read and write as much as I wanted, and always believing I could become a writer.

Markus, for reading every story I write and saying nice things about all of them. I love you.

About the Author

Elin Olausson is a fan of the weird and the unsettling. She has had stories featured in Curiouser Magazine, Luna Station Quarterly, and anthologies such as Dark Ink Books' *Unburied* and Scare Street's *Night Terrors Vol. 4*.

Elin's rural childhood made her love and fear the woods, and she firmly believes that a cat is your best companion in life. She lives in Sweden.